He leaned closer to her.

"I am not the big bad wolf looking to attack unsuspecting damsels like in the fairy tales, Shannon," he whispered.

She blinked. "If you're not a wolf, what are you then?" she asked sotto voce.

"I'd think of myself as one of the good guys who has never taken advantage of a woman."

Shifting slightly on her chair, she gave him a long stare. Shannon wanted to believe him, but it wasn't Joaquin who'd made her feel uncertain as to where their friendship would lead. She didn't trust herself around him. There was something about Joaquin that reminded her that she hadn't befriended or been involved with a man since her divorce.

And she couldn't deny there was a sensuous connection between them when their eyes had met across a room. Shannon had to continue to tell herself that she was immune to Joaquin—a man who made her feel things she'd forgotten existed whenever her traitorous thirty-year-old body reminded her that she'd once been a deeply passionate woman.

"That's good to know," she said, pretending to be interested in her salad tossed with light vinaigrette.

It was their last exchange as the conversations floating around the table focused on the château's ongoing restoration.

Dear Reader,

Welcome back to Bainbridge House.

It is time for a lot of changes to the historic château and in the life of Joaquin Williamson. The renowned landscape architect to Tinseltown's rich and famous willingly gives up his Hollywood lifestyle to return to New Jersey to oversee the restoration of the gardens on his family's estate before its grand opening as a hotel and wedding venue. But returning Bainbridge House's landscape to its original splendor won't be as challenging as convincing his sister's friend that his former celebrity status was just a foil to grow his business.

Ten years ago, up-and-coming actress Shannon Younger became embroiled in a scandal that resulted in her divorcing her popular actor husband. Despite switching careers, she still vows never to become involved with a celebrity. When she accepts the position of pastry chef for Bainbridge House and discovers she is not immune to Joaquin's charm, she extracts a promise from him that they can only be friends. She doesn't want another husband, while Joaquin reassures Shannon that he likes being single.

Once Shannon becomes a resident chef on the estate, her opinion of Joaquin changes and she questions whether she misjudged him as a media-seeking wannabe celebrity. Cooking together and hosting the Williamsons' movie nights bring Shannon and Joaquin even closer, shattering their promise to stay in the friend zone.

I hope you will enjoy *Say It Like You Mean It* as much as I enjoyed reuniting with the Williamson siblings as they fulfill their late father's wish to restore the estate, and along the way find their own happily-ever-afters.

Rochelle Alers

Say It
Like You Mean It

ROCHELLE ALERS

HARLEQUIN

SPECIAL
EDITION

HARLEQUIN®
SPECIAL EDITION™

Recycling programs for this product may not exist in your area.

ISBN-13: 978-1-335-59447-1

Say It Like You Mean It

Harlequin Enterprises ULC
22 Adelaide St. West, 41st Floor
Toronto, Ontario M5H 4E3, Canada
www.Harlequin.com

Printed in U.S.A.

Since 1988, nationally bestselling author **Rochelle Alers** has written more than eighty books and short stories. She has earned numerous honors, including the Zora Neale Hurston Award, the Vivian Stephens Award for Excellence in Romance Writing and a Career Achievement Award from *RT Book Reviews*. She is a member of Zeta Phi Beta Sorority, Inc., Iota Theta Zeta Chapter. A full-time writer, she lives in a charming hamlet on Long Island. Rochelle can be contacted through her website, rochellealers.org.

Books by Rochelle Alers

Harlequin Special Edition

Bainbridge House

A New Foundation
Christmas at the Château

Montana Mavericks: Brothers & Broncos

Thankful for the Maverick

Furever Yours

The Bookshop Rescue

Wickham Falls Weddings

Home to Wickham Falls
Her Wickham Falls SEAL
The Sheriff of Wickham Falls
Dealmaker, Heartbreaker
This Time for Keeps
Second-Chance Sweet Shop

American Heroes

Claiming the Captain's Baby
Twins for the Soldier

Visit the Author Profile page
at Harlequin.com for more titles.

Chapter One

Patrick Williamson signaled, changed lanes and then accelerated onto the freeway leading to LAX. "Are you sure you're ready to exchange palm trees and ocean views for sleet and snow?" he asked his brother.

"It's too late to back out now," Joaquin said, smiling. He'd sold his luxury condo in the Hollywood Hills to an international businessman, offering the current owner the entire contents of the three-bedroom residence to fast-track the sale. Then he'd moved in with Patrick as he prepared to ship his vintage car and personal possessions across the country.

Patrick shook his head. "I still can't believe that you're leaving California and moving back to New Jersey."

Slumping lower in the leather passenger seat in Patrick's pickup, Joaquin Williamson exhaled. "Believe it, bro. I promised Mom that I would overhaul the gardens at Bainbridge House, and there was no way I could continue serving clients here *and* oversee the project back east. I would've put off relocating until the summer if Taylor hadn't changed the timeline for the hotel's grand opening." What originally had been projected as a two-year timeline for restoring the sprawling property was recently updated to be completed in one.

Patrick smiled, steering with his right hand while he combed the fingers of his left through a wealth of reddish hair. At the same time, minute lines fanned out around his brilliant blue eyes. "That's because you're a control freak and you must micromanage everything, Joaquin. Even when you had a staff of experienced workers, you still had to reexamine everything they did."

Joaquin's smile matched his brother's. "I learned that from you."

Patrick nodded. "And I had an excellent teacher. If you'd worked directly with Dad, then you'd know where I got it from."

"From what I've heard about collaborating with Dad, I'm glad I didn't have to," Joaquin countered. What he did respect about their father was that he'd never brought his work home. Conrad Williamson may have put in long hours Monday through Friday at his Manhattan-based investment company, but he'd devoted every hour of the weekends to his wife and their children.

And despite sharing the same last name, Joaquin and his adopted siblings did not share DNA. However, there wasn't anything they wouldn't do for one another. And that included honoring their mother's wish to restore her late husband's ancestral home to its original magnificence. Joaquin's mantra was "family first and always."

He was looking forward to examining the estate's neglected formal gardens. Over the decades, resident caretakers had managed to keep the lawns and hedges free of weeds; however, that hadn't staved off the overgrowth of what had been carefully laid out flower beds.

What had initially been a residence for countless generations of Bainbridges beginning in the late nineteenth century was now slated to become a twenty-first century hotel and venue for weddings and private parties that could accommodate up to and including three hundred guests.

"I have to admit that I was shocked," Patrick said after a comfortable silence, "when Taylor asked me to allot funds to cover the payroll for around-the-clock workers, but then I understood once he told me he wanted to advance the date for the grand opening."

Joaquin let out an audible breath. "In order to have everything up and running by Memorial Day weekend, he needs the twenty-four-hour, five-days-a-week work crew."

The first week in January, his engineer brother Taylor, who had assumed the responsibility of overseeing the entire restoration, had returned from his honeymoon and started a video session to inform Joaquin and their veterinarian brother Tariq that he had updated the timeline for opening the hotel because of ongoing escalating costs of construction materials and supply chain shortages. Taylor had previously told their sister and professional chef Viola, after he'd conferred with Patrick, that he'd projected celebrating the grand opening this spring rather than the following year.

Patrick shook his head. "I still can't believe how fast the project is moving. When we went there for Taylor's Christmas wedding, only the ballrooms, kitchens and the suites on the second floor were completely renovated."

Joaquin nodded in agreement. Taylor had uploaded weekly videos of the work on the guesthouses and the installation of a second elevator. "When Mom showed us the property last year, not only were we shocked that Dad had spent the first twelve years of his life in a house with eighty-six thousand square feet, while none of us knew of his connection to the Bainbridges."

"Every family has secrets, Joaquin."

"I know that, but what I cannot understand, Pat, is why Dad told Mom about the property and not us. Why didn't he want his kids to know about his ancestors until after he'd died?"

Patrick's eyebrows lifted slightly. "That's because Dad was an extremely complicated man. What I still can't wrap my head around is that our little sister is going to become a married woman," he said, changing the topic.

Joaquin's dark brown eyes met his brother's blue ones. "Our sister will be thirty in a couple of years, so that doesn't make her so little anymore. I'm just surprised that she would fall for Dom because they seem like complete opposites. He's quiet, solitary, while Viola is so outgoing. And he seems quite content being the estate's caretaker."

"What you see in Dominic Shaw isn't exactly what you get."

"What are you talking about?" Joaquin asked.

"Dominic worked remotely for Dad's company after I moved out here to get involved in Andrea's family's winemaking business. He happens to have degrees in economics, accounting and finance."

Joaquin whistled softly. "Talk about family secrets. I had no idea that he'd worked for Dad or that he's a college graduate."

Patrick laughed. "That's because Dad had a mandate that he would never discuss business outside of the office, and it was one rule I followed to the letter. What I still can't get over is the notion that Viola is engaged to a man she just met."

"By the time they're married, they will have known each other nine months," Joaquin said in defense of their sister. Joaquin wanted to tell his brother if he had taken more time to get to know his ex-wife, he would not have married her. Viola had sent out a family group text that Dominic Shaw had proposed marriage on Valentine's Day and that she had accepted.

"Speaking of nine months," Patrick said, "Taylor and Sonja must be counting down the months when they're going to have their baby."

"I don't know about you, Pat, but I'm looking forward to becoming an uncle." Taylor and Sonja were expecting their first child in late May.

Patrick signaled again, changing lanes as the sign leading to the airport appeared in the distance. "Mom is going to be beside herself once she becomes a grandmother. She started talking about being a grandmother right after you married Nadine."

Joaquin had wanted to completely forget about the woman he'd married but knew that wasn't possible. Their brief marriage of less than two years had scarred him emotionally and made him wary of future relationships. He'd dated women but eschewed commitments, and this was something he'd professed before their initial encounter. Some were willing to accept his stance while others walked away, but not before thanking him for his candor.

"Well, Mom will get her wish once Taylor and Sonja have their baby." Their older brother had had a short engagement once Sonja Rios-Martin revealed she was pregnant, and they were married three months later in a Christmas-themed ceremony in a ballroom at Bainbridge House. "Speaking of weddings, have you and Andrea decided on a date?"

A frown settled between Patrick's eyes. "Not yet."

"What are you waiting for, brother? You've been engaged for more than a year."

"We'll marry when the time is right."

Joaquin stared out the passenger-side window at the passing landscape. He wanted to tell Patrick that if he didn't intend to marry Andrea, then he should end the relationship rather than string her along.

"If you say so, Patrick."

"What's that supposed to mean?" Patrick asked, visibly annoyed. His face flushed with high color.

"Nothing." Joaquin didn't want to get into an argument with his brother about his fiancée. He'd lost track of the number of times he'd wanted to remind him that he and Andrea Fincher were totally opposites. She was pampered and outgoing, while Patrick was quiet and controlled. She craved the spotlight while he preferred to remain in the background.

"How long do you think it will take before you miss partying with your wealthy clients?" Patrick asked, again changing the topic.

A hint of a smile lifted the corners of Joaquin's mouth. "You call it partying, to me it was networking."

"Being photographed with celebrities is what you call networking?"

Joaquin nodded. "Yes. Whenever a client invited me to their home for a dinner party and someone mentioned that I'd designed the exteriors, most times I was able to secure another commission. After a couple of years, I learned to turn it on for the paparazzi and turn it off whenever the cameras weren't around. Most of my commissions came from referrals, but there were a few I had to turn down."

He paused. "I made a name for myself in the architectural landscaping field and a lot of money along with that, but there were times when I was close to burnout from all the socializing. So when Mom told us about Bainbridge House last spring, it was a win-win to redesign the formal gardens."

His adopted father had been the last surviving descendant of Charles Bainbridge, who'd been commissioned to build the château during the Gilded Age. While all of Joaquin's siblings had signed on to work directly for Bainbridge House, the exception was financial wizard Patrick, who'd agreed to act as the chief financial officer for the restoration and when the hotel was fully operational. It was an undertaking he was able to accomplish not only electronically but also remotely.

Patrick gave Joaquin a quick glance before returning his attention to the road. "So, you're really serious about leaving Cali for good?"

Joaquin nodded again. "Very serious."

"Good for you."

Joaquin heard something in Patrick's voice that told him his older brother wasn't as comfortable with what would be his current lifestyle now that he and Joaquin would no longer live in the same state. Not only did Patrick live almost three thousand miles away from his family, but his relationship with Andrea had been less than satisfying. However, Patrick was emotionally less demonstrative than any of his siblings. He tended to hide his feelings behind a facade that all was right in his world. And Joaquin wanted to remind Patrick that there was the neglected vineyard on the estate.

Joaquin glanced at his watch. He had a little more than an hour to make his flight.

When he did arrive at Bainbridge House, he would assume residence in one of the six guesthouses on the property. Charles Bainbridge had had the guesthouses erected in a valley away from the main house to assure some of his guests' optimal privacy. Dom and Viola were living in one, and after renovating and updating three more of the remaining six, Taylor and Sonja had recently moved into theirs. Joaquin had agreed with his siblings that living in a guesthouse was preferable to occupying a suite of rooms in the mansion-turned hotel.

Patrick arrived at the airport, maneuvered up to curbside and got out at the same time Joaquin alighted from the pickup. He hugged his brother. "Thanks for everything."

Patrick thumped his younger brother's back. "Anytime."

Tightening his grip on the handles of his carry-on, he walked into the terminal. Rather than reconnecting with his extended family during the holidays, Joaquin would now see Taylor and Viola every day.

And Joaquin had not lied to Patrick when he revealed he'd tired of socializing. He'd had to be in party mode when he would've preferred to stay home and do absolutely nothing. And unlike Patrick, he was unencumbered. No girlfriend. No fiancée. And no wife. It was only after his marriage ended that Joaquin vowed never to be that vulnerable again.

He'd asked Patrick to handle the sale of his landscaping business, and now that he'd sold the condo, he was ready to return home. It had been years since Joaquin had thought of the Garden State as home, despite returning every year for the required family get-togethers. He'd left home at eighteen to attend college in California and stayed. Now, sixteen years later, he would reverse the trip. This time for good.

Shannon Younger sat on the window seat in the apartment above the garage at her parents' house staring at the rain lashing the windows as she waited for the steaming hot chocolate in an oversized mug to cool enough for her to take a sip without burning her tongue. She'd shampooed her hair and then applied a deep conditioner before covering her head with a plastic cap and then lathering her face with a cucumber mask.

She was grateful the manager of the DC restaurant where she filled in as needed in the kitchen had sent her a text the night before alerting her not to come in. She'd been able to sleep in late and share Sunday dinner with her parents. It was something she hadn't done often enough once she'd signed on to work every other weekend.

Working part time would not have been financially possible for Shannon if she didn't live at home with her parents. She'd offered to pay rent for the apartment, but her mother was adamant about taking money from her children—even if they were employed adults. Shannon had decided to offset their generosity by cleaning, doing laundry and occasionally cooking for her schoolteacher mother. She'd had to remind Marcus Sr. and Annette Younger it was the least she could do for their ongoing support as she awaited the position as an executive pastry chef for a New Jersey hotel the following year.

Shannon didn't mind being on call when she'd compared it to her last gig when she'd worked for a condescending caterer his staff referred to as *Beast*. But only out of earshot.

She'd had enough of his yelling and dictatorial mandates and finally resigned three days before the New Year. She knew she'd shocked the man when she'd sent him an email explaining that she would no longer work for him. Rather than reply to Shannon's email, he'd called her offering to double and even triple her fee, but he'd failed to understand that it wasn't about money. It was about respecting those working for him.

She'd endured intense instructors in culinary school because many were perfectionists and sought to bring out the best in their students. And it had paid off because she had graduated at the top of her class at Johnson & Wales University. Shannon had promised herself that if she ever had the opportunity to run her own pastry kitchen, she would not abuse her staff. A smile lifted the corners of her mouth. Running her own kitchen was no longer a pipe dream; it would become a reality next year. A lot had changed in her life since she'd walked away from her acting career and cheating actor-husband. That decision had allowed her to start over as a pastry chef.

It was as if Viola Williamson had become her fairy godmother, granting her most fervent wish. She was introduced to Viola at the Younger family's annual Halloween festivities last October by Dominic Shaw, a friend of her brother's. Viola had mentioned that she and her brothers had inherited a historic château and were currently refurbishing it to eventually open as a hotel and wedding venue.

She and Viola bonded at once; Viola asked Shannon if she would make the wedding cake and desserts for her brother's Christmas-themed wedding as soon as she found out Shannon was a pastry chef. Shannon had quickly agreed. It had been the first time she'd had the full responsibility of creating the desserts for a wedding. Viola even wanted to hire her as head pastry chef for Bainbridge House once the hotel was fully operational.

Her cell phone rang, and she swung her legs over the cushioned window seat and walked on sock-covered feet to the galley kitchen to retrieve it. She set the mug on the countertop. Reaching for the phone, she saw the name of the caller on the screen and smiled.

"Hello, Viola. Would you believe that I was just thinking about you?"

A laugh came through the earpiece. "I hope they were good thoughts."

"Of course they were."

"I'm calling to give you some good news."

Shannon's eyebrows lifted slightly when there came a pause. "Talk to me, Viola."

"Dominic Shaw and I are engaged, and we're planning to marry this June."

Shannon froze, then slowly folded her body down to a stool at the cooking island. "You're kidding?"

"No, I am not kidding. Dom is planning to ask your brother Marcus to be one of his groomsmen, so please don't say anything to Marcus until Dom speaks to him. My sister-in-law will be my matron of honor, and I'd like to ask if you would do me the honor of making the cake and desserts."

Shannon could not stop grinning. "Congratulations! And I am not going to say I knew it. Even though you'd admitted that you and Dom had only known each other for a couple of months, something told me Dom wasn't going to let you go."

"And I'm not going to let him go. Shannon, I'm not ashamed to admit that I'm crazy in love with him."

"Good for you and good for Dom. Do you plan to hold the wedding at Bainbridge House?" Shannon was happy that her brother's friend had been given a second chance at love.

"If the weather holds, then we're planning on a garden ceremony and outdoor reception."

It would be the second time Shannon would assume

the full responsibility of designing a cake and desserts for a Williamson wedding. She'd also done double duty of supervising the Bainbridge House kitchen, because even though Viola was the executive chef, she was also maid of honor for her best friend.

"If I didn't look like a hot mess right now, I'd FaceTime you so you could see me grinning like a Cheshire cat."

"Is that a yes, Shannon?" Viola asked.

"Of course it's a yes. When do you want to get together so we can talk about what you want?"

"You have to let me know when you're free."

"I am free this coming week."

"Good. A lot has changed since you were last here."

"I can't wait to see it."

"And there's a lot more, but I'll wait and tell you once you're here."

Shannon wanted to ask Viola if she and Dom were expecting a baby and if it was their reason for the short engagement, but she didn't want to overstep. Her eventual position as pastry chef at Bainbridge House meant Viola, as executive chef, would be her boss.

"Aren't you going to give me a hint, Viola?"

"Nope. You will see once you get here."

Viola was outgoing and incredibly talented, and she was what Dom needed to get over what he'd gone through with his ex-wife. "Oookaaay," she said, drawing out the word into two distinct syllables. "Now I'm going to spend the weekend wondering what you're hiding from me."

Viola's laugh came through the earpiece again. "The only hint I'm willing to give you is one I bet you're going to like."

Now Shannon's curiosity had gone from moderate to extreme, wondering just what it was that Viola was withholding from her.

"Now, you know you've ruined my day, because I'm going to rack my brain to trying to figure out just what it is you're not telling me."

"As I said before, I'm certain you're going to like what I have to tell you."

Shannon sighed. "If you say so." A beat passed before she said, "Is it okay if I come up on Tuesday?"

"Tuesday is perfect. How long can you stay?"

"I have to be back in Baltimore by Friday because I'm on call."

"That should give us more than enough time to decide what I want. Just text me when you get here, and I'll meet you at the gates."

She congratulated Viola again on her engagement and then hung up. The first time she'd come to the château, Shannon felt as if she'd stepped back in time to when Gilded Age nouveau-riche had flaunted their wealth with items she deemed wretched excess. How many dozen sets of dinnerware, silver and crystal did one family need? Bainbridge House contained more than one hundred rooms, and Sonja, Taylor's wife and the château's architectural historian and archivist, told her that Charles Bainbridge had employed a permanent staff of thirty to see to the needs of him, his wife, ten children and the estate.

Fast-forward 140 years, and once Bainbridge House celebrated its grand opening as a hotel, the Williamsons would have even more staff to run it twenty-four hours a day, seven days a week. Shannon had to admit that once restored to its original splendor, the estate would make one believe they had entered through a truly magical portal. And if Viola had hinted as to the changes since her last visit, then Shannon was looking forward to revisiting Bainbridge House.

Chapter Two

Tapping a button on the Honda Pilot's steering wheel, Shannon activated the Bluetooth feature and sent Viola a voice text message that she'd just left Sparta and that she would text her again when she was minutes from Bainbridge House. Viola replied to her text, saying she would be at the gate in a red pickup. This would be Shannon's second trip to the estate, and she was anxious to see Bainbridge House with updated changes.

She'd left Baltimore at eight that morning, and it had taken six hours to make the trip, which normally took four, because of icy roadway conditions along the New Jersey Turnpike.

She sent Viola another text when she saw the sign along the private road for Bainbridge House and turned onto the driveway leading to the estate where ten-foot stone walls and massive iron gates protected the property. The gates were open and she immediately spied the red vehicle. When Viola told her she would be waiting in a red pickup, Shannon hadn't thought it would be one that reminded her of a collectible vintage Tonka toy. She wasn't astute enough to identify or pinpoint the make, model and year of the truck, but she knew it was older. Bainbridge House was painted in green block letters and was superimposed over a banner of tartan plaid on the driver's-side door.

Shannon came to a complete stop, shifted into Park and tapped a button to lower the driver's-side window as Viola rolled down hers. "I would've been here hours ago if not for the weather," she explained as she spied the ring on Viola's left hand gripping the pickup's steering wheel.

Even from a distance, Shannon was able to discern the exquisite beauty of the large cushion-cut emerald surrounded by a halo of diamonds.

Viola smiled. "It doesn't matter as long as you are safe. I'm going to turn Lollipop around so you can follow me."

"Okay."

After Viola executed a U-turn, Shannon followed the little red pickup Viola had referred to as Lollipop along the cobblestone roadway lined with age-old trees. She was looking forward to when the trees were in full bloom; meanwhile, the snow on the naked branches and on the ground had turned the landscape into a winter wonderland. It had only been two months since Shannon last saw Viola and the Williamsons, but it felt much longer. She'd wanted to slow down and do some sightseeing, but Viola was driving too fast, and Shannon was forced to accelerate to keep pace.

When she'd come to Bainbridge House in December, she hadn't had time to tour the estate because she'd spent three days in the pastry kitchen baking for the wedding.

She'd devoted two full days to baking and decorating the wedding cake and the next two for desserts. For once, she hadn't been relegated to assistant, spending countless hours making marzipan roses, frangipani, leaves and ribbons. Designing a cake for the bride and groom that had exceeded their expectations was a personal triumph and validation that she was now able to supervise her own pastry kitchen.

The Honda rocked and shimmed over a rutted roadway as the land sloped into a valley, where she glimpsed stone structures with tiled roofs through the rapidly falling snow. From a distance, they looked to her like dollhouses. Viola slowed and then came to a complete stop alongside one of the houses and got out of the pickup at the same time Shannon shut off the SUV's engine and alighted from the door.

"Grab your bag. You're going to stay here with me and Dom this week," Viola said when Shannon hesitated.

"I thought I was going to stay at the château."

This was a surprise. Shannon and all the wedding guests had been put up in the renovated second-floor suites, and she was under the impression that she would occupy one during this visit. Walking around to the rear of the SUV, she retrieved a tote and wheeled carry-on from the cargo area, wondering how many more surprises she would encounter before returning to Baltimore. Her curiosity had always gotten the better of her. She always wanted to know who, what and when each time she was promised something new.

Viola shook her head. "Not this time. There is too much construction going on there around the clock. Once all the renovations are completed, you'll have your own suite of rooms at the château," she explained.

Now Shannon was totally confused. "What do you mean 'around the clock'?"

"Taylor hired a day, afternoon and night crew, so I doubt if you would get a restful night's sleep with all the drilling and hammering going on."

"Are you still living at your mother's condo?" She asked Viola.

Viola removed her ski cap and combed her fingers through her hair. The petite chef with a golden-brown complexion, curly dark hair and hazel eyes smiled. "After our engagement, I decided to move in with Dom."

Shannon's eyebrows lifted. "You're living here temporarily?"

Viola's lips parted when she smiled. "No. This is where we're planning to make our home."

She did not understand why Viola had elected to live in the caretaker's guesthouse rather than the château but decided not to pry. "By the way, I love your ring."

Viola stared at the outspread fingers on her left hand. "Thank you. Dom told me his father had given it to his mother when he'd proposed to her."

"It is beautiful." And it was. It was also very romantic that Dom wanted his fiancée to wear a family heirloom.

Viola knew she owed it to Shannon to give her an update about the ongoing restoration and how it would affect her future. When meeting her for the first time, she'd recognized Shannon as Shay—a talented actress who had made a name for herself on a popular television daytime soap. Tall, slender, dark-complected with delicate doll-like features and clear-brown eyes that sparkled like polished amber, the actress-turned-pastry-chef was a definite head turner. Shannon had let her hair grow out and had chemically straightened it. A modified pixie-cut was perfect for her small round face.

The moment she'd seen the desserts Shannon had created for the Younger's annual Halloween get-together, she'd known that she'd found her pastry chef.

When she'd asked Shannon whether she would be willing to become the hotel's resident executive pastry chef, she'd quickly accepted the offer. Aside from a generous salary, Shannon would have her own suite of rooms in the château in what had originally been servants' quarters. The miniscule spaces, located on the château's lower level, were renovated and enlarged into bedroom suites with en suite baths and sitting areas.

"After you're settled in, I'll give you an update on what has been going on at Bainbridge House."

Shannon pulled up the handles on her carry-on. "Where's Dom?"

"He and my brother went to look at greenhouses. Dom sent me a text just before you got here that they are on their way back. They will join us for either what will become a late lunch or early dinner."

"How many greenhouses do you plan to put up?" Shannon asked as Viola opened the solid oaken door.

"At least two and maybe even three. It took a lot of cajoling, but I finally convinced Taylor to go along with me to grow my own herbs and vegetables for farm-to-table dining. I told him it would save a lot of money if we could grow whatever we need on-site rather than buy produce from other local farmers. And there's the formal gardens and an orchard on the estate. Joaquin plans to cultivate exotic flowers and fruit trees for a year-round harvest."

Shannon laughed. "It's like one-stop shopping, where you don't have to leave the property to purchase produce and flowers."

Viola reached for Shannon's tote, anchoring the straps over one shoulder. "Girl, you just don't know the half of it. There's a lot more I must tell you, but that can wait until after you settle in. Come and I will show you to your bedroom."

Shannon didn't know what to expect, but the interior of the guesthouse, with an attached two-car garage, was deceptively large compared to the exterior because of its open floor plan. She didn't have time to examine the furnishings as she walked inside. A basket of dried herbs sat on a large, round pedestal table in the spacious foyer which opened into the living room with a sofa and overstuffed chairs and rough-hewn side tables from a bygone era.

She followed Viola up a winding wrought iron staircase to the second story and was shown a bedroom reminiscent of the ones in the château, but on a smaller scale. Looking at the French provincial sleigh bed, tables, chairs, armoire and highboy, Shannon felt as if she were revisiting the past. It was as though everything at Bainbridge House had been preserved for posterity.

"You and I will share the bathroom on this floor," Viola said. "Dom gets up early, so he uses the one off the kitchen. There's a supply of bath and hand towels, along with facecloths on a table, and you can also find bath accessories in the drawers under the vanity."

Shannon sighed audibly as she shrugged out of her puffy coat. "Do I have time to shower before lunch?" She craved a hot shower after being on the road for six hours, stopping once at a service station for gas, coffee and a bathroom break.

Viola nodded. "Of course. I've prepped everything, so I won't start cooking until you come down."

Shannon smiled. "Spoken like a true chef."

Viola laughed. "You can take the girl out of the kitchen, but you can't take the kitchen out of the girl."

"Word," Shannon drawled. She didn't feel as if she were truly alive until she spent hours in a kitchen cooking and baking. The space had become her happy place, where she challenged herself to concoct different cakes, pastries and confectionaries.

"I'll be downstairs, so you don't have to rush," Viola said as she turned on her heels and walked out.

Shannon opened a door and discovered a closet. She hung up her coat and unlaced her boots, leaving them on a shoe rack, before opening the carry-on and removing a large zippered canvas case with her grooming products and a terry cloth bathroom. Walking out of the bedroom and down the hallway, she found the bathroom and closed the door.

This bathroom had been updated to include double vanities, a soaking tub, a freestanding shower, a commode and a bidet.

Twenty minutes later, after brushing her teeth and showering, Shannon descended the staircase wearing black leggings, a white tailored shirt and black ballet flats. She heard voices coming from the kitchen and walked in to find Dominic Shaw and Joaquin Williamson sitting at the cooking island. When Viola had mentioned her brother, Shannon had believed she was talking about Taylor.

Dom's home was a combination of modern and rustic with double wall ovens, a microwave and a built-in stainless-steel refrigerator and dishwasher. Now she knew why Viola had chosen to live here rather than in a suite at the château. It embodied homeyness.

The kitchen was a chef's dream, with twin sinks,

plenty of granite countertops and a six-burner stove with a grill and range hood. A banquette under an oval stained glass window with enough space for six provided the perfect space to eat breakfast or end the day with coffee and dessert. The light from a trio of pendants above the island, reminiscent of Victorian-era gaslights, glinted off Joaquin's cropped curly black hair and Dom's lightly gray-streaked black waves.

Dom's large dark green eyes met hers as he slipped off the stool, flashing a white-toothed smile with his approach. "Welcome back to Bainbridge House."

Shannon pressed a kiss to his stubble as he folded her against his chest. "Thank you. And congratulations on your engagement."

Dom kissed her forehead. "Thank you. Did Marcus tell you that I want him to be one of my groomsmen?"

"No, he didn't. But I'm certain once he takes a break from doing taxes that he'll call me with the good news." Her brother's accounting firm was überactive during the months of January through May because of the tax season.

Taking her hand, Dom led her into the kitchen at the same time Joaquin stood. "I'm sure you remember Viola's brother Joaquin." Dom's cell phone pinged, and he reached for it in the back pocket of his jeans. "Excuse me, but I have to take this call," he said as he walked out of the kitchen.

Smiling, Shannon extended her hand to Joaquin. "It's nice to see you again."

Shannon wanted to tell Dom there was no way she could forget the man whose presence made her heart beat a little too quickly. To say he was tall, dark and handsome was an understatement. He was a head turner and neck breaker with his rich brown complexion reminiscent of whipped mocha, delicate features and large dark brown eyes. And his all-black attire made his presence even more dramatic. She'd lost count of the number of gorgeous men she'd met as an actress, but there was something about Viola's brother that was different, because he appeared totally oblivious of his good looks and his status as the go-to landscape architect to the stars.

However, Joaquin Williamson hadn't been subtle concocting excuses whenever he'd found himself in her pastry kitchen as she busied herself making wedding desserts. She'd found herself flattered by his attention, yet Shannon knew nothing would come from their mutual attraction. He would return to his festive lifestyle in Cali, while she would go back to the Charm City to work as a pastry chef before coming back to Bainbridge House.

There was also another reason she had no intention of becoming involved with Joaquin. He was a celebrity, as was her ex-husband, and because their romance, marriage and divorce had been played out in front of the cameras, Shannon had promised herself she'd never do that again. Never again did she want to become that transparent.

Joaquin did not want to believe he would see Shannon Younger this soon, but with the change in the timeline for the hotel's grand opening, it was obvious that Viola wanted her to come on board sooner rather than later. When he'd come to New Jersey for his brother's wedding, he was slightly taken aback once he realized the chef commissioned to bake the desserts wasn't a stranger. He and Shay, as she was known then, had been guests at the same dinner party hosted by a high-profile movie director.

He hadn't been able to stop staring at her despite her attending the event with the man who'd been her husband. And he hadn't been the only man mesmerized by the tall, slender woman with waist-length straight hair and a face and body that was certain to conjure up erotic dreams. Joaquin took her hand, smiling as his gaze lingered on her pixie hairstyle. It was of no import to him if Shannon had long hair, short hair or no hair. Joaquin still would think of her as stunning.

"Same here."

Joaquin didn't know why the two words of acknowledgment sounded stilted or rehearsed, but there was something about Shannon that had kept him slightly off balanced. Even though it had been obvious he'd come on to her last year, there was nothing in her demeanor that indicated she was slightly interested in his overtures. It wasn't that she wasn't friendly, but she was all business. After a while, he realized while he'd come to Bainbridge House for a family celebration, Shannon had been there to work.

"Oh, Shannon, now that you're here, you can help me to decide what to make for dessert," Viola said as she emerged from a far corner in the kitchen. She cradled several Mason jars against her chest over a black bibbed apron.

Joaquin's gaze swung from Shannon to his sister as he moved quickly to take the jars from her. "I'll take those." He silently cursed Viola's timing, because he wanted to ask Shannon how long she was staying. "By the way, what's for lunch?"

"It's too late for lunch," Viola countered. "I'm thinking of an early dinner."

He read the labels on the jars, noticing they were dated and filled with fruit. "What's for dinner?"

"Speaking of dinner," Dom said, preempting Viola's reply as he reentered the kitchen. "Taylor just called to say he and Sonja are coming over later to eat with us."

Viola bit her lower lip as if deep in thought. "Shannon, I hope you don't mind helping me now that I must change the menu."

"Of course not."

"I don't mind helping," Dom volunteered.

Viola smiled at her fiancé. "That's okay, darling. I believe Shannon and I can handle this."

Joaquin rested an arm on Dom's shoulder. "I suppose that is our cue to either watch television or get in a couple of games of pool while the ladies work their magic in the kitchen."

Dom narrowed his eyes at his future brother-in-law. "If you think you're going to hustle me in a game of pool, then you're crazy as a loon."

"Who told you that I'm a pool hustler?" Joaquin asked.

"Taylor. We had a wager, and I managed to beat him in three out of five games. After each game, we took a shot of your father's prized Balvenie Caribbean Cask fourteen-year-old single malt whisky, and that's when he told me you were good enough to be a pool shark."

"There will be no gambling and doing shots today, Dominic Shaw, because we have a guest," Viola called out.

Joaquin winked at Viola. "Shooting pool isn't gambling, sis."

"Let me warn you, Shannon, that every time Dom and Taylor shoot pool, there's always a wager," Viola said, frowning. "And it's just an inane excuse for them indulge in frat-boy craziness when they do shots."

"You could solve that problem if you get rid of the pool table," Shannon countered.

"Trust me, Shannon, it's something I've been thinking about," Viola said.

Dom shook his head. "Oh, hell no! I am not getting rid of my table. It's been in my family for years."

Joaquin glared at Shannon. "See what you've started."

He met Dom's eyes. "Once Viola gets an idea in her head, she's like a pit bull. She just will not let it go." He gave Viola a death stare. "Dom said he's not getting rid of his pool table, and that's that."

Dom flashed a Cheshire cat grin. "Thanks for having my back," he said under his breath.

"Come on, brother. Let's watch an encore of last night's basketball game. It's safer than pool because I don't need your sister getting on my case."

Joaquin followed Dom through the dining area and into an expansive space set up as a game room. He hadn't lied to Shannon about his sister's stubbornness. He didn't like calling out his sister, or taking sides, yet he knew as the youngest Williamson, and the only girl, their parents had indulged her to a fault. This wasn't to say that he hadn't also been guilty of giving in to Viola's whims. But Viola could also be too trusting and generous, and that prompted some men to take advantage of her.

However, Dom had admitted to him the only thing he'd wanted from Viola was her love and trust. And that it hadn't mattered that she was an heiress to an estate. It would be Dom's second marriage, and during the drive to look at greenhouses, the estate's caretaker had revealed to Joaquin the circumstances that had led to his divorce.

He and Dom had something in common, because he was the only one of Conrad and Elise's five children who'd been married, and in hindsight, Joaquin realized it was a mistake he did not intend to repeat. For Joaquin it had been once burned, twice shy. And now at thirty-four, he was free to live his life, and his sole focus was reconnecting with his siblings and overseeing the neglected gardens at Bainbridge House to fulfill their late father's final wish to restore his ancestral home to its original splendor.

Joaquin settled down on an overstuffed chair as Dom reached for the remote control to turn on the wall-mounted flat-screen to a sports channel. "How about a beer to tide us over until we eat?" Dom asked.

"Sure."

It'd been nearly a week since he'd returned to New Jersey and moved into one of the updated guesthouses on the property. Boxes labeled with their contents were stored in the smaller of the three bedrooms, yet he hadn't found it imperative to open all of them, while his Aston Martin Virage convertible was parked in the attached garage.

He'd arrived in time to see Elise Williamson off before she left the States for a four-week vacation in the French and Italian Rivieras. The tears he'd glimpsed in his mother's eyes when he'd walked into her condo had affected him more than he was willing to admit, when she'd whispered in his ear *You don't know how long I've prayed for you to come home.* He'd reassured his mother not only was he home, but it was to stay.

A feeling of peace swept over Joaquin at the same time a smile tilted the corners of his mouth. Living in the exclusive gated condo in the Hollywood Hills with on-site concierge paled in comparison to spending the afternoon and evening with family members he didn't get to see often enough. The sounds of laughter coming from the kitchen reminded him of his childhood—an incredible childhood he never would've experienced if he'd never been adopted by Conrad and Elise Williamson.

Dom returned and handed him a bottle of cold beer. "What did I miss?"

"Not much. The second half just ended."

Dom flopped down in a chair several feet away. "You didn't hear it from me, but your sister said she's glad you decided to come back to stay," he whispered conspiratorially.

Joaquin frowned. "Did she think I wouldn't?"

"Do not shoot the messenger. She meant after you restore the gardens, you would head back to California."

Joaquin shook his head. "That is not going to happen. My father was able to do in death what he hadn't been able to do in life, and that is to bring his family together to breathe life into his ancestral home. A home that is as much yours as the rest of us."

Dom gave him a sidelong glance. "Who told you?"

A sly smile flitted over Joaquin's features. "You mean about you being distantly related to my father?" Dom nodded. "Mom. She told me about the dustup you had with her before Taylor's wedding, when she saw you and Viola hugged up together."

Dom grunted under his breath. "That whole ordeal was hellish. Viola had not only moved out of Elise's condo and in with Taylor, but she'd refused to talk to her."

"That had to be serious."

"You do not know the half of it, Joaquin. I went to Arizona for a week, and once I got back, Elise apologized for calling me hired help and we're now remarkably close."

Reaching over, Joaquin touched his bottle to Dom's. His mother had called the estate's caretaker "hired help" when he was anything but. The blood of Charles Bainbridge ran in Dom's veins, and that made him more connected to the estate than any of Conrad and Elise's adopted children. "All's well that ends well." Halftime ended, and Joaquin forced himself to focus on the game instead of the woman in the kitchen with his sister.

He didn't know what there was about Shannon Younger that had him so intrigued, but he knew he had time to find out.

Chapter Three

"What's on the menu, chef?" Shannon asked Viola at the same time she slipped a black-and-white pinstriped apron over her head and looped the ties around her waist.

"I'd originally planned to serve a smoky ham and split pea soup with a salad and roast beef, blue cheese and bacon paninis, but with Taylor and Sonja joining us, we need to prepare something that will combine lunch and dinner."

"What about Italian?" Shannon suggested.

Viola's hazel eyes grew wide. "That's a great idea. I have enough chicken breasts to make francese and parmesan, and I know Sonja likes lasagna with sausage. And I also have a half dozen jars of tomato sauce in the pantry for the lasagna."

"If you have the ingredients on hand, then we can make all three to give everyone a choice. I'm willing to make the pasta for the lasagna and linguine with garlic and oil for the chicken parmesan and francese," Shannon volunteered.

Viola smiled. "Aren't you fancy? Making your own pasta," she said teasingly. She opened a drawer under the countertop, took out two large bandannas and handed one to Shannon.

"Me and flour are besties," Shannon confirmed with a wide grin, as she covered her hair with the bandanna.

"I took out some jars of canned apples and peaches to make dessert for dinner, but you're welcome to use them, that is, if you don't mind making dessert."

Shannon wanted to ask Viola if she was kidding. Making desserts was obviously her specialty. "Of course I don't mind. Even though I live in an apartment over the garage in my parents' house, I don't get to cook for them because my mother jealously guards her kitchen like a secret service agent protecting the president. What she will allow is for me to occasionally make Sunday dinner for her and Dad, so most times I just cook for myself."

A mysterious smile tilted the corners of Viola's mouth. "That's going to end once you come on board as the executive pastry chef when we host the grand opening during the upcoming Memorial Day weekend."

Shannon went still, her heart pumping a runaway rhythm in her chest as she replayed Viola's statement in her head. "Are you talking about *this* year's Memorial Day?" The query was barely above a whisper.

"Yes. Taylor has accelerated the timeline to complete the restoration because the cost of labor and construction supplies are escalating exponentially."

"So, that is what you meant about day, afternoon and night crews."

"Exactly."

Shannon watched Viola as she opened the refrigerator/

freezer and took out the ingredients they needed to make dinner for six. "I guess this means I'll have to come on board sooner rather than a lot later."

Viola handed her vacuum-sealed packages of chicken breasts labeled with the date. "If it's possible, I'd like you to be available before the middle of next month. We're going to have to put our heads together to create menus and taste-test everything. And because there will still be construction, you'll have to move in to one of the renovated guesthouses until you're able to live at the château."

The shock of relocating from Maryland to New Jersey in a matter of weeks assaulted Shannon like tiny missiles she couldn't dodge, because she'd resigned herself to believe she had at least a year. "How many guesthouses are on the estate?"

"Six. I'm living in one with Dom, and Taylor and Sonja are living in another. Joaquin moved into one last week. The remaining three are for my brother Tariq and hopefully Patrick, if he ever decides to leave California and move back, and my mother when she sells her condo to live closer to her grandchildren."

"So, all of your brothers prefer to live in the guesthouses rather than at the hotel."

Viola nodded. "None of us want to live under the same roof where we work. The guesthouses are an acre apart, which allows everyone a modicum of privacy. We grew up in a 5,000-square-foot farmhouse set on four acres in Belleville. The house had six bedrooms and seven baths, so we are used to having our own personal space."

When Shannon was introduced to Viola last fall, she had no idea that the woman who had enthralled Dom had inherited an estate with her brothers.

When she'd met Taylor Williamson for the first time, she was taken aback when she'd recognized him as the former high-profile male model T. E. Wills. And when she was introduced to Joaquin, Shannon wanted to tell Viola that she was more than familiar with the landscape architect. That they'd met each other at the soiree of a movie director, and she'd been mesmerized by his incredibly good looks and dark eyes that seemed not to look at her but through her. But once all the Williamsons were in attendance to celebrate the wedding of Taylor to Sonja Rios-Martin, Shannon realized that despite sharing the same name, they were not biological siblings.

Whooping sounds coming from the other side of the house shattered her reverie. It was obvious Dom and Joaquin were enjoying their game. "Not only will we have to create menus and taste-test the selections, but we'll also have to hire kitchen staff."

"You're right," Viola agreed as she added a package of sausage on the countertop next to the chicken breasts. She paused. "What do you think of the idea of staffing an all-female kitchen?"

Shannon let out a shriek before placing a hand over her mouth to keep from screaming out her approval. "I love it," she whispered.

Viola's smile was dazzling, her hazel eyes sparkling like polished jewels. "I was hoping you would agree. I've stayed connected with some of the women who graduated with me, and I have hinted about bringing them on board a couple of weeks before the hotel opens for business."

Excitement eddied through Shannon as she felt Viola's enthusiasm as surely as it was her own. "I'm still in touch with one pastry chef who I'm certain would be willing to move here from Silver Spring, Maryland."

"I ran this idea past Sonja, and she also agreed with me," Viola said as she lowered her voice. "We both know that the culinary arts have been and still are a male-dominated profession despite the increasing numbers of women becoming chefs, but I'm almost certain we're going to get some flack about being discriminatory."

"Can't you offset that by having a diverse waitstaff along with a sommelier and banquet manager?"

Viola flashed a smile. "Yes. And I also plan to hire a butcher."

Shannon's eyes shimmered in excitement when she said, "I remember seeing the photos of thirty-four women of color cadets posing in their uniforms with sabers as West Point graduates, and I was so overwhelmed with emotion that I started crying and couldn't stop. It was one of the most powerful photographs of women that I've ever seen. It's also on video, so I'll pull it up on my phone and show it to you later."

Viola took her cell phone off a shelf and handed it to Shannon. "I'd like to see it now." The seconds ticked as Viola stared at the screen. She appeared visibly moved when she turned off the phone and replaced it on the shelf. "That does it. We are going to have an all-female kitchen and to hell with those who have a problem with it."

Shannon could not stop grinning. In fact, she was still grinning as she followed Viola into the pantry.

"You have enough food here to feed several NFL teams."

Viola picked up a wicker basket and filled it with four jars of tomato sauce. "Dom and I go into town about once a month to shop for groceries and end up buying in bulk. Then when we get a measurable snowfall we just hunker down and cook for each other. And now that Sonja has just begun her last trimester, I've offered to cook for her and Taylor several nights a week."

"Do you ever go out to eat?"

"Yes. Occasionally, we drive into town to eat at Jameson's. It's a pub owned by Dom's friend J.J. If the snow stops and the roads are cleared by tomorrow afternoon, we can stop in. They're now offering an incredibly delicious lamb burger in addition to their angus burgers."

"I love lamb," Shannon confessed. "In fact, I prefer it to beef. Whenever I buy grass-fed baby lamb chops, I grill them with garlic and rosemary. And if I want to deviate from the norm then I add a honey habanero with crushed hazelnuts."

Viola closed her eyes. "Now you're singing my song. I happen to have a rack of lamb in the freezer. I'll make sure to defrost it, and we can have it before you leave. And speaking of lamb, the Bainbridges used to raise sheep on the property. They also had chickens, ducks and goats. Dom told me they had to get rid of the goats because they would chase the sheep and fight with the dogs."

"I can't imagine living in the same place all of my life where I'd been born and raised."

Viola removed a large canister of flour from a shelf. "I must agree with you about living here all my life. However, it's different with Dom. He loves it, even though he's lived here alone once his father and stepmother moved to Arizona several years ago. Personally, I would've gone stir-crazy staying here day to day without seeing or talking to another living soul."

"That's because you were raised with four brothers. There's just me and Marcus."

"By the way, do you miss acting?" Viola asked, changing the topic.

Shannon shook her head as she took the basket from Viola. "No."

"Is it because of what happened between you and your ex?"

Shannon met Viola's eyes, knowing if she wanted an

honest and open relationship with her, she needed to be forthcoming. "Yes. It wasn't only that he'd cheated on me, but once it'd become public, it was as if the entire world knew that Shay had been the last to know that her costar husband had gotten another cast member pregnant. What took the proverbial rag off the bush was that the writers wrote her pregnancy into the script."

Viola went still. "The writers and producers knew she was carrying your husband's baby?" she whispered.

"They had to know, Viola. What is the saying? The wife is always the last to know."

"How could they do that?"

"They did it because it boosted ratings. It had become a Brad Pitt, Angelina Jolie and Jennifer Aniston triangle played out in real time on a soap opera, and that's when I decided I didn't want my private life continually dissected in entertainment tabloids. My agent worked out a deal where I was able to get out of my contract, and as soon as that was settled, I concentrated on divorcing Hayden." What Shannon couldn't tell Viola was that her philandering husband hadn't wanted a divorce, because he'd claimed he'd been tricked into sleeping with his on-screen lover, but Shannon refused to listen to his lies and pleas for a reconciliation.

"One of these days, I'll tell you about the losers I hooked up with before I swore never again," Viola said as she led the way out of the pantry. "The scenarios were perfect for a reality show."

Shannon reentered the kitchen, smiling when she heard Joaquin and Dom shouting at the top of their lungs that one of the officials had made the wrong call when a player was fouled.

When she met and fell in love with Hayden Chandler, things moved fast. Although not paired as onscreen lovers, it was their off-screen relationship that had made headlines. After a six-month whirlwind romance, they were married, and the following year, she was nominated for a Daytime Emmy. Her fairy-tale world came crashing down once she'd discovered her husband's onscreen romance with a fellow actress didn't end when the director yelled 'cut.' Shannon was certain she could've endured the humiliation if it hadn't been played out in social media and become salacious fodder for TMZ

And once she'd made the decision to turn her back on a career she'd wanted since she'd first performed in a sixth-grade play, Shannon returned to Baltimore to plan the next phase of her life. She was twenty-two, divorced and solvent when she shed the persona of Shay the actress to embrace the real Shannon Younger.

Shannon's life changed again at twenty-three, when she applied to Johnson & Wales University. After earning a two-year degree in culinary arts and another two-year degree in baking and pastry arts, Shannon was ready to embrace her new career as a professional chef.

Shannon knew she was going to enjoy her tenure at Bainbridge House as she and Viola worked together effortlessly in the kitchen as if they'd orchestrated every move in advance. She poured flour on the countertop, formed a circle and cracked several eggs in the middle. She then gently mixed the flour and eggs into a ball, gently kneaded the dough and then rolled it out into a circle. Reaching for a dough cutter crimper wheel, she cut the dough into two-inch wide slices for lasagna noodles.

"I can't believe you make your own pasta."

Her head popped up, and Shannon saw Joaquin standing at the entrance to the kitchen, holding two beer bottles. She'd been so involved in making the pasta that she hadn't detected his presence. She smiled. "You don't have to drown your pasta with sauce when it's made with fresh dough."

Joaquin took a step inside the kitchen. "It's looks so easy when you do it."

"It is."

"If that's the case, then will you teach me how to make it?"

Shannon noticed that Viola had stopped pounding the boneless and skinless chicken breasts sandwiched between pieces of parchment she had placed on a cutting board and watched the interaction between her and Joaquin. "That can't happen because I'm only going to be here for a couple of days before I return to Baltimore."

A hint of a smile lifted the corners of Joaquin's mouth. "What about when you come back before our grand opening?"

Shannon met his dark eyes. "That all depends on when *you* come back." She'd assumed he would stay on at Bainbridge House, complete his project, and then return to California.

Joaquin smiled, showing a mouth filled with straight white teeth. "I am already back. Viola didn't tell you that I'm now living on the estate?"

"She did mention that you're staying in one of the guesthouses."

"I am not staying, Shannon. I'm now living in it. I don't want to infringe on your schedule, but anytime you're free, I'd like you to give me a few lessons. And I'm willing to pay you."

Shannon went back to cutting strips of dough. "That's not necessary," she said in a quiet voice, "because I don't think you could afford me."

It was obvious Joaquin wasn't expecting the rejoinder when he glared at her. "I'm definitely not a pauper, Shannon."

Her cutter halted in midair as she gave him a direct stare. "And neither am I, Joaquin, which means I don't want or need your money."

Joaquin's jaw dropped. "I—"

"That's enough, Joaquin," Viola said, interrupting whatever he intended to say. "Please get what you've come here for and stop bothering Shannon while she's prepping."

"I didn't know I was bothering her," he countered, frowning.

"He's not bothering me, Viola," Shannon said quickly, hoping to diffuse a verbal confrontation between sister and brother. "What else would you need me to assist you with?" she asked Joaquin.

"Biscuits. Whenever I make them for my eggs Benedict, they invariably come out like hockey pucks."

Shannon placed the strips of pasta on a floured board. She wanted to ask him why he used biscuits when the recipe called for English muffins. "We can talk about this later."

Joaquin nodded. "Thank you. Sis, where can I put these empty bottles?" he asked Viola.

"Leave them on the countertop near the sink. They'll have to be rinsed out before they go into the recycle bin in the mudroom."

Shannon waited for Joaquin to leave the kitchen, then turned her attention to Viola. "I don't mind showing your brother how to make pasta whenever I have some free time."

"Your free time is your own, Shannon, I don't intend to micromanage your life. All my brothers know how to cook, and I must admit very well."

"Who taught them?"

"My mother."

Shannon continued to cut dough into strips for lasagna as Viola revealed her mother had hired a woman to come to their home three days a week to clean and do laundry, but refused to employ a cook because she insisted on preparing meals for her family. "I don't know if she was paranoid about someone other than herself cooking for her children, but she made certain to prepare breakfast, lunch and dinner in between homeschooling all of us. Mama claimed she taught her sons to cook because she didn't want them to rely on a woman to feed them. Taylor makes the most delicious chicken and waffles I've ever eaten, and believe me, I've had enough of them to say that. And Dom is no slouch in the kitchen. He made shrimp and grits that were so lip-smacking good that I'm thinking about putting it on our Sunday brunch menu, along with Taylor's chicken and waffles."

"Brunch is my favorite meal."

"Mine too," Viola agreed. "Not to change the subject, but is there something going on between you and Joaquin?"

Shannon's hands stilled. "Why would you ask that?"

"I'd noticed a quite a bit of interaction between the two of you last year."

Shannon knew it was just a matter of time before the Williamsons discovered she and Joaquin hadn't met for the first time last December. "Joaquin and I were invited to the same dinner party hosted by a film director ten years ago. I was married to Hayden at the time, and Joaquin had attended with a young woman who had clung to him as if he were her lifeline. Even though we weren't formally introduced, I later discovered he'd designed the exteriors for the director."

"You never spoke to each other?" Viola asked.

"No," Shannon said, shaking her head. "So, when I realized who he was when I came here last year, I teased him, saying, 'We finally meet again.' And when he'd called me Shay, I told him that I'd left that life behind and that I'd like for him to call me Shannon."

Viola's eyebrows lifted. "I can't believe you two have history."

"Seeing each other across a crowded room isn't what I think of as history."

"There's no doubt you'd made quite an impression on Joaquin if he remembered you after ten years."

"What he may have been impressed with was the image of an actress who had recently earned an Emmy Award nomination."

"There was more than that, Shannon. Remember, Tinseltown is filled with actors," Viola stated.

"What are you trying to say?"

"My brother likes you."

Shannon felt a shiver of annoyance eddy through her. She didn't want Joaquin to like her, because despite his good looks and celebrity status, she'd vowed never to be taken in again by a man possessing those attributes. "His liking can never go any further than friendship."

"Then I predict you and Joaquin will get along well. I'd overhead him tell our mother that he doesn't want to get serious about a woman because he likes being single."

"Well, that makes two of us. And when it comes to marriage, I've been there, done that."

"Are you saying you'll never marry again?"

"I never say never, Viola. Love and life are strange and oftentimes very unpredictable. They will sneak up on you when you least expect. Right now, my focus is becoming executive pastry chef for Bainbridge House."

Viola rinsed and patted the cutlets dry, then placed them on a platter and seasoned them with salt and pepper. "That's what Dom and I agreed to when we first met, and look at us now. We're planning a wedding."

"You're planning a wedding because you fell in love with Dom and he with you. It took me a while after my divorce to realize I wasn't as much in love with Hayden as I was in awe with his image. He was older, erudite, drop-dead gorgeous, and had scores of women vying for his attention. I must admit, my ego overrode my so-called common sense when he asked if I would go out to dinner with him. Dinners led to sleeping together, and when he proposed marriage, I was in so deep that I couldn't refuse anything he asked."

"Was he your first serious relationship?" Viola questioned.

Shannon nodded. "Yes, in a sense, compared to my high school boyfriend."

"What he did was take advantage of you, Shannon. How old were you when you married him?"

"I'd just celebrated my twentieth birthday."

Viola slowly shook her head. "Young, innocent and unsuspecting."

"No, Viola. Young and stupid." She exhaled an audible breath. "Enough talk about my cheating ex. I'm finished with the lasagna noodles, so if you want to begin putting it together, I'll start on dessert before I make the linguine."

"What are you making for dessert?"

Shannon pointed to the jars of canned apples. "Handheld apple pies. I need a large cookie sheet."

Viola opened the door to a cabinet under the countertop. "One large cookie sheet coming up."

For the second time in less than three months Shannon shared a kitchen with Viola, and she was looking forward to the time when she would get up every morning and go into the pastry kitchen at Bainbridge House to bake bread and desserts for hotel guests.

The delicious mouthwatering aroma of the baked lasagna made with layers of thinly sliced sweet Italian sausage; spinach; marinara sauce seasoned with garlic, basil and oregano; ricotta and freshly shredded mozzarella cheese had filled the kitchen by the time Taylor and Sonja arrived.

Shannon greeted the obviously pregnant Sonja with a warm embrace. "You look incredible." Sonja wore a flowing knitted tunic top in a flattering orange over a pair of black leggings. Her curly dark hair was styled in a single braid and secured with an elastic tie, while her bare face radiated good health.

Sonja rolled her eyes upward. "Incredibly bigger than the last time you saw me."

"How are you feeling?"

"Great now that I'm not experiencing anymore nausea."

Taylor flashed a wide grin and folded Shannon against his chest. "Welcome back."

Shannon felt the power in the model-turned-engineer's lean body as he hugged her. "Thank you. How does it feel knowing you're going to become a papa?"

Taylor smiled, his dark eyes in an equally dark face shimmering with excitement. "I'm counting down the months." He sniffed the air. "Something smells good."

"We're having Italian tonight," Viola called out as she wiped her hands on the towel tucked under the ties of her apron. She hugged and kissed her sister-in-law and then her brother when he handed her a bag holding bottles of wine. "We're eating in the dining room tonight."

"I'm going to wash my hands and then set the table," Sonja volunteered.

"No, you're not," Viola countered. "The guys can set the table, so you go sit down and relax."

"That's all I do," Sonja said in protest. "I sit more than I stand."

Shannon met Sonja's eyes. "You'll treasure the times when you can sit, because after my sister-in-law became a mother, she was on her feet around the clock. Whenever I wasn't working, I'd go over and babysit so she and my brother could have a date night."

Taylor dropped a kiss on Sonja's hair. "Go and sit, sweetheart. There are enough dudes here who know how to set a table."

Viola pressed her palms together. "Dom will show them where to get everything, while Shannon and I finish up with dinner."

Shannon returned to the kitchen with Viola to boil the linguine and toss it with toasted garlic and extra virgin olive oil. Although she liked cooking for herself, it was different when putting together meals for others. It was as if she'd disappear into an alternate universe where everything she'd been taught came rushing back, and she was able to put her own spin on a particular recipe.

Viola's kitchen was a cornucopia of everything a cook or chef needed to concoct wonderful dishes. "I noticed you have lardoons in the fridge. Do you mind if I fry them up and add them to the salad?" she asked Viola.

"Girl, please. You don't have to ask. Just do you."

Shannon knew there were times when she tended to change a dish to make it more traditionally French or Italian, and the result usually garnered raves that buoyed her confidence. And despite being a professionally trained chef, it was baking desserts that took preference, while designing and decorating cakes were her passion.

Dom, Joaquin and Taylor had set the dining room table with seating for six with delicate bone china, silver and crystal stemware before she and Viola set bowls, platters, dishes and serving pieces on the table. Viola had set out a half carafe of nonalcoholic fruit punch for Sonja, while Dom uncorked bottles of rosé and white wine.

Viola sat at the end of the table opposite Dom, while Shannon sat next to Joaquin opposite Sonja and Taylor. Dom had filled their glasses, turned on an audio component, tuning it to a station featuring cool jazz before sitting.

Joaquin raised his glass, smiling. "Here's to long and lasting friendship."

She touched the fragile glass to his. "To friendship."

Both took a sip, their eyes meeting over the rim, and in that instant, Shannon wondered what was going on behind the dark eyes. His mouth was smiling, but there was something in his stare that unsettled her, and she wondered if it was curiosity; however, her woman's intuition communicated it was lust.

I can't, she told herself. There was no way she was going to fall under the sensual spell Joaquin Williamson projected by just existing, and now she chided herself for agreeing to teach him how to cook. However, she'd given her word, and those who knew Shannon Younger well were aware that she always kept it.

He leaned closer to her. "I am not the big bad wolf looking to attack unsuspecting damsels, Shannon," he whispered.

She blinked. "If you're not a wolf, what are you, then?" she asked sotto voce.

"I'd think of myself as one of the good guys who has never taken advantage of a woman."

Shifting slightly in her chair, she gave him a long stare. Shannon wanted to believe him, but it wasn't Joaquin who'd made her feel uncertain about where their friendship would lead. She didn't trust herself around him, because there was something about Joaquin that reminded her that she hadn't befriended or been involved with a man since her divorce.

And Shannon had to continue to tell herself that she was immune to Joaquin—a man who made her feel things she'd forgotten existed whenever her traitorous thirty-year-old body reminded her that she'd once been a deeply passionate woman who'd enjoyed sharing her bed with a man.

"That's good to know," she said, pretending to be interested in her salad tossed with light vinaigrette.

It was their last exchange, as the conversations floating around the table focused on the château's ongoing restoration.

Chapter Four

Taylor touched a napkin to the corners of his mouth. "I know once we open the hotel, the food will be phenomenal. Viola and Shannon, you two are extraordinary chefs."

"Hear, hear," came a chorus from the others at the table.

Shannon shared a grin with Viola. She had to admit the dishes were outstanding.

"Are you guys ready for dessert and coffee?" Viola asked, and her query was followed by moans and groans.

"Can we wait on that?" Taylor asked, "Because I'd like to give everyone some news about what Dom and I have agreed upon." He paused, then said, "Dom will become Bainbridge House's business manager. And that means he will be running the hotel."

Viola looked at Taylor and then her fiancé. "Did you know about this?"

Dom nodded. "Taylor and I decided this last year."

"And why didn't you tell me?" Viola asked.

"Taylor and I decided it would remain between us until the time was right," Dom said.

Taylor held up a hand, stopping Viola as she opened her mouth. "I don't want you to get into this with Dom, I was the one who'd asked him not to say anything. He will also manage the dining room staff and oversee the food and beverage and other supplies, which will leave you and Shannon to concentrate solely on cooking and supervising your kitchen personnel."

Viola narrowed her eyes at her fiancé before she glared at Taylor. "Brother, love, will Shannon and I have complete autonomy when hiring and or firing our kitchen staff?"

"Of course," Taylor said.

"Even if we decide to staff an all-female kitchen?" Viola asked.

"That's sexist," Joaquin said, frowning.

Shannon nudged him with her elbow. "Did you have any women on your landscaping crew?"

He lowered his eyes. "Well, no."

"If that's the case, then you can't have a problem with Viola and I staffing an all-female kitchen."

Sonja picked up her glass of punch. "I wholeheartedly agree with Viola and Shannon."

Taylor turned to look at his wife. "Did you put this bug in Viola's ear?"

Sonja's expression was unabashed innocence. "No. But she did hint that she wanted to hire some of the women she'd worked with, and I told her go for it."

"Chickens and greenhouses," Taylor murmured. "What's next?"

"What are you talking about?" Joaquin asked Taylor.

"Last year, when you were schmoozing with movie stars, Sonja started talking about raising chickens and putting up greenhouses on the estate, then our dear sister said the same as if they'd conspired against me. And now instead of two against one, Shannon had joined the conspiracy."

"Let it go, brother," Dom said in quiet voice, "and just roll with it. You of all people should know that once your sister gets something in her head, she refuses to relent. She couldn't stop talking about the old red pickup truck until I finally had it restored and gave it to her."

Viola flashed a Cheshire cat grin. "Lollipop is now *my* baby. Dom was very generous on Valentine's Day when he gave me Lollipop, a gold bracelet with a red pickup truck charm and an engagement ring."

"Nice move, Dom," Joaquin said under his breath.

He knew his sister could be a handful, but it was obvious his future brother-in-law knew what to do to make Viola happy. That was something Dom hadn't been able to accomplish with his ex-wife, and it was the same with Joaquin when he'd tried to give Nadine whatever she wanted, but it still wasn't enough.

He shook his head as if he could completely erase what he'd experienced with a woman who had made him question what he was doing and why. Nadine didn't like the studio apartment he'd rented, and insisted he purchase a one-bedroom in an upscale section of Los Angeles, but when he told her he couldn't afford it because he was still a college student, she'd refused to talk to him. He relented and after they'd moved into a larger apartment that left him living paycheck to paycheck. And what he'd refused to do was ask his father for more money.

However, the adage "act in haste, repent in leisure" did not apply to Joaquin Williamson. He'd married Nadine Phillips three months after meeting her for the first time, and divorced her less than two years later, citing irreconcilable differences. The breakup was amicable, and because there were no children or a division of property, he'd felt comfortable helping her father at his nursery while he continued to pursue his graduate studies.

"How does it feel to give up sunny California to become a Jersey boy once again?" Sonja asked as she gave him a direct stare.

"It feels really good," he said truthfully.

"When Taylor told me you were coming back sooner rather than later, I really didn't believe him," Viola said to Joaquin.

A frown settled between his eyes. "Why would you say that? You know I always keep my promise whenever I say something."

"It's just that you seem so anxious to get back to California whenever you came here for our family holiday gatherings," Viola countered.

"That's because I had a business to run. It's different now because I've sold the company and my condo, so there's nothing to go back to."

"Don't let Viola get to you, Joaquin," Taylor interjected as he smiled at his brother. "When I told our doubting sister that you were coming back to stay, she said she'd believe it when she saw it."

Leaning back in his chair, Joaquin stretched out his legs under the table and crossed his arms over a black waffle-weave sweater. "Neither rain, sleet nor snow will keep me from restoring the landscape to its previous grandeur. I'm also thinking about adding a few other features."

"Will you have to wait until the ground thaws completely before you begin the restoration?" Shannon asked him.

Joaquin turned his head to meet her eyes. "Actually,

no. I have the original blueprints for the garden and orchard, so I know what was planted if I want to replace them or introduce new plants." He smiled. "And I'll also try and make certain you and Viola will have enough fruit for your recipes."

Shannon returned his smile with a friendly one. "I'm going to need some edible flowers for the cakes I plan to make for weddings, and jams for high tea."

Taylor groaned aloud. "I didn't believe it when Viola talked about hosting afternoon tea."

"I think it's a lovely ritual," Sonja said as she folded her napkin and placed it next to her plate.

Taylor shook his head. "See what I've been talking about," he mumbled. "Once the three of them put their heads together about something, it's game on."

"Taylor wants no part of afternoon tea because he doesn't like cucumber sandwiches," Viola explained. "He claims cucumbers belong in salads."

Shannon was amused by the interaction between Taylor, his wife and his sister. It was clear they'd formed ranks to overrule him when securing whatever they wanted. "Cucumber sandwiches aren't the ones served at afternoon tea."

"What would you make?" Joaquin asked her.

"Of course, there will be the requisite tea cakes, but sandwiches could be crab and ginger triangles, deviled ham toasts, egg and sprout circles, avocado and bacon, spicy chicken sandwiches, and mini quiches just to name a few."

A smile spread across Taylor's handsome features. "Now you're talking."

"Is it because I mentioned meat?" Shannon teased.

"Damn straight," Taylor said. His smile was now a

full-on grin. "You can't expect a grown-ass man to survive eating food fit for rabbits."

"Here, here," chorused Dom and Joaquin.

Shannon shared a smile with Sonja and Viola, realizing if they were of one accord on a particular topic, the chances were they would be able to achieve whatever they wanted—if within reason. "I'm willing to predict that serving high tea in the solarium will become quite popular for some hotel guests."

Sonja pressed her palms together. "I'm going to sign up at least a couple of days a week just to eat the finger sandwiches and tea cakes. And if you're going to serve ginger, lemon or rose tea, then count me in."

"Are there going to be menu samples before the hotel's grand opening?" Joaquin asked.

Shannon laughed softly. "Yes. There will be a lot of samples."

Joaquin draped an arm over Shannon's shoulders. "I'm volunteering to be a taste-tester."

Dom raised his hand. "Me too."

"Yo!" Taylor shouted. "Count me in, too."

Joaquin dropped his arm, and within seconds, Shannon was able to feel more in control of her emotions. And whenever he stared at her, it was as if they were only two people in the room. It had happened a decade ago when they were with other people, then again when she'd come face-to-face with him during her first visit to Bainbridge House and now again.

Shannon didn't know why Joaquin's presence disturbed her, and she vacillated between wanting to figure out why and not wanting to know. There was no way she would allow herself to become sidetracked from her new position, and becoming involved with any of the single Williamson men would be history repeating itself.

left California for Maryland, Shan-
had sworn that she would never become involved
with someone she had to work with. And aside from
Joaquin sampling the dishes she and Viola would make,
there was no reason why they would have that much contact with each other. Most of her time would be spent in
the kitchens, while his was relegated outdoors, and for
Shannon, that was a definite win-win.

"Not to worry," Viola said, grinning. "There will be
enough samples to go around for everyone. And to make
it equitable, you'll be assigned a particular week, and
you will also be required to rate each dish you sample."

Shannon was looking forward to cooking and baking
what she and Viola would list on the breakfast, lunch,
dinner, high tea, brunch, bar, and happy hour menus. She
would have the sole responsibility of creating the dessert menu, along with her assistant's specialty cakes for
weddings and catered events.

"I'd like to be the first one to sign on for your desserts," Joaquin told Shannon.

"You're going to have to wait until I come back next
month." Shannon felt it necessary to give her restaurant
manager two weeks' notice that she would be relocating.

"Do you think it's going to pose a problem between
you and your boyfriend when you move here perma-
nently?" Joaquin asked her, his voice barely above a
whisper.

Shannon shook her head. "No."

"Why not?"

Shannon glanced around the table, wondering if anyone was eavesdropping on the interchange between her
and Joaquin, but the others were engaged in a lively debate about last week's Super Bowl. "I don't have a boy-

friend," she murmured. She couldn't tell by Joa~~~
deadpan expression what he was thinking. A beat passe~~~

"Oh, I see," he said.

A hint of a smile lifted the corners of Shannon's mouth, bringing his gaze to linger there. "Do you, Joaquin?"

He nodded. "It's just that thought you would be involved with someone."

"Is it because I'm not like a lot of women you've been photographed with who will do any and everything to get a man's attention." She knew she had struck a nerve with him when he gave her what she interpreted as a death stare.

"For your information, I don't have, as you put it, 'a lot of women.' And secondly, I didn't come home to get involved with a woman, especially not with one who has a tongue that is as sharp as a samurai sword."

It was Shannon's turn to glare at him. She did not think of herself as having a sharp tongue as much as she was frank and to the point. "If I'm going to get involved with a man, then it would never be someone like you. I'm so done when it comes to celebrities, and once I divorced my ex, I'd told myself, 'Never again.'"

"I'm not a celebrity," Joaquin said between clenched teeth.

"You don't think so? There have been countless pictures of you consorting with film and reality stars."

"That was networking for business."

"Yeah, right," she drawled.

He exhaled an audible breath. "I'm not going to argue with you but—"

"Then don't," Shannon whispered, interrupting Joaquin. She didn't want to hear anything he had to say about his celebrity persona.

Once the news was made public that Hayden Chandler had been sleeping with their costar, Shannon still had to be on set with her philandering husband and his real-life lover because of her contractual obligations. Her humiliation was exacerbated because the rival for her husband's affections was a popular actress with a massive social media following.

It had taken iron-willed control not to pull out every strand of hair in the other woman's head, but not before she made certain Hayden would never father another child. However, common sense prevailed once she realized they weren't worth her losing her freedom or self-respect. She had to talk Marcus and her father off the ledge when they'd hinted about confronting Hayden, and Shannon knew it would not have boded well for him.

Her mother and grandmother had preached relentlessly for her to let it go, but even after so many years Shannon found it difficult to do so. It wasn't as if she didn't like men. She just didn't trust them. And especially someone in the public eye, because she never wanted to be that vulnerable again if or when their relationship ended.

Joaquin's large dark eyes narrowed when they met hers. "Well, at least we know where we stand with each other. There will be no personal involvement."

Shannon nodded. "Nothing personal," she repeated.

"Is there a reason why we can't get along as friends? There will be occasions when we'll have to work together," Joaquin said.

The tension in Shannon's body eased with his query. And he was right. Their lives and future were inexorably intertwined, because both would live and work on the estate. "I don't have a problem with us becoming friends." Smiling, she extended her hand in a gesture of compromise, and she wasn't disappointed when he cradled it in his much larger one before bringing it to his mouth and placing a kiss on the back of her hand. "Friends it is," he said, smiling.

Someone cleared their voice, and Shannon saw Taylor and Viola staring at her and their brother. The siblings exchanged a glance she was unable to interpret, and she hoped what they'd witnessed wasn't what they believed was something more between her and Joaquin other than friendship and professionalism. He released her hand, and she rested it on her lap.

If Shannon were completely honest with herself, she could admit that Joaquin Williamson was someone she would permit herself to become involved with *if* he hadn't been touted as the landscape architect to the rich and famous. There were reports that he'd been mentored by famed landscape architect Claude Eccles, dubbed the twenty-first-century Frederick Law Olmsted. When the widowed, childless Eccles retired because of ill health, he transferred his client list to Joaquin, who in turn created a remarkably successful company of his own. And despite his high-profile visibility, Joaquin had managed to remain scandal-free. There were photos of him with several women arriving or leaving celebrity dinner parties and weddings, but neither he nor his dates were willing to be interviewed.

Shannon knew that would change once Bainbridge House celebrated its grand opening. The structure listed on the National Register of Historic Places and reopening as an upscale luxury hotel was certain to garner a lot of interest for those wishing to check in to a sixteenth-century French château that had been disassembled, transported and reassembled in New Jersey in the late 1880s.

Viola said Taylor planned to invite local elected officials and the press to the hotel's grand opening and had

Taylor reminded his siblings that they would have to be available for interviews.

Viola pushed back her chair. "There's a lot of leftovers, so whoever wants something, let me know."

Sonja rested her hand over her belly under the knitted smock. "I'll take a little of everything."

"What about you, Joaquin?"

"Let Sonja and Taylor have the leftovers. They have invited me to eat with them this week because I'm still unpacking and settling in."

"The door and the invitation are open if and when you decide to stop by and grab a bite, because I cook every day," Viola said, smiling. "After I pack up leftovers, Shannon and I are going to serve dessert."

"What's for dessert?" Sonja asked Shannon.

"Handheld apple pie."

"That's ingenious," Sonja said. "It's like eating an empanada."

Shannon sat up straight. "Do you make empanadas?"

"Chica please. I can't match you and Viola when it comes to gourmet cooking, but I'm no slouch when it comes to making dishes that have been passed down through generations of Puerto Rican women."

"Oh my gosh," Viola crooned. "You have to taste her pastelón."

A beat passed before Shannon asked, "Isn't that Puerto Rican lasagna?"

"Yes, it is," Sonja confirmed.

Shannon recalled seeing the dish listed on a menu when she'd visited a restaurant in DC featuring Latin dishes. "Is the recipe a family secret?"

Sonja laughed. "It was until I married Taylor. Even though I did give Viola the recipe, she still prefers that I make it."

"I'm not family, so I'm not going to ask for the recipe," Shannon said, "but I would like to sample it."

"I've used up all of my sofrito, so whenever I make up another batch, I'll make the pastelón," Sonja promised.

Shannon nodded. Despite being a classically trained chef, she was partial to dishes passed down through generations by home cooks. She'd preferred eating her grandmother's green beans with smoked pork and white potatoes to the one featured in the *Le Cordon Bleu Home Collection Cookbook*. The DC restaurant where she filled in part time had earned the reputation of serving some of the best soul food in the Capitol district. Their fried chicken, blackened catfish, smothered pork chops and side dishes of collard greens and sweet potato casserole were customer favorites, while she alternated with the other part-time pastry chefs making pies, cobblers and cakes.

She and Viola had talked briefly about the various menus but hadn't decided whether they'd wanted to offer casual dining for hotel guests and fine dining for catered parties. Shannon felt creating eclectic menus were more in keeping with a varied clientele and tastes.

"Have you ever made empanadas?" Joaquin asked Shannon.

She smiled. "Yes. I've made beef, chicken, and my personal favorite is Jamaican-style oxtail. Why are y'all looking at me like that?" Shannon asked when she noticed everyone staring at her.

"You make Jamaican oxtail?" Taylor asked.

She nodded. "Why?"

"I went to college in New York City, and on weekends, me and my buddies would travel to various boroughs to eat, and the first time we ordered Jamaican oxtail at this Brooklyn restaurant, we were hooked."

"Taylor's right," Viola agreed. "He's listed and rated every restaurant he's visited. And when I moved to Manhattan and went to many on his list, I must confess that he's right about most of them."

Taylor smiled across the table at Shannon. "I told Viola that I wouldn't interfere when it came to her setting up her kitchens, but I know I'd be happier than a pig in slop if Jamaican oxtail were on the menu. I don't care if it's the stew or empanadas."

"That would have to be Viola's decision, because I'm only responsible for what comes out of the pastry kitchen."

Viola waved her hand in a dismissive gesture. "Not true, Shannon. We're equal partners. The exception is the pastry kitchen, which is where you work your magic. I don't mind you training our assistants to make the oxtail where it can be listed on the dinner menu along with the appetizers. It will be added to the confirmed family dishes of Dom's shrimp and grits, Taylor's chicken and waffles, and Sonja's pastelón. Now, that leaves you, Joaquin, Patrick and Tariq, to offer your favorite family dish."

Shannon went still, not wanting to believe Viola had included her as a Williamson. "But I'm not family."

"You are if you're going to live on this estate and sit at *my* table," Dom said.

She met the dark green eyes, and Shannon felt as if her brother's friend was sending her not only a warning but a secret message, and she wondered if there was more to Bainbridge House's caretaker than he presented.

He'd been born and raised on the estate and had lived here his entire life, and in another four months, he would marry a woman who'd inherited the property. And if he'd originally been viewed as an outsider, that was in the past, because he was now Bainbridge House's business manager.

Forcing a smile, Shannon said, "Point taken." She pushed back her chair and stood. "I'm going to check on the dessert."

Viola also stood. "I'll help you."

She waited until she and Viola were in the kitchen to ask, "What did Dom mean when he mentioned me living on the estate while eating at *his* table?"

"That's something I'll tell you once we're alone," Viola whispered.

Shannon's curiosity was piqued the moment Viola hinted that it was something they would discuss when it couldn't be overheard by others. She was aware that most families had their secrets, and it was obvious Viola was willing to divulge one.

"Okay."

Chapter Five

Shannon sat on the passenger seat in the red pickup truck, staring out the windshield as Viola expertly shifted gears in the decades-old vehicle. Fully restored, it ran as smoothly as a new car being driven out of a dealer's showroom.

When she woke that morning, it was to a light dusting of snow on the ground, while rapidly rising temperatures made it feel as if it were May rather than February. After dinner, she had retired to bed and slept soundly throughout the night. The mattress's pillowtop, like the ones in the suites at Bainbridge House, had cradled her body like a glove, and she had to give the Williamsons credit for purchasing top-of-the-line bedding for their future guests. And once the château officially opened for business, Shannon was certain the accommodations would be comparable to elegant hotels around the world.

Viola downshifted as she approached a sharp curve along the narrow road. "I know you're curious about

Dom's comment about you living on the estate and eating at his table."

"I must admit, I have thought about it a couple of times," Shannon admitted.

"Dominic Shaw is a direct descendant of Charles Bainbridge and was a distant relative to my adopted father."

"You mean to say that he owns Bainbridge House?"

Viola shook her head. "Not outright. But once we're married, I plan to share half of my inheritance with him, which will give him partial ownership of the estate he rightfully deserves."

Shannon listened intently as Viola recounted the situation between her and Dom, and Elise Williamson once the older woman realized Viola and Dom were involved with each other. "It was the morning of Taylor and Sonja's wedding that Dom asked me to marry him, and when my mother walked into the kitchen to find us together, she berated Dom as hired help hooking up with her daughter to get her money. She had no way of knowing that Dom shared Bainbridge DNA when none of her children did, despite their being heirs to the estate."

"How far back does Dom's bloodline go?"

"He's fourth-generation Bainbridge. Charles Garland Bainbridge fell in love with one of his house servants, and she bore him a son. Although Charles married an heiress, he hid the fact that he'd fathered an illegitimate child with a fifteen-year-old girl. He was so obsessed with her that he set her up in a house on the estate to be close to her. He subsequently established an irrevocable trust to secure their son's future. The money in the trust covered property taxes and the salaries of future generations of resident caretakers for perpetuity."

"So, should I assume Dom knew about this?"

ter, that she was like a dog with a bone and wouldn't give up until she got the answer she wanted. "It's a yes."

"Good, because that's how it began with me and Dom. We started out as friends, and now we're engaged to marry."

"Good for you and Dom, because that's not going to happen with me and Joaquin. I don't mind being friends—"

"Friends with benefits," Viola said, interrupting Shannon.

"That's something I'm not willing to consider."

"Why not?"

"Because I have..." Her words trailed off.

"Because what, Shannon?"

"Because I've never been able to remain objective once I'm intimate with a man."

"How long has it been?"

A swollen silence filled the cab of the pickup as Shannon stared out the side window. "Eight years," she whispered, as she waited for a reaction from Viola.

"Forgive me if you feel I'm overstepping, but are you saying you haven't slept with a man in eight years?"

Shannon forced a smile. "There's nothing to apologize for, because as friends we should be able to be candid with each other. And that's exactly what I'm saying. I've dated a few guys since I've returned to the East Coast, but none lasted long enough for what I would consider serious enough for a commitment."

"Don't you have urges?" Viola asked.

"I used to, but that's in the past. You don't miss what you don't have."

She'd told Viola the truth about not wanting to sleep with a man. There had been a time after she'd discovered her husband's infidelity that her body had betrayed her. She'd wanted to sleep with him just to remind him of what he'd lost. It hadn't been easy, but as someone aware of the strong passions within her, Shannon had managed to turn off the switch in her head where she'd told herself that she didn't need a man in her life or in her bed.

"We're here," Viola said, shattering her musings, as she came to a stop in the lot behind row of two-story buildings.

When they walked into Jameson's, even though it was only midafternoon, Shannon discovered many of the booths and tables in the pub were filled with customers eating, drinking, and watching several muted televisions positioned over the wall behind the mahogany bar and in and around the dining room.

"This place has a nice vibe," she told Viola.

"I really like it. Dom and the owner went to school together."

A middle-aged woman seated them in a booth near a gas-lit fireplace and gave them menus. "Someone will be with you shortly," she said, smiling.

Shannon glanced at the menu. "You said the lamb burgers are good?"

Viola met her eyes. "They're delicious."

"I'd like for us to serve cocktail meatballs as appetizers for happy hour. It doesn't matter whether they are veal, lamb, beef or pork. They can be stuffed with different cheeses, and even prosciutto and bacon."

Viola flashed a wide grin. "We're going to have to compile an extensive list of selections before we decide what to keep or eliminate for each of the menus."

Shannon nodded. "We'll have almost three months, so that gives both of us enough time to finalize our menus. You'd mentioned hiring a butcher, so do you have someone in mind for that position?" Butchering and aging meat on the premises was not only cost-cutting but guaranteed the best quality and freshness.

"Yes. Even though the kitchens were updated, I did my homework about how I want it to be run. And that's when I contacted some of my cooking school colleagues about coming to work at the hotel. Once we get back, I'll show you the updates in the kitchens that were made since your last visit."

"So, the surprises keep on coming," Shannon teased.

Viola was engaged to Dominic Shaw and was planning a June wedding; the hotel's grand opening was scheduled for the Memorial Day weekend, and Joaquin had moved from California to a guesthouse on the Bainbridge House estate.

"Do you remember the architectural engineer Robinson Harris?" Viola asked. Shannon nodded. "Well, as the project manager, Robbie and Taylor decided to restore the outbuildings so they look exactly like they did in the original blueprints. Sonja has convinced Taylor to sell some of the items the Bainbridges collected over the years. Almost all are one-of-a-kind pieces. She had them appraised and authenticated, and some are valued at five and six figures."

"It sounds as if Bainbridge House will be somewhat of a museum," Shannon said.

"You're right about that. When our guests check in, they will believe they've stepped back in time but with modern amenities. Taylor and Robbie have reconfigured a space that had originally been for men to smoke cigars into a game room. There will also be a lounge off the lobby for those wanting to relax and watch television. We're going to set up another area where guests can listen to jazz as they order weekend brunch. One of the two dining rooms will have a full-service bar, and the other will be for intimate dining, much like a supper club."

"What about the ballrooms?" Shannon knew there were two ballrooms in the main house. The smaller one could hold at least fifty to seventy-five people, while the capacity for the larger one was more than twice that much.

"Taylor has decided to convert the ballrooms into restaurants and meeting rooms, and construction has begun on building a connecting structure behind the main house for a banquet room that can accommodate up to two hundred people. The real skill comes in matching the new construction to the original schematics, and that's where Robbie's ability comes in as an architectural engineer."

Shannon couldn't wait to see the recent changes since her last visit. "Do you think everything will be ready for the Memorial Day grand opening?"

Viola nodded. "So far, everything is on schedule. There are three eight-hour work shifts five days a week, so there is never a time when something isn't being worked on. Taylor had the barns and a few of the outbuildings demolished, and now they, too, are being rebuilt."

"So, you guys are really serious about having horses on the property?"

"Yes. When Charles Bainbridge built the château, he put in a bridal path for those wishing to ride. There is also a nine-hole golf course on the property, but Taylor wasn't certain whether he wanted to keep it, and because Robbie finally convinced him otherwise, that's going to be another project for Joaquin to take on."

"I must agree with Robbie's decision," Shannon said. "Corporations will host fundraising golf outings for their clients and employees. I think it would be a draw for a business conference lasting a few days when the attendees may want to get in a game of golf."

"You're right. Golf and tennis are always fun activities for those looking to unwind."

"Will the hotel have a tennis court and a swimming pool?" Shannon asked Viola.

"Yes. There will be indoor and outdoor pools, along with an on-site health club."

"Do you still play tennis?"

Viola shook her head. "No. I was extremely competitive growing up with four older brothers and challenged them whenever I could. But then I fell and broke my wrist trying to hit Patrick's vicious backhand volley and wound up spending the summer in the kitchen watching my mother cook. That's when I decided I wanted to become a chef."

Shannon's childhood was quite different from the Williamsons. She grew up with her brother and schoolteacher parents in a modest three-bedroom house in a middle-income Baltimore suburb. Her brother played hoops with his friends in their backyard and if they'd wanted to go swimming then it was in a pool at a city park. However, she didn't begrudge the Williamson siblings for being adopted by parents that had afforded them a luxurious lifestyle.

A server approached their table, introduced herself and took their order. Shannon had requested the lamb burger with loaded tater tots, while Viola asked for a bowl of chili.

While they ate and discussed future menus, a shadow fell over the table, and Shannon glanced up to find a tall man sporting a military crewcut. Then he hunkered down and smiled at Viola.

"Congratulations, beautiful. Dom gave me the good news about the two of you getting married."

A rush of color suffused Viola's face. "Thank you. J.J., I'd like you to meet Shannon Younger. She's going to be the pastry chef once the hotel opens for business. Shannon, this is Jack Jameson, the owner of this venerable establishment."

Shannon smiled at the man with friendly dark brown eyes. "It's a pleasure, Jack."

"It's J.J. to my friends. So, you bake?"

Shannon nodded. "That I do."

J.J. sobered. "I could use someone like you right about now. The company where I used to buy my desserts went out of business, and the one I use now leaves much to be desired. Most times I have to throw out what I order because there is so much leftover. J.J. reached out to grasp Shannon's hand. "Can I hire you to bake desserts for me?"

"I don't know—"

"You don't have to give me an answer now. I…" His words trailed off when one of the bartenders called out his name. "I'll be back later, Shannon," he said, standing upright. "Please think about it."

"That was weird," Shannon said under her breath when he left.

"Why would you say that? The man wants to hire you to make his desserts."

Shannon gave Viola an incredulous look. "Have you forgotten that I'm going to work for Bainbridge House and…"

Viola's eyebrows lifted questioningly. "And what, Shannon?"

The possibilities swirled around in her mind like the balls stamped with lottery numbers in a drum. She was scheduled to become a full-time employee for Bainbridge House, and it wouldn't pose a problem if she baked for the hotel and the pub at the same time. "What if I bake desserts for Jameson's under the label of Bainbridge House Bakery?"

Reaching across the table, Viola gave her a fist bump. "That's exactly what I was thinking. I told you before that I don't want to micromanage you. The decision will have to be yours and yours alone."

A spurt of excitement shot through Shannon as she thought about the varied desserts she would concoct for the pub, unlike the ones she'd created for Taylor and Sonja's wedding, which were much more decorative.

"I'm willing to do it!" She then sobered quickly. "Won't you have to run this by Taylor for his approval?"

Viola shook her head. "I'll let him know what we've decided, but it's Patrick who has the final approval. He will have to confer with J.J. about becoming a merchant willing to purchase our baked goods. Patrick usually will approve my requests, so there shouldn't be a problem setting up BH Bakery."

Things were moving so quickly that Shannon would have felt overwhelmed if she hadn't been so focused. She never could've imagined when Marcus told her he was inviting his college roommate to Baltimore for a family gathering that her life would change the instant Dom introduced her to Viola Williamson. And now, within two weeks, she would leave home once again and this time take up residence in a historic establishment as the hotel's executive pastry chef.

Shannon knew she and the other chefs would experience a modicum of nervousness and apprehension once Bainbridge House was open for business; however, she was secure enough to know that as a pastry chef, her desserts would please the eye and palate of the most discerning diner. After they had finished eating, J.J. returned to the table, and Viola told him she would get back to him about Shannon baking desserts for his pub after she'd spoken to her brother.

During the drive back to the estate, Shannon listened intently as Viola talked about the plans she and Dom were making for their wedding. The gathering would be like Taylor's and Sonja's with less than fifty guests.

Viola returned to the château and parked the pickup, then they got out and entered the château through one of several side entrances, but not before they'd left their winter jackets in the truck. Seeing and hearing firsthand the activity and noise made Shannon aware why she wouldn't have been able to sleep there at night. The marble floors were once again covered with protective floor covering to keep heavy machinery from damaging the polished stone.

"Wait here for me," Viola said, "I'm going to see if I can find Taylor to tell him about J.J. wanting you to bake for his restaurant."

Shannon watched Viola retreat as she walked, taking in the change to what had been the great room and was now a spacious lobby area. She hadn't taken more than three steps when she saw Joaquin talking to the project manager, Robinson Harris. She'd found the man with a nut-brown complexion and shaved head to be all business.

Joaquin turned and smiled when he saw her. She returned his smile with his approach. He wore a faded gray sweatshirt with black jeans and tan work boots. She felt a rush of heat in her face when their eyes met. Shannon did not know what it was about this man that stirred emotions she'd successfully ignored for years.

It was something she'd detected when she first saw

him across the room at that director's home and then again when she was formally introduced to him days before the Williamson–Rios–Martin nuptials. And now again. It wasn't what he said as much as it was what he didn't say. His stare disturbed her; as if his gaze stripped away the invisible protective shield that she had erected to protect her heart.

"Good afternoon, Joaquin."

"Good afternoon to you, too. Did you come alone?"

"No. I came with Viola. She wanted to talk to Taylor about something."

"Do you have any idea how long that's going to take?"

Shannon shook her head at the same time she looped the strap of her crossbody bag over her chest. "No, but she did tell me to wait for here, because she wants to show me the changes since my last visit."

"I can do that. I was just taking a break."

Shannon wanted to tell him that was something Viola had promised but didn't want him think she was attempting to avoid him—which in her head is exactly what she wanted to do at that moment. She was planning to leave Bainbridge House before the end of the week, and when she returned, she would be too busy to spend any appreciable time with Joaquin. Both would be busy with their own projects.

"What if Viola comes looking for me?" she asked, stalling for time.

Reaching into the back pocket of his jeans, Joaquin took out his cell phone. Seconds later, he showed her the screen. "I just sent Taylor a text to tell Viola that you're with me. Okay?" he asked, offering her his arm.

Smiling and resting her hand at the bend of his elbow, she nodded. "Okay."

Chapter Six

Joaquin placed his free hand over the slender fingers on his arm. "There's something I'd like to get your opinion on before I take you around."

She glanced up at him. "What?"

"You'll see."

Joaquin led Shannon into a space that had been converted from a storeroom to a makeshift office and closed the door, shutting out the sound of hammering and drilling. A long table held two desktop computers, three laptops and one printer. Gooseneck lamps with high intensity lighting illuminated the space. A single serving coffeemaker sat on a table in a corner. There was also a mini fridge. Metal tubes with blueprints were stacked in a tall wicker basket.

He pulled out a chair for Shannon, lingering briefly over her head as she sat in front of one of the laptops before he took the chair beside her. The subtle fragrance of her sensual perfume wafted to his nostrils, and Joaquin was able to detect notes of patchouli, jasmine, lemon and amber. It was the perfect complement to her body's natural feminine scent.

Slightly shifting the laptop, he booted it up and clicked on a program he'd uploaded with designs for the gardens, then turned it where she could view the screen. "What do you think of this one?"

Shannon stared at the image. "Isn't that the painting of Claude Monet's *Bridge over a Pond of Water Lilies*?"

Joaquin smiled. "Yes and no. It is reminiscent of Monet's painting, but it's what I want to replicate here on the estate."

Shannon turned to give him a direct stare. "There's a lily pond here?"

He nodded. "Yup. There are a couple of ponds. One with a waterfall and lilies and another that is home to ducks and swans. They are migratory but should return once the weather warms."

She blinked slowly. "You want to build a bridge over the pond." Her question was a statement.

"Yes. I'm going to have to discuss it with Taylor and Robbie to see if it's possible. It depends on if the ground can sustain the weight of the construction."

Shannon peered closer at the sliding images on the screen. "It would be the perfect location for a photographer to take pictures of a bride and groom and their wedding party."

Joaquin laughed softly. "You've read my mind. A stone path on the opposite side of the bridge will lead to a gazebo that will be constructed under wrought iron arches wrapped in climbing roses. That's another feature I would like to add to the harmony garden."

Her eyelids fluttered. "You're really going to call it the Harmony Garden?"

He registered skepticism in Shannon's query. "Can you think of something else to call it? A Zen garden is a place where one can come to relax and meditate, so what makes it so different from a harmony garden, where lovers can go to confirm their love for each other."

Shannon turned her head to conceal a smile. It was obvious that Joaquin Williamson was a romantic. Several beats passed, and then she said, "You're right. The Harmony Garden is a suitable name."

"Merci ma chérie."

"Vous êtes le bienvenu."

Joaquin gave her an incredulous stare. "You speak French?"

"A little."

"How much is a little?" Joaquin asked.

"Enough to order food, a hotel room or tell a cab driver where I'd like to go. I must confess, I understand more than I speak."

Joaquin angled his head. *"Où avez-vous appris la?"*

"I took French in high school. I also spent two months in France when I enrolled in courses to learn French and chocolate patisserie, and having a rudimentary knowledge of the language proved invaluable when communicating with many of the locals in villages miles from the major cities. Where did you learn the language?"

"My mother is fluent, and she would speak to us in English and French so that we were proficient in both languages."

"How often do you use it?"

"Not enough."

Resting her elbow on the table, Shannon cupped her chin on the heel of her hand. "It's the same with me."

"Although we probably won't get to see that much

of each other, there's no reason why we can't practice whenever we do."

Shannon's smile was dazzling. "I'd like that. But only if you don't speak so fast that I can't pick up what you're saying."

"I promise not to speak too quickly."

"Okay."

The Williamson family was unconventional. They'd grown up in a large house on four acres with enough room for everyone to have their own bedroom suites, and they didn't have to leave the property for recreation. And it was clear all were at least adequate cooks, Viola being the exception, and they were fluent in two languages.

Suddenly, she felt completely relaxed with Joaquin. He'd asked her opinion about his designs for the garden, and they were of one accord about the bridge spanning a pond filled with water lilies that was so reminiscent of the Impressionist painting.

Shannon was familiar with Claude Monet's masterpiece because she had fallen in love with the art of French Impressionist painters during her time there. She'd told herself once she purchased a house, she would dedicate a room to an art gallery with paintings by Monet, Cézanne, Degas, Renoir, Seurat and Toulouse-Lautrec.

"Have you visited France?" she asked Joaquin.

He nodded. "Only once. It was to visit the Palace of Versailles to see the gardens."

"I didn't get a chance to visit the palace while I was there," Shannon admitted, "but are the gardens that spectacular when seen in person?"

Joaquin powered down the laptop. "Spectacular doesn't begin to describe the gardens. I got to see them through the central window in the Hall of Mirrors, and it was awe-inspiring. I also went to England and Japan to study their gardens."

"Is that what you want for the gardens at Bainbridge House? For folks to be so overwhelmed with emotion that they don't want to leave."

Leaning back in his chair, Joaquin stared across the room. "That all depends on the individual, Shannon. We have five senses, and depending on what we see, hear, smell, touch or taste, we can react differently to stimuli. You are the perfect example of what I'm talking about."

"What about me, Joaquin?"

"When it comes to you, all of my senses are on edge."

Shannon felt a shiver of uneasiness eddy through her. Just when she'd felt completely relaxed and in control of her emotions, Joaquin's remark stripped away that confidence to make her feel at risk of falling under the spell he'd projected just by staring at her. It wasn't just his breathtakingly good looks; he projected an energy that pulled her in and refused to let go.

She'd been celibate for eight years—much too long for a woman who had thoroughly enjoyed making love with a man. Her mother and grandmother had preached that she had to let go of the resentment that one man had turned her into someone they didn't recognize whenever a man sought to get her attention.

And as much as she'd tried to explain to them that she didn't need a man to make her complete, both had ignored her protestations. It was her mother who'd recommended she go into therapy to rid herself of the anger that wouldn't permit her to move forward to even consider sharing her life and future with a man. Shannon knew Annette Younger wanted to see her daughter married with children, yet she knew that wasn't going to happen if she continued to live her life by her leave.

"What is it about me that makes you uneasy?" she asked after a pregnant pause. Joaquin smiled, his lids lowering and the expression so sensual that Shannon held her breath for several seconds.

"You must know that you're a beautiful woman, Shannon. When I saw you for the first time across the room at Carson Bennett's party, I was stunned."

A hint of a smile parted Shannon's lips. "I did notice you staring at me when you should've been giving your date all of your attention."

Joaquin frowned. "She wasn't my date. I'd just met her, and she'd introduced herself as Bennett's niece. I hope you didn't think me rude because you were there with your husband."

"Ex-husband."

"At the time he was your husband, Shannon. And I'm glad you got rid of him."

Her eyebrows lifted slightly. "You are?"

"Yes. If Viola had been in your place, and if that slug had done to her what he did to you, he would've gotten a good ass-kicking from each of her brothers. Even mild-mannered Tariq would've joined the beatdown."

"Now you sound like my father and brother. They had planned to fly across the country to jack up Hayden, and it took a lot of pleading from me for them not to come. If our marriage hadn't become headline news, it would've been different. It's the main reason why I refuse to get involved with a public figure. Once was enough for me." She paused. "What else is there about me that has you—as you say—'on edge'?"

It wasn't the first time Shannon had mentioned being a celebrity and public figure to Joaquin. Although he'd found himself attracted to everything about her, he did not plan to try and convince her to change her opinion of him. He was horticulturist/landscape architect Joaquin Manuel Williamson, and his sole focus was on his family and the estate they'd inherited.

And he had been forthcoming when he'd told Shannon she had him off-balance, but in a good way. "You have a wonderful voice," he said in a quiet tone. "It's a contralto that's sexy and sensual, and I would be able to recognize it anywhere. Then there's your perfume with notes of bergamot, peach, ylang-ylang, jasmine and lemon that are subtle *and* intoxicating."

"You can identify what makes up the fragrance notes in my perfume?" she questioned breathlessly.

He smiled, nodding. "I have a friend who's a perfumer and he used to quiz me about different blends."

"Did you pass his tests?"

"Not at first," Joaquin admitted. "It took years before I was able to differentiate between florals, woods and green notes." He placed his forefinger alongside his nose. "It's all about the olfactory nerves. Professional perfumers are gifted with an incredible sense of smell."

"You've explained how I look, sound and smell. What about the other two senses?"

"If you're asking how you feel, then I would have to say wonderful. When I held your hand, it was soft and silky, and it's apparent when looking at your face that you take loving care of your skin." Her flawless sable-brown complexion radiated good health.

Shannon lowered her eyes. "I must admit, I spend a lot of money on self-care products."

"Then, it's money well spent," Joaquin said. "I must forfeit the last sense of taste, because as friends, we shouldn't be kissing each other."

Shannon gave him a long, penetrating stare, then nodded. "You're right. Kissing on the mouth is a line we cannot cross if we want to remain friends."

"What if you decide to cross that line, Shannon? How would that change things between us?"

"Nothing's going to change, Joaquin, because I don't intend to cross that line."

Shannon's statement about not crossing the line was what Joaquin needed to prove his priorities. He hadn't returned to New Jersey to become involved with a woman, but with a mission that required his attention around the clock.

"And neither do I," he said with enough confidence that he'd begun to believe it.

"If Robbie gives you the go-ahead to build the bridge, will it be completed before the grand opening?" said Shannon, bringing the topic of discussion back to the garden.

"It shouldn't take more than a couple of weeks from start to finish. The gazebo can be constructed in a day or two. I..." Joaquin's words trailed off when his cell phone rang. He answered it after the second ring. "Yes, I understand. Don't worry, sis. I will take care of everything."

"Is something wrong?" Shannon asked him when he set the phone on the table.

"The alarm at my mother's condo went off, and the security people called Viola to come and check out her place. There wasn't a break in, but they wanted her to reset the code. She's driving over with Dom, and she wants me to stay with you until they come back. She also said to tell you that Taylor says it's a go on the pub's desserts."

Clasping her hands together in a prayerful gesture, Shannon smiled and sighed. She would begin making desserts and highlight her creations months before the hotel's grand opening.

"Is that good news?" Joaquin asked.

Shannon unclasped her hands. "It's wonderful news."

She told Joaquin what had happened at Jameson's when she and Viola had gone there for lunch."

He angled his head. "Bainbridge House Bakery? I like the sound of that."

"Viola said if Taylor approved it, then it would be up to Patrick to give it the final word."

"You don't have to worry about Pat. There isn't anything he would deny Viola."

"Why would you say that?"

"Patrick is a CPA and oversees the finances for the restoration. Taylor has a budget for construction costs. It's the same with me when it comes to landscaping, while Tariq can only spend so much on the number of horses he can purchase. However, the exception is Viola. Her budget is limitless. He told her she can outfit her kitchen however she wants. In other words, she has blank check for equipment, appliances, food or personnel needed to run the hotel kitchens."

"Why is she the exception?" Shannon asked Joaquin.

"Because she is Viola Williamson, Shannon. My parents doted on her because she was the only girl, and I'm not ashamed to say that her brothers, me included, have continued the practice. But to be realistic, a hotel's kitchen is just as important as the hospitality an establishment offers their guests. Taylor and Patrick want the Bainbridge House to be a four-star hotel. The difference that makes Bainbridge House unique is because it's listed on the National Register of Historic Places. People in the States travel to Europe and choose to stay in a castle or château because they want to feel as if they are a part of the past but with modern amenities."

"I agree when you say that," Shannon said, "because during my stay in France, I did get to tour and eat at a couple, and I must admit that the food was phenomenal because they only used fresh ingredients. Viola and I both agree that eating an omelet made with eggs laid that morning are a totally different experience from eating store-bought eggs."

Joaquin gave her a sidelong glance. "So, you're really serious about raising chickens on the property?"

"If we are going to grow our own vegetables and have an on-site butcher, why not have free-range chickens? And it isn't as if they're going to be the only animals on the estate."

"Horses are different, Shannon."

"No, they're not, Joaquin. An animal is an animal, whether large or small. And if you're going to have a resident vet, I don't see the problem in having a few dozen laying hens."

He narrowed his eyes. "How much is a few dozen, exactly?"

She shrugged her shoulders. "That is yet to be determined. Viola told me there was a time when the Bainbridges had chickens and sheep on the property. There were also goats, but they had to get rid of them because they would chase the sheep and fight with the dogs."

"Are you seriously thinking about having sheep, too?"

Shannon shook her head. "No, because that will have to be Viola's decision. I'm only responsible for the pastry kitchen."

"But you are a chef?"

"Yes, but my specialty is making desserts."

"What's the different between a baker and a pastry chef?"

She met Joaquin's large dark eyes, and she detected amusement in the glossy orbs. "Bakers make cakes and pies, and a pastry chef makes desserts."

Attractive lines fanned out around his eyes when he

smiled. "And your desserts for my brother's wedding were definitely works of art."

Shannon inclined her head. "I try."

"Don't be so modest. You do more than try, Shannon. The wedding cake was spectacular with layers of red velvet, pistachio, and white cake covered with white chocolate. And in keeping with the Christmas theme, you made eatable red-plaid ribbons that you'd wrapped around each layer. I still have pictures of the dessert table on my phone."

"Your brother's wedding was very special for me because it was my first time making all of the desserts."

"And you'll have to do it again when Viola marries Dom."

"By that time, I'll have an assistant. If Viola wants flowers on her cake, I'll have to decide whether to make them by hand or use Russian piping nozzles."

"What are those?"

Reaching into her crossbody bag, Shannon removed her cell phone and pulled up a video with a chef decorating cupcakes with flowers using different piping nozzles. "It would take me days to make those flowers by hand when they can be piped in mere minutes," she said as Joaquin stared at the screen.

"That's incredible. The flowers on her cake can match those in her bouquet."

Shannon shared a smile with Joaquin. "We haven't discussed her color theme or what kind of cake she wants. But I noticed the tartan banner painted on the doors of Viola's pickup, so maybe she would want to incorporate that into the color scheme."

"The Bainbridge name is Gaelic, meaning 'bridge of bright water.'"

"So, that's why Dom had the tartan plaid painted on Lollipop."

"Dom told me he's Scottish on his father's side and Irish on his mother's."

"That's a lot of plaid to choose from," Shannon teased.

"And whatever colors they choose, I'll try to get co-ordinating flowers."

"Are you going to grow them yourself?"

Joaquin nodded. "I'll cultivate them in the greenhouse because, right now, the planting season is too short to pick them for a June wedding."

"It looks as if Bainbridge House will become one-stop shopping for an on-site wedding. The bride can choose whether to have a ballroom or garden ceremony and reception. She can also select her flowers, cake, menu and secure lodging for her family and guests without ever leaving the estate."

"You're right about that, Shannon. I know that you, Viola, and your staffs will do the *damn* thing when it comes to throwing down in the kitchens."

Shannon laughed because Joaquin sounded like someone hyping it up for a pep rally. "We do okay." Joaquin draped an arm over her shoulders like he had done at dinner the night before. This time, she wasn't bothered by the gesture because they'd established the ground rules for their friendship.

Leaning closer, Joaquin pressed his mouth to her ear. "You do more than okay. Now are you ready to see some of the updates since you were last here?"

She sucked in her breath, holding it for three seconds before letting it out. Joaquin's warmth and the scent of his cologne elicited a yearning she'd long thought dead. He was kissing her ear and not her mouth, but the effect was the same. It was a tender gesture that hinted of intimacy.

"Oui, monsieur."

"Allons, ma belle."

Shannon forced herself not to react to his "Let's go, beautiful." And if she were completely honest with herself, she would admit that whenever Joaquin stared at her, she felt something that she hadn't felt in years: desire. He was the first man since her divorce that had her wondering what it would be like to sleep with him.

Then she had to remind herself that he was her boss's brother, and with them both living on the property, it would prove disastrous if they got involved and then decided to break up. She'd always wanted her own kitchen since graduating cooking school, and now that it was a reality, she didn't want or need any distractions, no matter how much she'd felt herself attracted to the most sensual man she'd ever met.

Joaquin had claimed she had him on edge, and he had no way of knowing it was the same with her. Just meeting his eyes and listening to the timbre of his low velvety voice or staring at the long slender fingers of his masculine hands was a shocking turn-on. Joaquin Williamson was the epitome of tall, dark, handsome and sexy. He'd claimed being photographed with beautiful women was a form of networking, but for whom? She was certain women were standing in line waiting for him to notice them and felt lucky to have him ask them out.

Shannon knew she had to be careful, incredibly careful, not to fall under the sensual spell Joaquin emanated whenever they shared the same space. He stood and eased back her chair as she rose to stand. Reaching for her hand, he laced their fingers together and led her out of the office.

Chapter Seven

Shannon hadn't realized her mouth was gaping when she saw the obvious changes in the lower-level kitchen. A butcher shop had been constructed with an expansive room for aging meat. A smoker and wood-burning oven were also new additions. She turned to see Joaquin leaning against the prep table.

"What do you think?" he asked.

"It's incredible," Shannon replied.

"I agree."

The updated commercial kitchen has been outfitted with every appliance needed to serve the hotel's guests. She walked into the adjoining pastry kitchen and smiled. There was also a new addition: another wood-burning oven. Shannon's imagination was working overtime thinking of making pizza with an endless variety of toppings.

She returned to where Joaquin now sat perched on a

stool. "Are you going to give me a hint as to new changes in the first-floor kitchen?"

Slipping off the stool, Joaquin extended his hand. "Come with me and I'll show you."

The kitchen on the first floor, although half the size of the other one, was outfitted with everything Viola and her staff needed to serve hotel guests. Shannon smiled when she saw several espresso machines, an ice cream maker and another one for making gelato.

"Well, dessert lady," Joaquin teased, "does this meet with your approval?"

She turned and met his eyes. "Yes, it does. I love making gelato."

Joaquin smiled. "And I love eating it. In fact, I prefer it to ice cream."

Shannon also loved the intense flavors of gelato because it had less butter fat than ice cream. "Are there any other changes since my last visit?"

Joaquin reached for her hand again. "Yes. They are still converting the bedrooms into suites on the third floor, and the ones in the turrets will become honeymoon suites. Taylor said construction on the barn and stables will begin sometime next month, along with the new banquet rooms."

"What about the changes in the solarium?" she asked.

"Glass to replace the broken or cracked ones are on back order. As soon as they are replaced, I'll outfit it with trees and plants that will resemble an indoor oasis."

"What made you decide to become a landscape architect?"

Joaquin smiled. "I suppose it is the same as why you decided to become a pastry chef, Shannon."

She glanced up at him. "And that is?"

"Creativeness. You love making beautiful desserts,

while I love to design gardens. A field of wildflowers growing in abandon is awe-inspiring, but when you take those flowers and blend them with ornamental grasses and an outcropping of rocks, they become a part of a landscape to be admired for generations."

"Do you plan to make a lot of changes to the gardens?"

Joaquin shook his head. "Not to the original blueprint for the gardens around the château, but I'm thinking about making modifications to the orchards and the property near the ponds. And before you ask, it shouldn't take that long, because next month, I'm going to advertise for experienced landscapers to come on board to help with the project." He paused. "What about you, Shannon? Do you have someone in mind as your assistant?"

Shannon had made a mental note to contact her former cooking school friend about coming to work at the hotel as her assistant. Mara Lewis had talked about leaving DC after a heartbreaking split with her long-term, live-in boyfriend.

"Yes. Once I go back to Baltimore, I'm going to call her and ask if she would like to work with me."

"How many assistants do you think you're going to need?" Joaquin asked Shannon.

"I'll begin with one, and once business picks up, then I'll probably hire another one even if it's a part-time position. I would prefer if she were local because she would not be faced with packing up her life and relocating."

"You still intend to staff an all-female kitchen?"

"Yes." Shannon narrowed her eyes at Joaquin. "Why do I get the impression that you still don't like the idea of Viola and I having kitchens staffed by women?"

"Please don't get me wrong, Shannon. Now that I've thought about it, I believe it is genius when it comes to marketing the hotel. I'm certain advertising an all-female kitchen at a luxury hotel will garner a lot of attention."

She wanted to tell Joaquin it was not a gimmick. All he had to do was look at his sister's tenure at a Michelin-star restaurant where she'd been systematically passed over for promotion in lieu of male chefs who had been hired after her.

"Viola and I did not decide on an all-female kitchen to garner praise in the media. It's just that we've been shut out of so many professions that I think it's time for us to level the playing field. Women during my mother's and grandmother's generation were encouraged to become teachers, nurses or even social workers, not professional chefs." Shannon did not want to remind Joaquin that his own mother was a teacher and that her parents were also teachers. "What Viola and I intend to do is give women chefs the opportunity to exploit their classical training, and the result will make the kitchens at Bainbridge House comparable to the one at Le Bernardin."

Joaquin lowered his head and pressed a kiss on her hair. "I like the sound of that."

"You like it because it will put Bainbridge House in the forefront, or that your employees are unique?"

"It has everything to do with Bainbridge House, Shannon, and anyone involved with it. And that includes you. I made a promise I would help my siblings fulfill a dream my father had about restoring his ancestral home."

"So, it's about family, Joaquin."

He gave her a long, intense stare. "It's always been and always will be about family, Shannon. None of us share DNA, but we're closer than many who do, because there isn't anything we wouldn't do for one another. And now that includes Sonja and Dom."

Shannon nodded when she wanted to tell Joaquin the

Williamsons were no different from the Youngers. Her parents, grandparents, her brother, his wife and their children were one cohesive unit, and there wasn't anything they wouldn't do for one another.

"There's not much more we can see here without interfering with the workers, so would you like to go and see the ponds?"

"Yes," she said quickly, then paused. "But that's going to pose a problem, because I left my coat in Viola's pickup truck." Even though the temperatures were above freezing, it still wasn't warm enough for her to venture outdoors wearing only jeans and a pullover sweater.

Joaquin led Shannon around a tangle of wires in the hallway to a side door. "Come with me to my place. I have a ski jacket that you can wear. It's going to be too big, but it will keep you warm."

She wanted to tell Joaquin it wasn't necessary that she go to his house with him, but then she didn't know how long it would take for Viola to return to the château. And she'd also realized they were practically shouting at each other to be heard over the incessant drilling, welding and hammering. Within seconds of walking outdoors, Shannon felt the chill. The temperature had dropped noticeably. What had begun as a warm springlike late morning was now more like a typical northeast February winter afternoon. Joaquin opened the passenger door to a late-model Infiniti QX50, and helped Shannon in before he rounded the SUV and sat behind the wheel.

"Nice ride," she said, smiling.

"It's Sonja's," Joaquin said as he tapped the Start Engine button. "Taylor leased it for her when she lived in a rental, but now that she's living on the estate, she rarely drives it."

Shannon glanced at his profile. "So, now it's yours?"

Joaquin shook his head as he put the vehicle in Reverse and slowly maneuvered out of the space between two pickups. "No. I had my car shipped here from Los Angeles."

"Ferrari or Benz?" she teased, smiling.

"Neither. I have a 1992 Aston Martin convertible."

Shannon wondered if Joaquin was a fan of James Bond movies, because the vehicle was driven by the popular fictional British agent. "Wouldn't you prefer to a more up-to-date model?"

Tiny lines fanned out around Joaquin's eyes when he smiled. "I happen to like old cars because of their designs, and when I heard someone talking about selling the convertible, I asked to see it. I must admit, it wasn't much to look at, but I offered the owner much more for it than it was worth and then paid someone to restore it."

"How does it run?"

"Like a dream. The original owner hadn't put too many miles on it, so with regular maintenance, I can look forward to driving it for many more years."

"Would you consider selling it if someone offered you twice or even three times more than its value?"

"Nope. It took me a long time to find a vehicle I really like driving, so if someone wanted to offer me an obscene amount of money for it, I would still turn them down. One of these days, I'll take you for a drive, and you can judge for yourself why I like it so much."

Shannon wanted to ask Joaquin if he would be willing to let her drive his car and knew instinctually that he would turn her down, because she was more than familiar with men who thought of their cars as their babies. It had been that way with her ex. She suspected he loved his classic Mercedes Benz more than he'd loved her or any woman.

"Can you drive a standard shift car?" Joaquin asked, as if hearing her thoughts.

"Yes. Why?" She'd learned to drive at sixteen when visiting her grandparents in North Carolina. Her grandfather had owned several farm vehicles with standard transmissions, and it had taken two days for her to become adept at shifting gears before stalling out.

"Maybe I'll let you drive so you can see what I'm talking about."

Shannon stared out the windshield as Joaquin drove away from the château. "I'm looking forward to it."

"What are you thinking about?" Joaquin asked after a comfortable silence.

"This is the first time I've seen the estate grounds. When I came here last year, I spent all my time in the kitchen at the château, and when I arrived yesterday, Viola was driving too fast for me to take in the landscape."

Joaquin decelerated. "It is a little overwhelming. I got here last week, and it took me two days to drive around to take in everything. A football field is approximately an acre, so the estate could cover nearly four hundred football fields."

"Viola mentioned there is a vineyard on the property. Do you intend to revive it?"

"That would depend on Patrick."

Shannon shifted to stare at Joaquin. "Why Patrick?"

"Because he's the vintner."

"I thought he was estate's accountant."

"That too, Shannon. Pat got involved with a girl whose family are wine growers and have vineyards on Long Island and in the Napa Valley. And when Andrea was urged to come to California to help her uncles, she asked Pat to come with her. My brother had fallen in love with her, so he agreed. They were engaged a few months later, and it didn't take Pat long to learn everything there is to know about the winemaking business."

"Has he said anything about coming back to revive the winery?"

Joaquin grunted under his breath. "I would never try to predict what Patrick Williamson would or would not do. Please don't get me wrong, Shannon. I love Patrick, but he is the most complex of any of my siblings. He will show you only what he wants you to know about him. I suppose he's more like Dad than any of us, because there was a time when they did work together. Once he graduated college, he went to work for my father at his investment company, and both were like covert agents, because they never talked about what went on in the office."

"Maybe they did that to protect the integrity of their clients."

"You're probably right. I hadn't thought of it that way."

Joaquin knew he could be critical and opinionated, but discussing things with Shannon had allowed him to rethink some situations. What he said about her decision to hire only female chefs was sexist, but it had come out before he had been able to censor himself. Not only wasn't he sexist, but he encouraged Viola to become a professional chef.

While he'd found himself rethinking his opinions and his willingness to compromise with Shannon, Joaquin realized that hadn't been possible with Nadine. Even if his ex knew something was black, she'd refused to agree with him. Once he'd decided to end his marriage, he had become recalcitrant almost to a fault when dealing with women. It had become his way or no way. The exceptions were his mother and sister.

Joaquin didn't know why he'd developed another stance with Shannon, except that he'd wanted her to like him enough that they could become more than friends. However, he knew he had to take it slow with her, because she still viewed him as a celebrity. He'd been playing a role he'd become very adept at. Yes, he'd purchased a condo in an exclusive LA neighborhood that afforded him the privacy he sought, because anyone coming to see him had to be announced to be permitted entry into the building. And whenever he'd ventured outdoors, he was unrecognizable when wearing a baseball cap, dark glasses, faded jeans and old running shoes.

Joaquin occasionally dated once his divorce was finalized, but the liaisons were always short-lived, because as Claude Eccles's protégé, he'd been totally focused on his profession. Everything changed once Eccles retired and Joaquin had assumed his client list. Most times when he'd been seen out and about, it was with up-and-coming actresses. A few he saw more than once, but at no time had they interested him enough to become romantically involved. There were women he did date who wanted to stay out of the spotlight, and those were the ones he continued to see.

He hadn't lied to Shannon when he admitted her presence kept him on edge. She was a woman who intrigued him as no other had before. It wasn't just her delicate beauty but her carefree spirit. That there was more to the actress-turned-pastry chef than she'd presented to the public.

She'd been a talented actress who was able to morph into whatever role she was given, but when faced with the scandal that her husband had cheated on her, she refused to be interviewed and continued to act alongside her duplicitous husband until she was eventually written out of the script. Even when she'd been pursued by paparazzi, Shannon did not attempt to conceal her identity but went about her day-to-day life like an ordinary Angeleno.

Fast-forward ten years, and Joaquin did not want to believe the actress known as Shay had come to Bainbridge House to bake desserts for his brother's wedding. And seeing her close up confirmed what he'd felt when staring at her across a crowded room, unable to take his eyes off her. There had been a vaguely sensuous longing that had disturbed him. And he'd asked himself over and over, why this woman and not some of the others? Why had he found himself enthralled with a married woman?

He'd heard men talk about a woman who was the one—the one they knew they'd wanted to spend their lives with. Joaquin didn't know if Shannon was the one, because she said they would always remain in the friend zone. He drove off the rutted road and came to a stop alongside his home. Dom told him all the roads on the estate were scheduled to be repaired a month before the hotel's grand opening.

"Don't move," he said to Shannon. "I'll help you out."

Shannon waited for Joaquin to come around and open the door of the SUV. Their eyes met when his hands circled her waist as he held her effortlessly off her feet. "You can put me down now."

He nodded, smiling. *"Oui, mademoiselle,"* he said, lowering her until her feet touched the ground.

There was something so mischievous in Joaquin's smile that she found herself grinning. *"Merci."*

Placing an arm around her waist, he led her up the stone path to the house and opened the door.

She'd noticed that Viola hadn't locked the door to her

home, and it was the same with Joaquin. "You don't lock your door?" she asked.

"No. Even though you probably don't notice them, there are cameras throughout the estate that are monitored by an off-site security company. No one coming or leaving the property will go undetected."

She walked into the living room and felt as if she were looking at history with an overstuffed off-white leather sofa with scroll arms, and matching chairs with toile de Jouy print throw pillows. During her two-month visit in France, Shannon had come to recognize Louis XV–style rococo chairs and Aubusson carpets.

"Your home is beautiful."

Joaquin nodded. "Thank you, but I can't take credit for any of the furnishings. When Taylor sent me photos of this place before the renovations, I told him I only wanted him to update the electricity and plumbing. Once I saw that the furniture were reproductions of a mix of French and English, I realized I preferred the more mid-1770s French styling."

"Were all of the furnishings left here once the guest-houses were closed up?"

"Yes. Dom said after his father retired as the caretaker, he'd continued the practice of making certain every piece of furniture on the estate was covered and that the rugs and paintings were crated."

Shannon didn't know why, but she thought Joaquin would have preferred a more contemporary living style. "Do you have a pool table?" she asked.

A hint of a smile played at the corners of Joaquin's mouth. "I'm seriously thinking about buying one."

"Where would you put it?" There was no space in the living room, and what Shannon could see through the partially opened pocket doors leading to the dining room.

She wondered if there was another room on the first floor where there would be enough space for a pool table.

"I was thinking about putting it at the rear of the house but then changed my mind. Come with me and I'll show you."

Again, Shannon was mildly surprised when she stood in the middle of a large space at the rear of the house that doubled as a sunroom. A round table with six chairs were positioned in one corner and in another a pair of cushioned rockers, a love seat and several chairs with matching toile de Jouy pillows and cushions. She'd thought of it as the perfect place to begin and or end the day. She didn't know why, but at that moment she wondered how it would be to live with Joaquin. To go to bed and wake up with him and for them to share breakfast in the sunroom. She dismissed the thought as soon as it entered her head, because she'd told herself they could not and should not become more than friends.

"Why do I get the feeling that this house is so much larger than Dom's?"

"That's because it is almost a thousand square feet larger. Sonja told me that Charles Bainbridge had the caretaker's house built for his mistress and son to live in, but once he began hosting guests, he would put them up on the third floor in the château while his family were assigned the second-floor bedrooms. After some time, he decided to have the guesthouses built for those traveling with their valets and ladies' maids. The help was put up in the two bedrooms on this floor and were relegated to using a small bathroom that is located off the laundry room, while their employers and children stayed in the three upstairs bedrooms. I've planned to convert one of the bedrooms on this level into an office, and the other will be a theater and game room. And if I do decide to purchase a pool table, then it will go in there."

"It sounds as if you have everything planned for your future at Bainbridge House."

Joaquin nodded. "I've had almost a year to think about it, Shannon. When my mother told us about this property, and then when we came to see it, I knew what I wanted to do. At the time, I still had several ongoing commissions, but once they were completed, I began the process of selling my business and condo."

Joaquin had to sell his home and business, but those weren't prerequisites for Shannon. "My life is less complicated than yours because I live with my parents and work part time. I want to give my employer two weeks' notice that I will be leaving before I move here next month. Viola told me that I will live in one of the guesthouses until my apartment at the château is completed."

"I've seen the plans for the apartments, and I think you'll like living there."

"How many apartments do you plan to have? Shannon asked, because she wanted to know who else other than herself would live at the château.

"There will be at least four. Right now, there's just you and Robbie. However, Taylor did mention hiring a permanent security person and having them live on-site. Why don't you look around while I go upstairs to find that ski jacket for you? We should leave soon because I want you to see the some of the property before the light begins to fade."

Shannon took Joaquin's suggestion and found herself in the kitchen. She found it almost impossible to contain her excitement when she stared at the expansive space that was a chef's dream. A vaulted beamed ceiling set the stage for an updated kitchen in hues of monochromatic grays and blues. If she hadn't been a chef, Shannon would have thought of the space as over the top for a bachelor, but then she recalled Viola saying that all her brothers were more than adequate cooks. She recognized the brand of the built-in French door refrigerator-freezer with an exclusive five-door convertible drawer and dual ice maker. Double dishwashers, eye-level ovens, an eight-burner stovetop under a massive copper range hood and a quartz-topped island with six stools. A perfect stage for cooking and entertaining. Shiny brass knobs on the stove and handles on the cabinets and drawers provided a dramatic contrast to the varying shades of blue.

"You like the kitchen?"

She turned to find Joaquin at the entrance to the kitchen. He'd put on a puffy vest over his sweatshirt. "I love it. Are all the kitchens in the other guesthouses like this one?"

Joaquin walked in holding a ski jacket. "I don't know. I haven't seen them. When Taylor asked me what I wanted in here, I sent him a picture of the kitchen in my condo."

"There's no doubt that you can do some serious cooking in here."

"That's what I'm hoping once you teach me to make biscuits."

"Is that all you want me to teach you?"

"That's only the beginning. I would like you to show me how to make pasta."

"What else, Joaquin?" she asked, holding back a smile as he helped her into the jacket.

Lowering his head, he pressed his mouth to her ear. "Pie crusts, donuts, bread and—"

"Wait a minute," Shannon said, interrupting him. "How did we go from biscuits to baking bread?"

"Flour and I don't get along, so if I can learn to make

a biscuit that doesn't resemble a golf ball, then I'm willing to try other things."

"Are you saying that you and flour are on a break?" she teased.

He smiled, flashing toothpaste-ad white teeth. "That's exactly what I'm saying."

"Once I get the two of you back together, then I'm going to have you make your eggs Benedict for me."

He bowed his head. "It would be my pleasure."

"And if you want to make bread, then you need to buy a heavy-duty stand mixer with a paddle for mixing and a dough hook kneading."

"I'll ask Viola to order it for me," Joaquin said, as they left the kitchen.

Shannon gave him a sidelong glance. "Once I come back, I'm going to be busy making desserts for the pub and testing recipes for the menus, so that will only leave the weekends for your lessons."

Joaquin nodded. "I don't plan to work weekends, so whatever you decide is okay with me."

Shannon wanted to tell Joaquin that it was more than okay with her. Although they'd agreed to stay in the friend zone, a sixth sense told her it wasn't what Joaquin wanted for them. And if she were truly honest with herself, she wanted more than friendship, too.

Then, she recalled Viola saying that she and Joaquin would get along well because he didn't want to get serious about a woman and liked being single. Well, she also liked being single, and now at thirty, she felt mature enough to know to end a situation if or when it became detrimental to her. She would spend one more day at Bainbridge House before leaving to return to Baltimore for the next two weeks—enough time and distance for Shannon to forget about the man who made her feel things she didn't want to feel. That whenever he stared at her, she was reminded of how long it had been since she'd been made love to.

All Joaquin had to do was stare at her, and she felt as if he could see through what she'd attempted to conceal from him. She liked Joaquin Williamson. A lot. However, Shannon wasn't certain whether he liked her the way a man liked a woman, or if he was intrigued with the actress known as Shay. Well, Shay was gone, never to be resurrected, and once she made the decision to walk away from her acting career, Shannon had not experienced one iota of regret. She'd been able to scratch the acting bug, and now she was ready to embrace her new calling as a head pastry chef.

"Where are we going first?" Shannon asked Joaquin as he got into the SUV beside her.

"I'm going to take you to see the ponds. And if there is still enough daylight, then the orchards and vineyard."

"It's too bad I won't get to see the ducks."

"They'll probably come back around the time you return."

Shannon wanted the two weeks to pass quickly because she was looking forward to starting over at Bainbridge House. And once she settled into the guesthouse as her temporary lodgings, she truly would leave her past behind to begin her life anew.

Chapter Eight

Shannon didn't want to believe the property had geese *and* swans. The large, graceful birds were one of her favorites, along with peacocks. Moving from Baltimore to Bainbridge House was like going to an amusement park that was full of unexpected surprises. Winter hadn't lessened its grip on the northeast, yet it did not detract from the landscape with the perennials lying dormant and awaiting the arrival of spring to bring forth their blooms in an array of magnificent colors.

She stared out the windshield as Joaquin drove over the orchards and pointed out the number of trees that would yield enough harvested fruit for pies and desserts and for canning the following year. Late afternoon shadows had begun to blanket the landscape when Joaquin returned to the château as the workers for the four to midnight shift were arriving. Shannon saw Viola's red pickup pulling into a space next to a work van.

"Viola's back," she said to Joaquin as he shut off the engine.

"Perfect timing."

Shannon got out and waited for Viola's approach. "How did it go with your mother's alarm system?"

Viola rolled her eyes. "The technician said there's something wrong with the connection and the entire system must be rewired. Dom's staying over tonight because the company has arranged to come early tomorrow morning." She leaned closer. "How was it hanging out with Joaquin?"

"Nice," Shannon said, lowering her voice as Joaquin came over.

Viola looped her arm through Joaquin's. "Thank you for looking after Shannon while I was gone. I'm going to take her back to the house, and you're welcome to come, too."

Joaquin pressed a kiss on Viola's hair. "Thanks, kid, but I promised Taylor and Sonja that I would hang out with them tonight."

Shannon took off the ski jacket and handed it to Joaquin. "Thanks for the jacket."

He met her eyes. "Will I see you tomorrow?"

"I plan to be on the road before noon."

He took a step and kissed her cheek. "Get back safe, and I'll see you again when you come back next month."

Shannon nodded and smiled. She wanted to tell Joaquin that she'd enjoyed spending the afternoon with him and that she was looking forward to doing it again. She was also looking forward to when she would return to Bainbridge House and begin the next chapter of her life and career.

"That's a promise."

Turning on her heel, she followed Viola to Lollipop

and got in. "Don't get you dare get any ideas about me and Joaquin," Shannon said when Viola stared at her with a mischievous grin.

Viola started the pickup. "I don't know what you're talking about."

"Yeah, right. Why did you ask me how it was hanging out with your brother?"

"I was just asking because of the way he was staring at you."

"And that was?"

"Like he was mesmerized, Shannon. I don't get to see Joaquin as often as I would like, but I know there is something about you that makes him less uptight than usual. Even when he'd come home for family holidays, he was wound so tight that none of us could get him to relax. He claimed it was because he wanted to get back to his business, but I always thought it was because of a woman. And whenever I asked him about who he was seeing, he would say, 'No one in particular.'"

Viola's mention of a woman had aroused Shannon's curiosity. "He's never introduced a woman to your family?"

The lengthening silence inside the pickup was deafening before Viola said, "No."

There was something in Viola's tone that communicated to Shannon that women in Joaquin's past was not a topic for discussion. "I got to see the ponds and orchards," she said, deftly changing the topic.

"When I moved here last summer, everything was still lush. The fruit and berries were ripe and ready for picking," Viola said as she maneuvered out of the lot. "I told Joaquin that I wanted to plant some strawberries and blueberries, but he told me it would take at least two to three years for blueberry plants to grow."

Blueberries were always a favorite for Shannon. "That means we'll have to buy them if we want to offer blueberry muffins or pancakes."

Viola moaned under her breath. "I love blueberry muffins."

"I occasionally will make a variety with sour cream and top them with Swedish pearl sugar."

"Oh, my goodness, I can just imagine the mouthwatering aromas coming out of your kitchen when you bake for the pub. Speaking of Jameson's, Patrick sent me a copy of an email he sent to J.J. outlining a contractual agreement."

"Damn," Shannon drawled. "That was quick."

"Patrick doesn't believe in wasting time. He has your banking information when he paid you for making the wedding desserts, so you can expect to be placed on the payroll the first day you get back."

Shannon nodded. Things were happening faster than she had anticipated. Not only would she become a permanent Bainbridge House employee, but she would also take up residence, albeit temporarily.

She wasn't certain how her parents would react to her moving in two weeks; however, she hoped to reassure them that they would see her more often, because New Jersey was a lot closer to Maryland than California. And once Bainbridge House opened for business, she planned to invite them to stay.

Marcus Younger ran a hand over his face. Shannon knew she had shocked her parents when she told them she would be moving within two weeks, but she could not have anticipated the news would affect her father harder than her mother.

"You're like a vagabond, Shannon. It is as if every ten years, you get itchy feet and must leave home."

Annette Younger placed a hand on her husband's arm. "Let it go, Marcus. I know we were expecting Shannon to be with us for at least another year, but she's a grown woman who must live her life without seeking our approval."

Shannon wanted to tell her father that as it was, they did not get to see each other every day. He left the house at dawn to drive to a high school in New Carrollton, where he taught chemistry and coached the football team, while her mother was an assistant principal at a local Baltimore elementary school.

"I know that, Netta," Marcus said, calling his wife by his pet name for her, "but why so soon?"

Shannon met her father's dark eyes. "Because the restoration has been fast-tracked to be completed this spring rather than ahead of next year."

"When will we see you again?"

Shannon gave her father a reassuring smile. "When the hotel opens, and you can come to check in as a guest. The grand opening is Memorial Day weekend, and I expect you and Mom to be there."

Annette smiled. "Don't worry, honey, we'll be there with bells on. Now, don't let your father spoil your joy just because he doesn't want to lose his baby girl."

"Dad's not losing me, Mom. It's just that he's so used to me being here that he doesn't want to accept the fact that I won't be around to make his favorite chicken fried steak and biscuits smothered with sausage gravy."

Annette glared at her husband. "I thought the doctor told you to watch your cholesterol."

Marcus lowered his eyes. "I only have it when you go visit your folks in Silver Spring."

"Daddy!" Shannon gasped. "Why didn't you tell me that your doctor wants you to monitor your diet?"

Her parents had recently celebrated their fortieth wedding anniversary and were still passionately in love with each other.

"It's not that often that I ask you to make it for me," Marcus rationalized.

"Marcus, I don't plan to spend my golden years taking care of a man who is too hardheaded and stubborn to follow what the doctor tells him what he shouldn't be eating."

"What happened to 'in sickness and in health,' Netta?"

Shannon wanted to laugh at her father's crestfallen expression, but his elevated cholesterol was no laughing matter. "Dad, don't try and put a guilt trip on Mom. Listen to your doctor and cut out the foods he recommends that you *not* eat. I'm scheduled to work this weekend, so I'm going to my place to get a jump on packing. And, Mom, I know you don't like me in your kitchen, but I'm going to cook every night until I leave."

Annette's light brown eyes filled with moisture. Shannon knew her mother was putting up a brave front, because she had also gotten used to having her daughter live under their roof. Pushing back her chair, Shannon walked out of the kitchen, down a hallway and to the door that led to her apartment.

Shannon sat across the table on a screened-in balcony of an apartment with views of Rock Creek Park, sipping cappuccino while Mara Lewis complained incessantly about her ex-boyfriend and how he'd blindsided her when he told her he was moving out because he'd fallen in love with another woman.

She waited for her friend to pause, then said, "It's

time to let him go, Mara. I know it hurts, but he's not worth crying over something you knew wasn't going to happen."

She'd met Mara when they were both students and roommates at Johnson & Wales in Charlotte, North Carolina. Shannon bonded quickly with the perky natural blonde with sparkling sapphire-blue eyes.

Mara blotted the corners of her eyes with a napkin. "I know, Shannon, but every Christmas and Valentine's Day, I expected him to give me a ring, but nothing. I'm going to be thirty-five next year, and my biological clock is ticking."

"Women are having babies in their late thirties and even in their forties, so you shouldn't be so fixated on your biological clock."

"You can say that Shannon because you're only thirty."

"I would say and feel the same way if I was thirty-five or even forty."

"Don't you want children?"

Mara's question gave Shannon pause. When she'd married Hayden at twenty, she hadn't considered motherhood because of the impact it would have had on her life and career. "Maybe one of these days," she said, "but right now becoming a mother is not a priority for me."

Mara ran her fingers through her chin-length hair, holding it off her forehead. "You don't realize how jealous I am of you, Shannon. I know you don't like to talk about it, but you've really gotten your life together after your divorce."

Shannon shuddered visibly as a shiver of annoyance eddied over her. Mara was right. She didn't like talking about her aborted acting career or the scandal that had plagued her high-profile marriage and subsequent divorce. And she didn't come to see Mara to witness a pity party but to ask her friend if she would be willing to become her assistant once Bainbridge House opened for business.

"It has taken a while, but now I'm ready to fulfill my dream to run my own kitchen," she said after a noticeable pause.

A frown flitted across Mara's features. "What are you talking about?"

"I've been hired to work as head pastry chef at a hotel in New Jersey, and I would like you to be my assistant." Mara had secured employment with a celebrity caterer in the capitol district since graduating culinary school.

Mara's jaw dropped as a rush of color suffused her pale complexion. "You're kidding, aren't you?"

"No, I'm not," Shannon said. She told her about Bainbridge House and the grand opening scheduled for the upcoming Memorial Day weekend. "I don't know if you're willing to relocate, but the offer will be open until the beginning of May. After that, I'm going to contact several cooking schools to interview potential pastry chefs."

"You won't have to do that Shannon, because I'm your girl. Don't you remember when I said that we should open a business together?"

Shannon smiled. "I do remember, but at the time, I thought it was just bravado because we'd scored perfect points when we made that vanilla sponge cake with strawberry meringue."

"I still remember the reaction from the other students when we set it on the judging table. It was so quiet that you could hear a rat piss on cotton," Mara said, grinning, "until Chef took a bite of the cake and started moaning. That was when the knives came out and everyone gave us death stares."

Shannon's grin became a full smile. "We became the

dynamic duo with that creation. But then, you were always on point when it came to working with chocolate."

"I love working with and eating chocolate. Whenever Jordan and I had an argument, I'd bake up a batch of chocolate chip cookies or a salted-caramel chocolate cake and binge for days. Then he'd pour fuel on the fire when he began with the fat jokes." Mara's eyelids fluttered. "I don't know why, but this is the first time that I'm glad to be rid of him."

Shannon had always thought that Mara could've easily been a full-figure model. "Good for you." She wanted to tell her friend that letting go was a process, that it would take time to get used to sleeping alone.

"Yes," Mara sighed. "Good for me. I'm going to accept your offer, because there's nothing keeping me here. I'm going to list this condo with a realtor even before moving back to Reston, where I'll chill on my parents' horse farm until it's time for me to become a Jersey girl."

Shannon exhaled an inaudible breath of relief. Although she'd wanted to hire Mara as her assistant, she hadn't been certain if the woman would be willing to move from DC. And she knew it would not have been possible if Mara was still dating Jordan.

Shannon took a chance when she called Mara to ask if she could discuss a project with her without disclosing any details. She knew her friend was still emotionally fragile after her recent breakup, yet knew she'd had to meet with Mara in person. Knowing she would have an assistant was an important detail she could eliminate from her to-do list before the hotel's opening.

She had packed all her clothes and personal items, and loaded the boxes into the Honda's trunk. Her parents had also resigned themselves that she was moving and that she was only a four-hour drive away. Shannon was also anxious to return to New Jersey because Patrick had finalized the contract between Jameson's and Bainbridge House Bakery and J.J. had asked that she deliver desserts for the pub's annual St. Patrick's Day celebration.

And as promised during her stay in Baltimore, she'd taken over her mother's kitchen, preparing health-conscious meals. She was looking forward to working with Mara, and as a team, she was confident they would concoct spectacular desserts comparable to the chefs who were employed by past generations of Bainbridges.

Chapter Nine

Shannon slowed as she spotted the road sign indicating the approach to Bainbridge House. What she was experiencing was very different from when she'd come to the estate two weeks ago, because this time it wouldn't be to visit but to stay.

Viola had messaged her that her guesthouse had been cleaned from top to bottom and aired out before her arrival. She had also sent Shannon videos of the various rooms and reassured her that there was an ample supply of linens for the bath and bedrooms, and she had also supplied the kitchen with dishes and cookware.

Shannon was grateful that the guesthouse was move-in ready, and it would take only a few days to unpack the boxes with her clothes and personal items she'd collected over the years. There had been an upside to living over the garage apartment in her parents' house because of the limited space. Her apartment had had enough space for a sofa bed, a bistro table with two chairs, and a bookcase doubling as a stand for a television that had been filled with magazines and cookbooks.

Her father had called her a vagabond, and despite wanting to deny it, Shannon realized she had moved around a lot during the three decades. She'd been born and raised in Maryland, then at eighteen, she'd moved to California. After a few years, she returned to Maryland before moving to North Carolina. After graduating culinary school, she'd returned to Maryland, and now she was going to be a New Jersey girl. She hoped this would be her last move.

There were times when she'd felt that she was searching for something beyond her reach. She had become a pastry chef, yet the positions she had secured hadn't felt fulfilling until she made the desserts for Taylor and Sonja Williamson's wedding. It was then Shannon had known for certain that she needed to run her own kitchen. And it was at the wedding that she'd also done double duty as pastry chef and head chef, supervising the kitchen because Viola had also been Sonja's maid of honor. The experience was enough to give Shannon the confidence to bake desserts for the hotel and assist Viola when needed.

Mara had surprised Shannon when she called her the day before to say her father and at least a dozen of his business associates were planning to come to the grand opening, after she'd told her parents there was a golf course on the property. Shannon knew she had to talk to Joaquin about revamping the links in time for the grand opening. A smile parted her lips as she tried to imagine the hotel's grand opening with the banquet Viola had planned for the media and elected officials.

Viola and Dom were sitting in Lollipop waiting for

her when she drove through the gates and came to a stop next to the pickup.

"Welcome home," Dom said through the open driver's-side window.

Shannon smiled. "Thank you."

"Follow me and I'll take you to your guesthouse."

Shannon had been inside Dom's and Joaquin's homes, and when she walked into the space that she would call home for the next three months, she felt as if she'd entered a portal that transported her back more than a century, when the nouveau-riche went to extremes to emulate European royalty.

"Nothing is personalized because Taylor's not certain whether Mama or Patrick plan to move here," Viola said, as she stood off to the side in the living room.

"It's still incredibly beautiful," Shannon said at the same time Dom walked in carrying the boxes she'd loaded in her SUV.

Viola smiled. "I'm glad you like it. The house has Wi-Fi, central heating and cooling, and Dom installed a generator a couple of days ago. On the dining room table, there's a set of house keys and a remote device for the front gates. Security systems are scheduled to be installed in all guesthouses before the roads are paved sometime in April."

Shannon walked past the dining room and into the all-white kitchen. The pristine palate was interrupted by stainless-steel Sub-Zero, Wolf, and Cove appliances. It was obvious the Williamsons had spared no expense when upgrading and updating the kitchens and bathrooms in the guesthouses because they did not have to purchase furnishings and accessories to decorate their homes. A collection of gleaming copper pots and pans, dinnerware and crystal were displayed in a cupboard spanning an entire wall.

"I went grocery shopping yesterday and bought a little extra to put in your fridge and pantry," Viola said.

"We were definitely thinking alike, because I'd stopped at a supermarket near Sparta to buy a few groceries, and the first thing I need to do is get the perishables out of the car."

"Don't worry about that, Shannon. That's why I asked Dom to come with me, so he can unload everything. Do you want me to stay and help you unpack?"

Shannon shook her head. "No, thanks. It shouldn't take me long to put everything away. It looks like a lot of boxes because I decided to pack light."

"Okay. I'm going to leave you to settle in, but if you need help, just send me a text. Oh, by the way, dinner is at Taylor's place. Sonja is making pastelón."

"Which house is theirs?" Shannon knew how to get to Viola's and Joaquin's homes, but because the guesthouses were built on one-plot acres, she still hadn't familiarized herself with every structure on the estate.

"Not to worry. I'll have Joaquin pick you up around six. His house is closest to yours."

Shannon wondered if Viola had deliberately selected her to live in this guesthouse because she was hoping something would develop between her and her brother. Well, that wasn't going to happen, because she hadn't come to Bainbridge House to begin an affair with Joaquin.

After Shannon called her mother and left a voicemail that she'd arrived safely, she emptied the grocery bags into the refrigerator and freezer, and other staples in the pantry alongside what Viola had bought for her. She then concentrated on unpacking her clothes and hanging them in massive twin armoires that took up more than half a wall in the master bedroom. The en suite bath was as elaborate as the other furnishings in the house with a freestanding tub with decorative curved legs and gleaming brass fixtures. There was another full bathroom in the hallway outside two other bedrooms, and a half bath between the kitchen and pantry. She'd discovered a laundry room behind a door facing the pantry with a washer and dryer.

Shannon had to remind herself not to get too used to living in the grand guesthouse, because she was eventually going to move in to an apartment in the château. However, she'd planned to enjoy it for now. It had taken her less than three hours to put her personal stamp on her new digs, so she prepared to take a leisurely bath before deciding what she could make to take Taylor and Sonja's for dinner.

Dressed in a pair of loose-fitting lounge pants with an oversized tee, Shannon took out a package of ground lean pork, beef and veal, which she planned to make into honey garlic meatballs.

She'd just gathered the ingredients for the sauce when the doorbell chime echoed throughout the house. Shannon glanced at the clock on the microwave. It was minutes before five. Viola had said Joaquin would pick her up at six. Wiping her hands on a dish towel, she walked out of the kitchen to answer the door.

Joaquin smiled at Shannon when she opened the door. It had been two weeks since he last saw her, and during that time, he'd often thought about her. At times a little too often. He handed her a large shopping bag. "I know I'm early, but I wanted to bring you something as a housewarming gift."

Shannon peered inside the bag. "It's beautiful, but I'm afraid I don't have a green thumb, so chances are it will be dead before I move into my apartment."

He smiled. "You don't need a green thumb when it comes to succulents. They are some one of the hardiest house plants you can own."

Shannon opened the door wider. "I'm forgetting my manners. Please come in."

Joaquin wiped his feet on the thick straw rug outside the door and walked into the entryway. Several sweet-grass baskets lined the mahogany drop-leaf table, along with a stack of books and magazines.

"Are these yours?" he asked, pointing to the baskets. He'd asked because they could've been some of the artifacts collected by the Bainbridges over the years.

"Yes."

"They are exquisite. These are more spectacular than some of the others I've seen when I went to Charleston."

"You've been to the Low Country?" Shannon said.

"Yes. One of these days, I'll tell you about my travels."

"I know we're expected to go to Taylor's at six, but I'm still making the sauce for my meatballs."

"Were we supposed to bring something?" he asked.

"No. It's just that as a Southern girl, I was raised never to go to someone's home empty-handed."

Joaquin followed Shannon as she made her way to the kitchen. "But now you're a Jersey girl."

Shannon smiled at him over her shoulder. "Only on the outside. Where do you recommend I put the plant?"

"Anywhere there's indirect sunlight. You should water it when the soil is dry to the touch."

She removed the potted plant from the bag and set it

on the kitchen windowsill. "It looks nice there. Thank you again, Joaquin."

He nodded. "You're welcome."

"Do you have to leave now?"

"No. Why?"

Shannon smiled. "Because I'd like you to be my sous chef."

Joaquin was hoping she would ask him to stay. "What do I need to do after I wash my hands?"

"I want you to finish forming the meatballs."

He peered into a large glass bowl filled with tiny meatballs. "Is this one of the dishes you want to put on the menu?"

"I'm considering it," Shannon said. "But there are a few others I'm thinking about putting up for contention. I'm going to show you how to form the meatballs before you brown them in a frying plan for about ten minutes to get some good color on them while I finish putting the ingredients together for the sauce."

"You're going to cook the meatballs in the sauce?"

"Yes. It will take less than half an hour before they're cooked through because of their size."

Joaquin leaned over the cooking island. "I told you I'd like to volunteer as one of the judges for your dishes."

She gave him a skeptical look. "Do you really believe that you can be impartial?"

"Of course." He placed a hand over his heart. "You really wound me when you believe I'm not trustworthy."

"Stop with the melodrama, Joaquin," Shannon said, laughing, "and go wash your hands so we can get this done before we have to leave."

Shannon was given a hint of what she would come to expect when working with Joaquin once she showed him how to make biscuits. He was a quick study. Sharing cooking duties with a man was a new experience for Shannon, because Hayden had employed a full-time cook and housekeeper.

"Would you like to sample one?" Reaching for a fork, she speared a meatball and handed it to Joaquin once the meatballs were fully cooked in the honey garlic sauce.

He plucked the meat off the fork and popped it into his mouth. "Oh, sweet heaven. That is delicious."

"It's the sauce that gives it an Asian flavor."

Joaquin moaned. "I could sit here and eat this entire bowl."

"You can have another one while I go upstairs to change. Once they're completely cooled, you can cover the dish with the lid. One, Joaquin," she stressed as she turned on her sock-covered feet and walked out of the kitchen.

She quickly changed into a pair of black stretchy pants with a matching long-sleeved top and then pushed her feet into black low-heeled booties. Peering at her reflection in the mirror over the vanity, Shannon fluffed up her hair with a small round brush. Earlier that year, she'd decided to let her hair grow because it would prove easier to just style it in a twist or ponytail. The waist-length straight hairstyle that had become a trademark of her former career as Shay was gone.

Shannon opened the armoire where she'd stored her fall and winter clothes and selected an off-white puffer. Spring had put in an early appearance in Maryland, while winter still hadn't released its grip on the Garden State. While they waited for the meatballs to cook, Joaquin had revealed that the greenhouses were delivered, and within days, the electrical and irrigation systems were scheduled to be installed.

She thought Taylor's decision to fast-track the restoration was a stroke of luck for her. Now she wouldn't have to wait a year before she became an employee at Bainbridge House. And each day brought her closer to the dream she'd had the first day she walked into Johnson & Wales as a culinary student. Shannon could hear her grandmother's voice in her head telling her it wasn't enough for her to work in a bakery but to own a bakery. That she would never experience ultimate fulfillment until she controlled her own destiny.

Well, Grandma, you're about to get your wish, because your grandbaby girl is going to supervise her own pastry kitchen.

Shannon found Joaquin in the kitchen sitting on a stool at the island flipping through one of her cooking magazines. He was also wearing black slacks, a sweater and boots.

"I'm ready."

The two words were pregnant with a sense of strength that made her feel invincible. She'd left home at eighteen to chase a dream, believing if she worked and studied hard, she could become an accomplished actress. She'd fulfilled that dream when she was nominated for an Emmy, unaware her success would be short-lived. If it hadn't been for the support from her family, Shannon knew she would've dissolved into a maelstrom of anguish and despair that would probably linger for years.

Her parents and grandparents had preached to her while growing up that she was a descendant of survivors and that she would survive the media firestorm that had turned her life upside down. However, it had been her training as an actress that had permitted her to get into character as someone who could ignore their existence. Shannon had decided to remain in California until her divorce was finalized before returning home because she'd equated running away as an act of cowardice. And for Shannon, being a coward was not an option.

Joaquin slipped off the stool and picked up the covered casserole dish with the meatballs. Smiling, he said, "Let's ride."

"Did you drive over?" she asked him.

"Yes. Can you drive a stick shift car?"

Shannon nodded. "Yes."

"I'll act as your navigator when you drive my car to Taylor's place." Cradling the dish to his chest, he reached into the pocket of his slacks and handed her a set of keys.

A jolt of excitement eddied through Shannon as her fingers closed over the keys. She left the house and went completely still when she saw the forest-green sports car with a tan leather interior. She opened the driver's-side door and buckled the seat belt at the same time Joaquin slipped in beside her. Inserting the key in the ignition, Shannon shifted into gear and slowly let out the clutch as she depressed the gas pedal, smiling as the car moved smoothly forward.

"Nice," she whispered when she shifted into second gear. "Did I pass your test?" she asked Joaquin.

He gave her a sidelong glance. "Did you think I was testing you?"

"Yes."

"I'd never do that."

"Why?"

"Because I want you to be able to trust me. If we're going to be friends, then there shouldn't be ulterior motives behind what we do or say."

Shannon wanted to tell Joaquin that it wasn't going to be that easy for her. She hadn't realized it until years later that she was gullible when it came to trusting men she was dating. She'd dated a boy in high school and was totally unaware that he was also seeing other girls at the same time. There were rumors about his cheating, yet she had chosen to ignore them because she was in love.

It was different with Hayden, because not only was he older and erudite, but he'd promised to protect her from what he'd deemed predators preying on young actresses looking to make it in the film industry. He'd promised to love and protect her, but in the end not only had he deceived her, but their marriage had become public fodder. And despite divorcing Hayden she still had trust issues when it came to forming relationships. In as much as she wanted to give into her feelings and trust Joaquin something wouldn't permit her to do so.

"Tell me when it's time for me to make a turn," Shannon said, totally ignoring his reference to her trusting him.

"Continue down this road, and once you pass a weeping willow tree, turn right and you'll see Taylor's house."

Shannon downshifted as she drove over the rutted road to a house in the distance. Viola had mentioned the roads would be the last to be repaired because of the heavy machinery coming and leaving the estate. She pulled in behind the red pickup, shut off the engine and gave Joaquin the keys. "Thanks for letting me drive."

He winked at her. "Anytime you want to take it out on the road, just let me know."

She wanted to tell him that *if* she did have time to indulge in driving for pleasure, it would only happen on weekends. Shannon had carefully planned her schedule to test recipes and bake for the pub. She had less than ten days before she was to deliver St. Patrick's Day–themed dessert to Jameson's.

The front door opened, and Taylor emerged from the

house at the same time Shannon alighted from the sports car. She had come to like and admire the model-turned-engineer whose laidback persona had put her immediately at ease. He appeared totally in control of spearheading the complete restoration of the château, which had been vacant for more than half a century.

"Welcome home," Taylor said, smiling.

It was the second time that day that someone had welcomed her back, verifying that Bainbridge House was now her home. "Thank you."

Taylor patted Joaquin's back before he dropped an arm over Shannon's shoulders and pressed his mouth to her ear. "You know you didn't have to bring anything. Sonja and Viola have everything covered."

Shannon smiled up at him as he escorted her into his home. "I figured they would, so I decided to make appetizers." She sniffed the air. "Oh my goodness! Something smells delicious."

"That's the pastelón," Taylor said. "Sonja just put it in the oven."

"It's been a while since I've eaten pastelón," Joaquin remarked as he followed them into through the expansive entryway and through the living and dining rooms.

Shannon glanced at the dining room table set for six before walking into the kitchen. She smiled when she saw Viola tearing lettuce leaves and placing them in a large wooden bowl. Dom was adding liquids to a blender, and Sonja sat on a barstool at the island slicing melons for a fruit salad. A song from the soundtrack of *Saturday Night Fever* blared from hidden speakers.

Viola noticed her first and picked up a remote device to lower the volume on the music. "I recognize that casserole dish. What did you make?"

"Honey garlic meatballs."

Sonja wiped her hands on a dish towel. "Do you mind if I have a few?"

Shannon set the dish on the countertop. "Of course. There's enough for everyone to have some before dinner."

Viola opened an overhead cabinet and took out six small dishes and filled each with meatballs. Shannon watched the reactions of Taylor, Dom, Sonja and Viola as they ate what she hoped would become her contribution to the hotel's appetizer menu.

Sonja slowly shook her head. "Damn, girl. These are addictive. You can't just eat one."

"I agree," Dom said. "They have to go on one of the menus."

Viola met Shannon's eyes. "Do you want to submit these meatballs as a family favorite?"

Shannon was temporarily at a loss for words. She wasn't a Williamson or a Bainbridge, yet Dom and Viola's family had embraced her as a member of their family. "Yes, and thank you."

"No, thank you," Taylor said before he popped another meatball into his mouth. "These are incredible."

"Amen," Joaquin intoned.

"What else do you make using a honey garlic sauce?" Sonja asked Shannon.

"Chicken wings, bite-sized spareribs and baked pork bites."

Excitement lit up Viola's hazel eyes. "I've got an idea. What if we offer three honey garlic chicken wings, three pieces of spareribs, three meatballs and three pork bites and called them the Dirty Dozen?"

Shannon laughed. *The Dirty Dozen* was one of her grandfather's favorite movies. Grandpa Younger was obsessed with anything related to the military. He had enlisted in the army at eighteen, served four years and used his GI benefits to purchase a house built on three acres to expand the family farm.

"I like it."

"So do I," Joaquin confirmed.

Viola pressed her palms together. "That does it, Shannon. You'll be given credit for the Dirty Dozen."

Nothing in Shannon's expression revealed what she was feeling at that moment. The Williamsons adding her name to a dish on their dining menu was something she could not have imagined when she'd agreed to come on board as the hotel's pastry chef.

"I don't know if Joaquin told you," Taylor said, breaking into Shannon's thoughts, "but the family has a tradition of setting aside Saturday nights as movie night. Whoever is hosting will prepare dinner and select the movie. March is musicals, so Sonja and I have selected *Saturday Night Fever*."

"Next week is ours," Dom said. "We've selected *Grease*."

"What say you, brother?" Viola asked Joaquin.

Shannon noticed Joaquin staring at her. Did he expect her to agree to host it with him? "*Westside Story*." She'd said the movie title without giving it much thought.

Joaquin winked at her. "You heard Shannon. It's *Westside Story*."

Shannon wanted to remind Joaquin that they were friends and not a couple, like Taylor and Sonja, or Viola and Dom. That they must remain in the friend zone, because to cross or blur that line was not an option. At least not for her.

Chapter Ten

Shannon sat at a table sharing a meal with the Williamsons. Conversations were light, teasing and occasionally self-deprecating, and after taking a single forkful of the Puerto Rican pastelón, she knew why it would be listed on one of the hotel's restaurant menus. The contrast of sweet, salty and savory were a perfect combination for layers of thinly sliced sweet plantains, sofrito-infused ground beef, and cheese.

Viola indicated the family favorite menu would be divided into starters or appetizers, entrées and desserts. Shannon had unexpectedly contributed the Dirty Dozen as an appetizer, but she still had to come up with several desserts.

"Is it true that you have a commitment for an assistant?" Dom asked Shannon.

During the drive from DC to Baltimore, Shannon had called Viola to tell her that she'd found her assistant pastry chef and wanted her to begin the second week in May. Viola had teased that Shannon was way ahead of her, because she still had to contact several of her friends to find out whether they would be willing to come and work at Bainbridge House.

Shannon nodded. "Yes. I got a firm commitment from Mara Lewis. We were roommates in cooking school. Her father is a VP at a major pharmaceutical company and Mara has convinced him to attend the grand opening. She said he's bringing at least a dozen of his colleagues who are golfing enthusiasts."

"That does it, Joaquin," Taylor said. "You're going to have to get the links in shape before we open for business."

Joaquin knew he had been put on the spot. When he'd asked Taylor about the neglected golf course, his brother had been ambivalent as to whether he wanted to refurbish it. Now that Shannon mentioned potential guests wanting to golf, that meant he had to survey the landscape and put it back together.

He'd interviewed more than a dozen workers and had tentatively selected half to become a part of a landscaping crew he needed to restore and maintain the property. He had set up a schedule for removing overgrown weeds from the orchards and flower beds. A thorough cleaning of the ponds was necessary before the ducks and swans returned, and he'd urged Robbie to sign off on erecting the bridge and gazebo in the Harmony Garden within the next two weeks.

Joaquin had also painstakingly identified every flower, fern, tree and grass on the estate, and had also purchased large planters and urns, chairs and benches for areas he'd wanted to set aside for those wishing to rest after a leisurely stroll. He'd discovered a formal limestone parapet with potted plants, a row of fruit trees and exuberant mounds of perennials, annuals and herbs.

Now that the greenhouses were up, he'd planned to meet with his sister and Shannon to confirm what they wanted to grow. Cultivating fruit and vegetables and dwarf trees in a controlled environment like greenhouses protected them from blight, parasites and occasional wildlife. Bainbridge House was built close to the Dryden Kuser Natural Area, the highest point in New Jersey, and Joaquin had caught glimpses of rabbits, a few feral cats and several deer close to the property line.

"Taking care of the links will become a priority," he said to Taylor.

"What about the vineyard, Joaquin?" Sonja asked.

He gave his sister-in-law a direct stare. "That all depends on Pat."

"But what if he decides never to come back?" Viola questioned.

It was a question that had plagued all the siblings. It was as if Patrick had resigned himself to living in California and eventually marrying his fiancée. "I don't know, Viola. What do you think, Taylor?"

Taylor slumped lower in his chair. "I've been contemplating bringing in a professional taster to judge the quality of the wine, and if he gives it a thumbs-up, then I'm willing to hire a vintner."

"I'm keeping my fingers crossed that when Patrick comes back next month for Easter, we can convince him to stay," Viola said.

Joaquin wanted to tell his sister that was wishful thinking. He had come to know Patrick better than most of his siblings once Patrick moved to California. A month rarely passed when they didn't get to see each other. Most times, Joaquin drove to Napa Valley just to kick back and relax to escape the bright lights of the City of Angels.

"The best thing you can do, Viola, when it comes to Pat is let him be."

Viola narrowed her eyes. "What aren't you saying, Joaquin?"

"Don't try and put any pressure on our brother. I believe it's the reason why he hasn't married Andrea. Whenever I visit Pat, she complains that he's taking too long to set a date, and I try to tell her to let it go, but she just won't listen."

"I just wonder if she's coming with him," Viola mumbled loud enough for everyone sitting at the table to hear.

"We'll find out once he arrives." Joaquin wanted to tell his sister to forget it. He knew Viola was upset with Andrea because she'd made a scene when she'd come to Bainbridge House for Taylor and Sonja's wedding, and insisted to be moved into another suite from the one she was sharing with Patrick because she didn't like it. The impasse ended once Patrick told Andrea he had no intention of moving his things to another suite because he was jetlagged and needed to sleep.

"Are you going back to Baltimore to share Easter with your family?" Taylor asked Shannon once there was a lull in conversation.

Shannon felt all eyes on her. "No. My parents are teachers, and this year, they are planning to take their grandchildren on a cruise during spring break."

"Then you can celebrate with us," Joaquin said.

"Are you inviting me?"

"Of course, he is," Viola confirmed. "Mama insists we all get together three times a year so that no matter where we are on the planet, we always make it home."

"Be careful, Shannon, " Sonja warned, smiling, "because you'll wind up becoming a Williamson. I never knew when Viola introduced me to her brother that I'd end up married to him."

Viola laughed. "It wasn't my intention to play matchmaker, but I'm glad that not only are you my friend, but you're now my sister."

Sonja rested a hand on her belly. "And as soon as I push out this baby, you'll be an auntie."

Shannon wanted to tell Sonja that she had no intention of becoming a Williamson. She did not mind bonding with the family, but nothing beyond that. "Do you know what you're having?" she asked Sonja.

The architectural historian shook her head. "No. I told Taylor I want it to be a surprise."

"It's hardly going to be a surprise, sweetheart," Taylor replied. "Either we're having a boy or a girl."

"It doesn't matter whether it's a boy or girl, because Mama claims she's going to send engraved announcement cards to all her friends and invite them to a dinner party to celebrate her becoming a grandmother," Viola said jokingly.

Shannon laughed. "That sounds serious." She recalled that when her mother had claimed grandmother status for the first time, it was as if Annette Younger could not help herself when what seemed like every month, she would show photos of her grandbaby to all her colleagues, and her husband finally told her she had to stop.

Viola rolled her eyes. "You don't know my mother. She's been complaining to us that all her friends brag about having grandchildren while her kids were punishing her because they were anti-marriage. She claims the gods must have forgiven her because she will now celebrate the marriage of two of her children and the birth of her grandchild in less than a year."

"That's because your mother is a drama queen," Dom deadpanned.

Viola gave him a death stare. "I know you're not about to bad-mouth my mother again now that you say y'all are besties. Mama came to you to apologize for what she'd said about you, and instead of accepting her apology, you got her so drunk that she could hardly stand up straight."

"You must be kidding," Joaquin countered.

"You have to be kidding, Viola, because I've never seen our mother drink more than one glass of wine," Taylor said.

"She didn't until my love convinced her to do shots," Viola crooned.

Shannon gasped. "Oh no! You didn't, Dom," she chastised in a hushed voice. "I thought you'd stopped doing shots after what you'd experienced at my brother's wedding."

"What did he do?" Viola questioned.

Dom glared at Shannon. "I don't think we need to rehash that."

"I think we do," Joaquin chimed in, "especially where it concerns our mother."

"Are you going to tell us what happened, Dom, or should Shannon?" Viola said, continuing with her questioning. She turned to look at Taylor, who was struggling not to laugh. "And what are you sniggling about, brother?"

Taylor put up both hands. "Nothing."

"Damn it!" Dom whispered through clenched teeth. "I know if I don't talk about it now, Viola will never allow me another day of peace. And do you want the abridged or unabridged version?"

"Stop stalling, Dom," Viola warned.

A swollen silence filled the room as everyone stared at Dom. When Shannon noticed the flush suffusing his face, she was sorry she'd mentioned the incident because of her fondness for her brother's friend.

Dom cleared his throat. "I was a groomsman in Shannon's brother's wedding party that was held at a mansion overlooking Chesapeake Bay. The reception had ended, and Marcus and Chynna had left for their honeymoon, when some of the guys gathered in one of the suites and decided to do shots. I stopped after the eighth one because after that, everything became fuzzy. But I do remember getting into a taxi that took me back to my hotel, and when I woke up around noon the next day, I was still wearing my tuxedo. Instead of checking out, I stayed in Baltimore for a couple of days because I was too sick and hungover to drive back here. That's when I vowed never again."

Taylor coughed into his fist, garnering a withering green-eyed glare from Dom.

"Okay I'm guilty of doing shots again, but only as a wager."

Shannon listened intently, along with the others, as Dom revealed that Taylor had challenged him to a game of pool, and with a bottle of aged scotch as the prize for the winner. They'd played the best of five games, and after the end of each one, they would take a shot. Dom won three games to Taylor's two.

"After five shots I was three sheets to the wind," Taylor admitted, "while my soon to be brother-in-law sitting here grinning like a Cheshire cat reacted as if he'd been drinking apple juice."

Viola landed a soft punch on Dom's shoulder. "Are

you engaged in some sort of conspiracy to get my family drunk?"

Dom feigned a grimace. "I didn't force your brother to drink, Viola, because after all, he is a grown-ass man capable of making his own decisions and hopefully accept responsibility for them. And it was Elise who'd said even though she rarely drank, she needed something stronger than coffee or tea once I'd offered her something to drink. She also insisted I refill her glass, and after the second time, that's when I decided to call you to come get her." He paused. "Now, can we please put it to rest that I'm responsible for enticing Williamsons to indulge in drunkenness?"

"Dom, are you certain you still want to become a part of this family?" Sonja asked him.

The estate's caretaker smiled. "So certain that I'd charter a private jet to fly me and Viola to Las Vegas so we could elope tonight. But that's not going to happen because I don't need another dustup with Elise when she's cheated out of becoming the mother of the bride."

"I guess that settles that," Joaquin said, extending his water glass to Dom. "No more talk about shots, and I for one am proud to call you brother."

Taylor also raised his glass. "That goes double for me, Dom."

Viola looped her arm through her fiancé's as she glared at her brothers. "Y'all are all over thirty, and it's time to give up the frat-boy games. And out of deference to my sister, who's carrying my niece or nephew, I suggest whenever we get together, we serve mocktails until after Sonja has her baby. Does anyone have a problem with that?" Her query was followed by a unanimous chorus of nos from the assembly.

Sonja inclined her head. "Thank you. I don't know

about everyone else, but I'm ready for dessert. Shannon, will you please help me serve the flan?"

"Of course."

Shannon stood in the kitchen with Sonja and carefully inverted the dish with the crème caramel custard pudding. She cut slices and placed them on dessert plates while Sonja filled the coffeemaker with grounds.

"I didn't expect dinner conversation would become so intense," Sonja said as she removed containers of milk and cream from the refrigerator.

Shannon nodded in agreement. "I really like Dom, but I blame myself for mentioning him doing shots at my brother's wedding."

Sonja made a sucking sound with her tongue and teeth. "Don't even go there, Shannon. If it didn't come up now, it would've somewhere down the road, because Viola did hint at Elise being under the weather after her reconciling with Dom. It's nice to see that they are getting along now that Viola is engaged to him."

"When is Elise scheduled to return from her cruise?"

"Taylor said she's expected back the last week in the month. She plans to spend April, May and June stateside before possibly taking off again mid-July."

"She really must like cruising."

"Like, Shannon? She loves it. Elise told me that she'd wanted to cruise once her children were adults, but her husband refused to go with her because his parents had died in a boating accident. But now that she's a widow, she's making up for lost time."

Shannon placed the dessert plates on a large tray. "I've read about folks who live on cruise ships. All-inclusive living fees include access to food from restaurants and bars, laundry, gym and medical checkups."

"How much will that set someone back?" Sonja asked Shannon.

"About thirty thousand a year. And that averages out to twenty-five hundred dollars a month. It's a bargain if your rent is two thousand a month, while an extra five hundred won't begin to cover the cost of food, laundry, a gym membership and doctor visits for urgent care."

Sonja busied herself heating milk for cups of cappuccino. "That is a bargain."

"It is for anyone who's able to work remotely."

"Have you ever thought about working for a cruise line?" Sonja asked Shannon.

Shannon pondered the question for several seconds. "To be honest, I did at one time. Even before I'd graduated from culinary school, I'd made a list of places where I'd considered working, and a cruise ship was one of them because I would've been able to work and visit different countries at the same time."

Sonja slowly shook her head. "As an army brat, I've had more than my share of living on bases in different countries."

"You didn't like it?"

"What I didn't like was not sustaining friendships. Living on base and my father being transferred every two or three years was not conducive to lasting friends. Speaking of friendship, I hope you won't hold it against me when I mentioned you becoming a Williamson."

Shannon waved hand in a dismissive gesture. "There's no need to apologize, Sonja. I'm beginning to think of myself as an unofficial Williamson, because my appetizer and probably a dessert will be listed on the family menus."

Sonja gave her a sidelong glance. "So, you don't think it's because we're trying to hook you up with Joaquin?"

"No! Why would you say that?"

"I don't want to overstep, but whenever I see you and Joaquin together, I notice there's something going on between you two that you're attempting to hide from the rest of us. I was even surprised when Taylor mentioned it to me. And most times, he's so involved with the restoration that he doesn't seem to notice much else."

"Maybe it's because Joaquin and I have decided we are going to be friends."

"Is that what you want?" Sonja asked.

"It's what we both want, Sonja. Living on the same property and occasionally working together isn't the best fit for a relationship if we were to break up. It was different for you and Taylor because you didn't live together until your engagement, and it's the same with Dom and Viola."

"You and Joaquin are living on the estate but aren't living together, so there's goes your argument. I'm going to ask you one more question, then I'm going to get out of your business."

Shannon smiled. "What is it?"

"Would you ever consider becoming romantically involved with him?"

"No." She'd said no when she'd wanted to say never. Taylor entered the kitchen, and Shannon was grateful for the interruption. She handed him the tray with the desserts. "You can take these. Sonja and I will bring the coffee."

Shannon knew she could easily get used to watching movies on Saturday nights with the Williamsons. They'd gathered in the living room, and claimed a sofa, chairs and love seats to watch the large flat-screen mounted over the fireplace. Soundbars positioned around the space made her feel as if she were in a movie theater.

She'd seen *Saturday Night Fever* years ago, but just watching John Travolta act and dance was a reminder of her days as a high school musical theater student. When she'd moved to Los Angeles, it was to enroll in the Stella Adler Academy, where she credited the training she received as responsible for turning her into a multidimensional actress. Viola had asked if she'd missed acting, and her reply had been no, but if she were truly honest with herself, then the answer would have been a resounding yes. Shannon missed studying her lines while totally immersing herself into a character when she didn't know where Shay began and the fictional character ended.

"Have you thought of what we're going to prepare when it comes our turn to host movie night?" Joaquin asked Shannon as he drove her back home. He stopped in front of the house and turned off the engine.

Shannon glanced at his profile, marveling at the perfection of his even features illuminated from the gaslight-inspired lanterns flanking the front door. "I was thinking of a buffet, because it is less formal than a sit-down dinner. That way everyone can choose what they want to eat."

Joaquin smiled. "I like your idea. Maybe we should get together in the coming days to figure out what we want."

She nodded. "Okay. I'd also like to create a real movie theater atmosphere when we offer movie night gift tubs. The tubs can be filled with popular candies and packages of microwave popcorn."

"Listen to you," Joaquin said, grinning. "You really know how to make a gathering festive."

"It comes from hosting themed holiday parties. My family put on a Halloween party last year, and Dom brought Viola with him for his plus-one, and that's when we bonded once we discovered we were both chefs. She helped me make Halloween-themed cookies, cupcakes, a large orange pumpkin cake with alternating slices of devil's food and buttercream frosting. Viola had carved small pumpkins and squash with mad, bad and frightening faces before lighting them with battery-operated candles."

"I still can't believe just you and Viola made all of the food and desserts for Taylor and Sonja's wedding."

"That's because we're a dream team, Joaquin. And it helped that the wedding was small; otherwise, we would've needed assistants."

"And now you have an assistant. By the way, how many pastry chefs will you need once the hotel is fully staffed?"

"Mara and I will be full time, while I anticipate hiring one recent culinary graduate trained in French patisserie and another as a chocolatier part time."

Joaquin moaned, and Shannon couldn't stop the rush of heat sweeping over her body, bringing soft flutters in the region between her thighs. She wanted to get out of the car and inside the house before she embarrassed herself.

"I love chocolate," he said.

"If that's the case, then I'll be certain to make a variety of petit fours as dessert for our movie night."

"What do you plan to make?"

A beat passed before Shannon said, "I'll make a few with crystallized ginger, orange almond paste, Black Forest, raspberry brandy, coffee and cognac, rum and orange marmalade, and nougat and amaretto. I will use liquor-flavored extracts for the brandy, cognac, rum and amaretto."

"Will they be similar to the desserts you plan to serve for afternoon tea?"

"Are you asking because you plan to sign up for afternoon teas?" she asked, answering his question with one of her own.

Joaquin gave her a quick glance. "I have to sign up?"

"Of course," Shannon countered. "Viola and I will have to know how much to prepare. It will not be a good look for the hotel if we run out of sandwiches and desserts."

"I'll sign up if you have sandwiches with meat."

"You're as bad as Taylor," she chastised. "What's up with you guys and your obsession with meat?"

"There was a time when I was in college when I'd decided I wanted to become a vegetarian, but the result was I rapidly began dropping a lot of weight."

"How much weight did you lose?"

"Twenty pounds."

Shannon gave him an incredulous look. "Twenty pounds is a lot of weight, Joaquin."

"I suppose it was for me because when I enrolled in college, I was as tall as I am now, and I weighed one-seventy-five."

"One-fifty-five is much too thin for someone with your height."

"I hadn't realized it then, but at that age, kids do a lot of stupid things."

"Thank you."

"For what?" Joaquin asked.

"For letting me drive your baby."

"Anytime you want to drive it again, just send me a text."

"I don't have your number, and I left my cell phone in the house."

Reaching across her body, Joaquin opened the glovebox, took out his phone and handed it to Shannon. "You can put your number in the Contacts."

It took less than a minute for her to input the information before handing him the phone. "All done," she said as she unbuckled her seat belt.

"Don't move. I'll walk you in."

"That's not necessary, Joaquin." She'd locked the door before leaving and felt confident no one had broken in.

"Okay. I'll wait here until you get inside."

Leaning to her left, Shannon kissed his cheek. "Good night." She knew she'd shocked him with the gesture when he went completely still before she got out of the car.

She opened the door, walked in and caught a glimpse of Joaquin sitting behind the wheel and staring out the windshield at her. She waved and he returned it. Shannon closed the door and locked it.

"I like him," she whispered.

In that instant, Shannon knew she had to stop lying to herself.

Chapter Eleven

Shannon woke at dawn but decided not to get up, because for the first time in months, she wasn't on call. Turning over, she went back to sleep and hours later, pangs of hunger forced her to get out of bed. She had managed to unpack most of her clothes and put them away, but she still had to set up her computer, printer or television. What was the rush?

She'd anticipated spending no more than three months living in the guesthouse before moving into her apartment at the château, so her stay was temporary. Viola revealed that every structure on the property had been rewired and was Wi-Fi accessible, so Shannon decided the sunroom would be the perfect area to set up her electronics.

"Oh no," she groaned as she picked up her cell phone off the countertop and saw the low power indicator on the screen. She hadn't charged the phone since before leaving Baltimore. Shannon slipped a pod in the single-serve coffeemaker before she went back upstairs to retrieve the phone's charger.

Twenty minutes later, Shannon sat at the breakfast island, having drunk a cup of coffee and eaten two slices of wheat toast with peanut butter, and scrolled through her emails. She had several missed calls from Mara, along with her voicemail. Mara had asked that she call because it was important she talk to her. There was also a text message from Joaquin.

She dialed Mara's number, her heart beating fast, because Mara had called three times. "Please let it not be bad news," Shannon whispered as she counted off the rings before there was a break in the connection. "What's up, Mara?" she asked when she heard her friend's hoarse greeting.

"I don't know what's wrong with me, Shannon."

"What are you talking about?"

"Jordan called me this morning to say he wants to get back together."

Shannon swallowed an expletive as she shook her head. She did not want to believe Mara was panicking because she didn't know how to proceed with her emotionally abusive ex. "What is it you want to do, Mara?"

"I don't know."

"You don't know, and I don't know what to tell you," Shannon countered.

"What would you do if you were in my situation?"

"Do you want the unvarnished truth, or do you want me to tell you what you want to hear?"

There was a lengthy pause on the other end of the connection, then Mara said, "I need you to be truthful."

"You're deserve more than a man who decides to trade you in when he believes he's found someone better. I know you're freaking out because you want a baby, but I suggest you forget about this jackass and move on."

"I hear what you're saying, Shannon, but I wish you were still in Baltimore so I could hang out with you for a few days just to get away and clear my head."

"Why don't you drive up, and I'll show you what to expect once you come on board."

"Really?"

Shannon smiled. "Yes, really, Mara. Things are slow here on the weekends, so today and tomorrow works for me."

"Thanks, friend. Send me the address, and I'll see you later. Hopefully I'll be able to check out the neighborhood, where I can either rent an apartment or purchase a condo."

Shannon hung up, wondering if once Mara saw Bainbridge House, it would get her out of her funk about Jordan. What she couldn't believe was the audacity of the man playing with Mara's head. Hopefully, that would all come to an end when Mara moved to New Jersey.

She sent Joaquin a text asking him to call her when she found the box with her computer and printer. Her phone rang as she was booting up the desktop. Joaquin's name popped up on the screen, and smiling, she activated the speaker feature.

"Good morning, my friend."

"Good morning to you, too. What's on your calendar today?"

"My assistant is driving up this weekend to check out accommodations before she comes to work for us." Shannon didn't want to tell Joaquin that Mara was attempting to straighten out her personal life before she became a Bainbridge House employee."

"Good for her, because our grand opening will be

here before we know it. I'd sent you a text because I'd like to set up a time when we can meet for my biscuit-making lesson."

Shannon paused. She wanted to convince Mara to stay over until Monday so she could show her where they would be working at the château. "What about Tuesday evening?"

"Sounds good. Your place or mine?"

"Your place, Joaquin. By the way, did you buy the mixer?"

"Yes. Why?"

"Because I'm also going to show you how to make bread. And don't worry about the ingredients. I'll bring everything."

"What time do you want me to come by and pick you up?"

Shannon smiled even though Joaquin couldn't see her. "There's no need to put out a trail of breadcrumbs like Hansel and Gretel for me to find my way back to your home," she teased. He laughed, and her smile grew wider when the deep, sensual sound came through the speaker.

"Do you realize Gretel was a murderer when she pushed the witch into the oven, killing her?" Joaquin asked.

"We can debate ad nauseam about the brutality in childhood fairy tales. My sister-in-law refused to read many of the Grimm's stories to her children because some of the plots were so dark."

"That's something we can talk about when we get together."

"Okay. I'll see you Tuesday."

"Tuesday it is, and dinner is on me."

"You're cooking?"

"Of course, I'm cooking, Shannon. I'm nowhere as

accomplished as you or Viola, but I do know how to rattle a few pots."

"If that's the case, then I'll bring dessert."

"Good. Enjoy your time with your friend, and I'll see you Tuesday."

Shannon hung up and returned to the task of hooking up her printer and television in the sunroom.

Later that evening Shannon sat up straight when Mara drove through the open gates and came to a stop next to the Honda. Mara had called her when she'd left Sparta, New Jersey, and Shannon had stayed on the line with her, giving her detailed instructions as to which local and private roads to take to arrive at Bainbridge House.

She smiled down at Mara when she lowered her driver's-side window. "Welcome to Bainbridge House. You can follow me once I turn around." Shannon started the Honda's engine, then executed a U-turn and drove slow enough for Mara to follow her.

As they cruised along the roadway lined with lampposts reminiscent of Victorian gaslights, she noticed some of the trees were displaying buds, and she was looking forward to when they were in full bloom and the gardens were awash with color from flowers, ferns and grasses.

Shannon glanced up in the rearview mirror and smiled. Mara had slowed considerably. Her friend's reaction was like hers when she'd come to Bainbridge House the first time this past Christmas, when seeing the magnificent pink-hued French-inspired château.

Viola said that Taylor had attempted to retain most of the château's original character during the restoration and had made minimal changes to modernize the lobby area, restaurants, lounges and meeting rooms. Project manager and architectural engineer Robinson Harris had designed the new ballrooms to mirror the original ones. Joaquin mentioning the grand opening was fast approaching made Shannon aware that everything had to be completed before mid-May. The last two weeks in May would be a dress rehearsal for Memorial Day weekend, the official kickoff of the summer season.

And by that time, the kitchens would have to be fully staffed.

Running a hotel the size of Bainbridge House was no doubt daunting, but Taylor had reassured everyone that he was up to the task, because he planned to interview and hire experienced staff as the hotel's general manager, while Robbie would oversee engineering. Taylor claimed he was still attempting to convince Patrick to return and join him as the CFO and assistant general manager.

Shannon knew she only had a few months before she would move in to her apartment at the château. The two-bedroom suite located on the lower level would be as luxurious as those on the second and third floors. The plans indicated sitting areas, en suite bathrooms, a utility kitchen for her to prepare her meals and soundproofing to counter the noise from the lower-level kitchens.

Shannon stopped in front of the house, cut off the engine, got out and waited for Mara to alight from her two-seater MG roadster. The classic car had belonged to Mara's grandfather, who'd gifted her the vehicle after she graduated culinary school.

Shannon hadn't known anything about Mara Lewis before they became roommates. It had taken a week before Mara had opened about giving up her position at the FBI as a forensic accountant, because investigating white collar crime had lost its appeal, and as a pastry chef, she was able to develop her inner creativity struggling to break free. And that freedom was on full display whenever Mara decorated a cake.

"Why didn't you tell me this place looked like this? It's incredible," Mara said."

Shannon smiled. "I wanted to surprise you."

Mara's eyes sparkled like polished sapphires. "*Shocked* would be a better word. I can't believe you're going to work and live here."

"Don't forget, you're going to work here, too, that is, if you're still willing to become my assistant."

Mara sobered. "I gave you my word that I'm willing to become your assistant."

"What about Jordan, Mara?" She wanted to remind her friend about her frantic telephone call about her ex wanting to reconcile.

"Please don't mention that slug, Shannon," Mara spit out, scowling. "As I was driving here, I thought about what I've had to put up with over the years, and none of it was good. I did all the giving and never got anything in return. And not just money but emotional support. And to prove that I'm so done with him, I blocked his number, and I told my father that he wasn't allowed access onto the property if he came looking for me."

"Good for you. Now grab your bag, and I'll show you to your bedroom before we have dinner and talk about how we're going to run our pastry kitchen."

Mara's mouth gaped when she followed Shannon into the entryway. "Oh my gosh!"

"What's the matter?"

"Do you realize this table is a genuine antique? And the rug is an Aubusson."

Shannon knew Mara would've been able to identify the furnishings because her mother was a professional interior decorator. "I suspect every piece of furniture on the estate is an antique or an exquisite reproduction."

"I'm willing to bet that when my mother comes here for the grand opening, she's going to begin cataloging everything."

"Your mother is coming?"

"Mother wouldn't miss it. She loves golfing as much as my father. Dad would never admit it, but his wife is a better golfer than he is."

Shannon hoped the weather would cooperate to coincide with the hotel's opening for their guests to take advantage of the links and the outdoor swimming pool. "What did your folks say when you told them you were moving to New Jersey?" she asked as she led the way up the staircase.

"Mother was little upset because she wouldn't see me as often, but Dad said he's glad I could finally get away from Jordan."

"Are you saying that your father didn't like your boyfriend?"

"Dad hated him. He said if he was certain it wouldn't be traced back to him, he would've put out a hit on Jordan."

Shannon stopped at the top of the staircase and met Mara's eyes. "Did you tell him about your relationship with Jordan?"

Mara nodded. "Yes. It was only after I gave up the condo and moved back home that dad admitted that he'd hired a private detective to investigate Jordan and discovered I wasn't the first woman he'd scammed."

"But I thought after he'd broke up with you that he was dating a politician's daughter."

"He was. What Jordan didn't know was that my father and his new mark's father were college frat brothers. His new hustle was shut down before he was able to execute it, and that's when he called to talk about us getting back together. I freaked out because despite knowing he's a dog, I still have feelings for him."

Shannon wanted to tell Mara that it would take time for her feelings to change and hopefully fade completely. It had been that way with Hayden, because despite his duplicity, she still had been in love with her husband.

"Your bedroom is across the hall from mine. You'll have at least an hour to relax before dinner is ready."

"I'm going to unpack, take a quick shower, then I'll come down to help you."

Shannon mulled over what Mara had revealed about her father hiring a PI to do a background check on her boyfriend, and she was glad that he had, because she knew Mara was still vulnerable and could possibly become involved with Jordan again.

Weeks before the hotel opened, it was incumbent on her to have a staff she could depend on. Mara would spend two, maybe even three days with her and have Mara sign a contract for employment. And no doubt Mara's skill in cake decorating would be on full display whenever a couple booked their wedding at the historic site.

"Brother, are we boring you?" Taylor asked.

Joaquin smiled and shook his head. "No."

"Well, you haven't contributed more than ten words to our discussion, and time is winding down to when we expect to be fully staffed in less than ten weeks."

"Could it be that your brother is distracted because he can't keep his mind off a certain pastry chef?" Dom teased.

"Watch your mouth, Dom," Joaquin warned, frowning.

"What's the matter, Joaquin? Are you being defensive because you know what I'm saying is true?"

"You need to stay out of my business, Dom."

"That's where you're wrong, brother," Taylor said. "We need to be fully staffed before the grand opening."

Joaquin realized his distraction had begun ten years ago when he first saw Shannon and then again when she'd come to Bainbridge House to bake desserts for his brother's wedding. And it had intensified once again now that she was living on the estate. Initially, it had been her natural beauty that had attracted him, as it had many other men that night.

He liked that she hadn't been impressed with his pseudo celebrity status while she'd reached superstardom with her Daytime Emmy nomination. And when she greeted him with "Good morning, friend," it was as if she was deliberately reminding him they were only friends. If he were truthful, he would admit his thoughts about Shannon were far from friendly, and what he wanted to do with her was undeniably much more so.

"Sorry about that, Dom," Joaquin said.

"No need to apologize brother. When do you want to install the irrigation system in the greenhouses?"

"Monday. Once that's done, I want to wrap the trunks of trees along the garden paths with tiny white solar lights."

Taylor's eyebrows lifted slightly. "That's a lot of trees, Joaquin."

Joaquin smiled. "And hundreds of thousands of lights."

Taylor nodded. "Consider it done. Robbie said he's ready to build the bridge over the pond, and once that's done, he'll erect the gazebo."

Dom ran a hand over his hair. "Viola keeps talking about holding our wedding in the garden, so I know she's going to love posing for pictures on the bridge and in the gazebo."

"I thought I heard my name," Viola said, as she walked into the living room.

Joaquin draped his arm over his sister's shoulder when she sat next to him. "That's because your fiancé was talking about wedding photos."

"What about them?"

"Taylor said Robbie and his men are ready to build the bridge over the pond. After that, they'll put up the gazebo."

"Are you guys staying for dinner," Viola asked.

Joaquin removed his arm from around his sister's shoulders. "I'm going home because I have a few more plans to look over."

Taylor stood. "I promised Sonja that I would take her out tonight. She's been complaining that she's experiencing cabin fever, and it's been a while since we've had a date night."

"Joaquin, are you sure you want to go home, because if I don't have to cook, Dom and I are going into to town to eat at Jameson's, and you're welcome to join us."

"Thanks for the offer, but I'm going to pass tonight."

"I'm letting everyone know that we're having brunch here tomorrow at eleven. So Dom and I will expect to see you guys."

Joaquin met Taylor's eyes. "Has our dear sister always been this bossy?"

"You've been away for a long time, so you're not aware that she's become a drill sergeant."

Standing up straight, Joaquin executed a snappy salute. "May I be excused, ma'am?"

A rush of color darkened Viola's golden-brown complexion. "That's not right. I'm not that bossy. Tell him, Dom."

Dom averted his eyes. "No comment."

"I think it's time for me to leave," Joaquin said under his breath.

He drove back to his house, recalling how different his weekends were when he'd lived in Los Angeles. There had always been an event listed in his planner, along with an endless roster of people he could call if he craved company. And he was never at a loss for female company if he didn't have a date for a particular affair.

But for him, it had become a game that he'd learned to play quite well. And despite having several relationships lasting at least a couple of years, neither he nor his exes ever talked about it publicly. Joaquin knew he'd become an anomaly, because no one, other than his family, ever knew of his prior marriage. He'd been a college student when he'd married Nadine in Puerto Rico and dissolved their union with a quickie divorce in Mexico less than two years later.

When he'd admitted to Viola that he liked being single, it had been a half truth. There was something about Shannon Younger that made him wish he could retract those words. He liked her—enough to want to become involved. What he liked most was that he could be himself in her presence. And for the first time in a very long time, he could just be Joaquin Manuel Williamson, third son of Elise and the late Conrad Williamson, and brother to Taylor, Patrick, Tariq and Viola.

He parked his car in the garage, went into the house and retreated to his office. Joaquin had come to enjoy his new home. Whenever he looked out a window to see trees and grass, he harkened back to his boyhood growing up in the large farmhouse set on four acres in Belleville, New Jersey. There wasn't a need for him to make friends because he had his sister and brothers. And they didn't have to find a park to play in, because everything they needed was on the property: an in-ground pool and basketball and tennis courts.

There had been times when Joaquin craved his own alone time, and this was when he'd retreat into his bedroom and either read or listen to music. However, he had come to know that spending too much time alone wasn't good, because he tended to dwell on how he had become a statistic in New Jersey's foster care system as a two-year-old.

Elise had told him, as she had all her adopted children, why she had signed up to become a foster mother and her decision to adopt them. Joaquin had been too young to remember the trauma he'd endured before the state's Child Protective Services had taken him from his birth mother; it was when he'd celebrated his tenth birthday Elise revealed that after years of being abused by her live-in boyfriend, she'd died under mysterious circumstances.

He turned on the laptop and pulled up a program with a blueprint of the landscape. There was a wooded area near a rock wall where he wanted to build a short flight of connecting steps to a higher terrace as a multilevel stage to display potted plants of white lilies, ivy, petunias, santolina and Canterbury bells. The landscape would be reminiscent of one he'd completed for a client in Berkeley with plants and cacti native to the area.

Joaquin stared at the screen for more than two minutes without moving. Dom was right. He was distracted and knew he had to get his act together, or he would not make his deadline to restore the gardens before the Memorial Day weekend. Taylor had suggested they have a dress rehearsal the weekend before. And that meant every employee would be tested. And no one, including the Williamsons, was exempt.

Chapter Twelve

"What the heck is that?" Mara asked Shannon when her cell phone began buzzing.

She reached for the phone and stared at the screen. After breakfast, she and Mara had gone into the sunroom to relax before Shannon took her on a tour of the property. She had also planned to drive into town so Mara could meet with a real estate agent about possible rentals and/or house sales.

"It's a weather warning alert. There is a prediction of a nor'easter with at least three to four inches of rain. There's also a mention of flooding."

"When?

Shannon glanced at the phone again. "Tomorrow morning." Meteorologists had predicted warm temperatures for Sunday but wind and rain for Monday.

Mara unfolded her legs. "I'm sorry, Shannon, but I'm going to leave before the weather gets bad."

Smiling and successfully concealing her disappointment, Shannon nodded. "That's okay. Anytime you're ready to come back, just let me know."

"You're the best. Meanwhile, I'm going online to look for someplace to live around here."

"If you don't find anything before you're hired, then you can always stay with me. I told you that I'll have a two-bedroom apartment in the château, so I won't mind having you as a roommate until you find a place. It will be like old times when we roomed together at Johnson & Wales."

"Thanks, but I don't want to impose on you. I'm certain I'll be able to find something close by."

Shannon wanted to tell Mara that she was being silly talking about imposing. Her friend was generous almost to a fault, and that was the reason her boyfriend had taken advantage of her. The first time she gave him an expensive gift for his birthday, he'd subsequently given her a shopping list of what he wanted for his next birthday.

"Don't stress yourself about trying to find a place, Mara, because we need to be completely focused once we begin working. My boss is getting married at the end of June, so we'll have a month to confer with her about what she wants for her wedding desserts."

"Has she decided what type of cake she wants?"

"Not yet. And because you are the Picasso of cake decorating, that will be your responsibility while I take care of the other desserts."

A rosy flush swept over Mara's features. "You really want me to make the cake?"

"Girl, please," Shannon drawled. "Stop being so modest. You know you're the second coming of Sylvia Weinstock."

Mara lowered her eyes. "I try."

"You do more than try. And false modesty isn't becoming, Ms. Lewis," Shannon teased.

"On that note, I think I better go upstairs and pack. I'll text you once I get home." She took several steps, then stopped. "Thank you, Shannon, for helping me get my head together."

Shannon wanted to tell Mara that she hadn't done anything, that her friend had to acknowledge that she'd spent too many years with someone who wasn't good to her and that *she'd* taken the initiative to exorcise Jordan Hitchcock from her life.

Forty-five minutes after Mara left to return to Virginia, Shannon got a call from Viola.

"Taylor called to tell me that he's suspended all work on the château until the storm passes."

"Do you think it's going to be like Superstorm Sandy?" she asked Viola.

"I don't think anyone knows until it hits, but because we're not along the coast, we don't have to concern ourselves with flooding. But it's downed trees that has Joaquin worried."

"Hopefully, there won't be a lot of property damage."

Shannon wanted to tell Viola that if there was damage, then Joaquin better start pruning and planting. It would be less time-consuming and costly to clean up rather than replant.

"Let's hope you're right, Shannon. Are you sure you don't mind being alone during the storm?"

"I'm good, and I'm not worried about the power going out because we all have generators."

"If you say so. Taylor said he's going to tell Joaquin to check in on you because you're going to be alone."

"That's not…" Shannon's words trailed off when she realized Viola had hung up on her.

She didn't need someone to babysit her because she lived alone. However, when Shannon thought back, she realized it was the first time she hadn't shared a domicile with another person. When she'd left home after graduating high school and moving to Los Angles, it was to share an apartment with another aspiring actress before she married Hayden. She'd moved back to Baltimore to live with her parents for a year following her divorce before going to stay on her grandparents' farm in North Carolina. And she'd shared an apartment with a roommate during her four years at Johnson & Wales, the last two with Mara.

When she'd celebrated her thirtieth birthday the day before Halloween, she could not have envisioned how much her life would change. Not only had she been offered a position she aspired to since graduating culinary school, but she could control where she wanted her life to go.

Shannon left her phone on the table in the sunroom and turned on her computer. She had set up a schedule, listing the ingredients she had to have on hand to bake desserts for Jameson's St. Patrick's Day celebration.

Although it would be months before the hotel opened, Shannon wanted to make samples of chocolate candies, French bread, cookies, cakes and pastries, and a shiver of excitement eddied through her when she thought about the number of desserts she and her staff would make for weddings, corporate parties and of course afternoon tea. Making the petit fours for Joaquin's movie night would serve as an introduction.

And because she had the rest of her day to herself, Shannon decided to clean the house and put up a couple of loads of laundry. She'd just finished folding the clothes she had taken out of the dryer when the doorbell rang.

Peering through the security eye, she saw Joaquin staring at her. Shannon opened the door and smiled when she noticed him cradling a mixer against his chest. "What are you doing?"

"I decided to bring the mixer over because I thought we could get a jump on my lesson before the storm hits. After that, I'll probably be up to my eyeballs cleaning up downed limbs and other debris."

She opened the door wider. "Come in and put it in the kitchen." Shannon curbed the urge to laugh and to ask Joaquin if it was so critical that he learn how to make biscuits.

"I left the rest of our dinner in the car," he said over his shoulder as he walked past her.

"Our dinner?"

"Yup. I did promise to make you dinner."

Shannon followed him, silently admiring how his slim-fit jeans hugged his firm hips. He may have been a scrawny college student, but the man standing in her kitchen claimed a well-toned physique that was certain to make a woman give him a second and maybe even a third look.

"You're going to make dinner for me tonight?"

"Yes. For you and your friend."

"Mara left."

Joaquin gave her a direct stare. "What happened? I thought she was going to hang around to look at properties."

"She was until there was the report of the nor'easter. Mara lives in Virginia, and she wanted to go back home before the roads flood."

Joaquin flashed a lopsided grin. "Well, I guess it's just going to be the two of us."

"You're really full of yourself, aren't you?"

His grin faded. "Why would you say that?"

"Because you were so certain that I would be amenable to having dinner with you tonight." However, she did remember Viola mentioning that Taylor was going to have Joaquin check in on her. Though, checking on her didn't necessarily translate to them sharing dinner.

"I sent you a text to tell you I wanted to switch from Tuesday to tonight, and if you didn't have a problem with it, to text me back in an hour."

Shannon was glad for her darker complexion when she felt a wave of heat in her face. "I didn't see the text."

"Where's your phone, Shannon?"

She groaned inwardly. "I must have left it in the sunroom while I was doing chores around the house and didn't hear the ringtone.

"Do you always misplace your phone?"

"Not really. I don't get that many calls, so I see no need to have it glued to my hand."

"Am I forgiven?"

"For what, Joaquin?"

"For showing up unannounced."

There was something so boyishly charming about his expression that Shannon knew she couldn't remain annoyed with him. "Yes, you are forgiven. Why don't you go and get the rest of your stuff out of the car so we can get this party started."

Joaquin congratulated himself on his good luck as he returned to his car, because he hadn't anticipated finding Shannon alone when she'd told him her friend was visiting her. And he hadn't said anything to Viola when he'd gone to her house for brunch, because he'd assumed she had invited Shannon, and she'd declined because she was entertaining company.

He also had been forthcoming, wanting to switch the days because he wasn't certain whether he would be available to spend any time with her once the storm passed. When he'd gotten the alert on his phone, he'd tuned to the Weather Channel, and meteorologists were reporting that with strong winds coinciding with high tides, weather conditions were ideal for a potentially powerful storm.

Taylor canceling work at the château for several days would allow the workers to concentrate on cleaning up property damage once they returned. It would also give Joaquin time to survey the landscape before planting new shrubs and trees. And he was glad that construction on the bridge and gazebo hadn't begun, because if damaged or destroyed, he would have to order more building equipment.

Joaquin knew there would come a time when he probably wouldn't get to see much of Shannon. The exception would be Saturdays. Movie night was a holdover from his childhood when his father left his Manhattan office early to begin the weekend with his family. He religiously devoted Friday night, all day Saturday and Sunday to be with his family.

Conrad would walk into the house and greet his wife and each of his children with a kiss on the cheek. Even when they were teenagers, the practice continued. The one time Tariq complained about a man kissing him, Conrad quietly explained there were many cultures where men exchanged hugs and kisses, and it didn't make them less masculine. And now that they were adults, he and his brothers continued to hug when greeting one another but saved the kiss on the cheek for Viola.

He went back inside and discovered that Shannon had slipped on an apron over her long-sleeved tee and jeans.

She'd fashioned a bandanna into a headband and had tied it around her forehead. He'd noticed that whenever she cooked, she always wore an apron and head covering.

Joaquin set a large canvas bag on the floor near the breakfast bar. "Do I need an apron and bandanna?"

Bending slightly, Shannon removed an apron and bandanna from a drawer under the countertop. "Yes, if you're going work in my kitchen. The apron is optional if you don't mind getting flour on your clothes, but covering your head is mandatory. There's nothing worse than finding someone's hair in your food."

"I'll take both."

She smiled. "I was hoping you would say that. Now, what did you bring for dinner?"

"I thought we could do biscuits with fried chicken and sausage gravy."

Her eyebrows lifted. "I thought you wanted to substitute biscuits for the English muffins when you make eggs Benedict."

"I do. But it's been a while since I've had fried chicken, so we're going full-on Southern with the sausage gravy."

Shannon gave him a skeptical look. "Don't you think this should be a dish for brunch?"

"That's what I'm hoping. If it comes out well enough, then I want you and Viola to consider it for the brunch menu."

"Oh, I see," she said, smiling. "This is going to be your taste test?"

"Yup. I've got the fried chicken and gravy down pat, so all I need is the biscuit."

Reaching into another drawer, Shannon took several pairs of disposable gloves, then washed her hands in one of the two sinks. She beckoned him. "Suit up, wash up and let's go."

* * *

Shannon sat in the alcove with Joaquin savoring the peppery white sausage gravy slathered over a thinly sliced fried chicken breast sandwiched between layers of a flaky buttermilk biscuit. The slight bite of the pepper and the sage and fennel in the sausage gravy was the perfect complement to the chicken Joaquin had marinated with creole seasoning.

"This is definitely a winner, Joaquin."

"So, I get an A?"

"It's an A-plus. Do you think you can duplicate making the biscuits?"

"Maybe. I never thought to use frozen shredded butter in the dry ingredients."

"Just make certain to use the large holes in the box grater, then pinch the pieces until all the butter is well coated with the flour mixture. Do this for about thirty seconds before you add the buttermilk." Whenever Shannon bought butter, she would freeze some for future cooking and baking.

"I can't believe you make it look so easy."

"I told you before that flour and I are besties. I'm going to put the unbaked biscuits into a resealable freezer bag for you. You can them keep in the freezer for at least two months."

Leaning back in his chair, Joaquin crossed his arms over his chest. "I doubt if they will last that long."

"Aren't you going to share them with your other family members?" Shannon asked.

"If they come around, then yes. If not, then no."

"Weren't you taught to share?"

"Yeah, but there are some things I refuse to share."

Propping her elbow to the table, Shannon rested her chin on her cupped hand. "Would you care to elaborate?"

A beat passed, then Joaquin said, "I'm talking about a relationship."

Shannon paused. "What about it?"

"If I'm involved with a woman, then it can only be the two of us, because I don't want a third person in my bed."

Shannon lowered her arm as she registered what she interpreted as a challenge in his statement. "In other words, you expect her to be loyal to you?"

"It has nothing to do with loyalty, Shannon. It's all about trust. I want her to trust me not to cheat on her and vice versa."

There was another noticeable pause before Shannon asked, "Have you had a woman cheat on you?"

"Yes. More than a few times."

"Have you ever cheated on a woman?"

"If I were in a serious relationship, then never."

She wanted to ask him what he considered serious but decided the conversation was becoming too personal, and she chided herself for asking if a woman had cheated on him. And he didn't have to interrogate her about her past because those following her on social media knew that her husband had not only cheated on her but had gotten another woman pregnant.

"If we were to become involved with each other, I would never cheat on you," Joaquin said after a noticeable pause.

"I thought we'd agreed to be friends."

He nodded. "We did, but what if circumstances change, and we become more than friends?"

The silent voice inside Shannon screamed yes, if only to relive the intimacy she'd denied herself for years. There were occasions when she'd wanted to go out with a man and just sleep with him as a reminder that she'd enjoyed being loved and making love.

"Is that what you want, Joaquin? For us to sleep together?" He gave a long, penetrating stare that made her feel slightly uncomfortable.

"Don't put words in my mouth, Shannon. If I wanted to sleep with you, then I'd just come out and say it."

"I'm sorry."

He shook his head. "Don't ever apologize for something you feel or say. I'm not going to lie and say I'm not attracted to you, because I am. You intrigued me the first time I saw you, and I've become more intrigued each time we share the same space. I don't know what it is about you, but you're different from any woman I've ever met."

"Is it because you regard me as an enigma, while you're trying to figure out why I married a much older man?"

"Why you married Hayden Chandler is none of my business, because that is your past. I just want to discover who the real Shannon Younger is."

"What you see is what you get."

He shook his head again. "I beg to differ with you, because there are times when you are quiet and reflective and others when you're open, teasing and almost coquettish. Which one are you, Shannon?"

"All of them, Joaquin, because isn't that the reason why you're intrigued with me?"

"Maybe *intrigue* is the wrong word. Maybe I should've said you enthrall me."

"I'm that beguiling?"

"You have no idea."

Shannon thought Joaquin was coming on a little too strong, but something told her that he wasn't attempting to sweet-talk her to get her into bed with him, that he wouldn't have a problem getting most woman to sleep with him.

"I'm not going to lie and say that I don't like you, but I want us to take it slow. And it's not as if I'm going anywhere, because I do live here."

She didn't want to lie to Joaquin because she'd been lying to herself for weeks, or maybe even months. The moment she'd walked into Bainbridge House and realized he was the same man she'd stared at across a room so many years before she did not want to believe he was the brother of the woman who'd hired her to become the hotel's pastry chef. She did not know what there was about him that made her feel things she did not want to feel because she knew she wasn't willing to act on them.

However, in the months following the wedding Shannon had thought about Joaquin, wondering what there was about him that made her want more than friendship. That she wanted them to be friends with benefits.

His impassive expression did not change when he said, "How slow?"

"As slow as it takes," she said, refusing to be pressured. She'd allowed one man to overwhelm her with his looks, money and charm, and she had vowed never again. And Joaquin Williamson was a trifecta, because he possessed all three.

"Okay. It's a deal."

Shannon was slightly taken aback that he'd agreed so quickly, and unknowingly he'd gone up exponentially on her approval meter. "Now that we've settled that, have you thought of what you want to serve for your movie night?"

"*Our* movie night, Shannon."

"Okay," she conceded, "*our* movie night."

"You said you want a buffet, so maybe we could serve finger foods."

"Wait," she said, pushing back her chair to stand. "I want to get pen and paper to write down what we decide." Shannon returned to the table and took a sip of sweet tea. "What do you want to make?"

Joaquin felt as if he'd won a small victory when Shannon had agreed to see if they could take their friendship to another level. It wouldn't necessarily involve them sleeping together, but he wanted to be able to call her up and ask her out on a date. Or if she would be willing to come to his house to share a meal, watch a game on the TV or even a movie. She'd asked that they take it slow, and he would.

"I like working with chicken, so I'd like to make Korean-style fried chicken wings with gochujang sauce."

"Oh no, you didn't say Korean fried chicken. Have you ever eaten at Bonchon?"

"More times than I can count. Their chicken is addictive. One bite and you're hooked." Joaquin grinned. "Anytime I was near Brentwood, I'd stop in and order some."

"I'd ordered their chicken a few times in DC, and like a homing device, I wound up driving there at least once a week until I told myself enough."

"So, is that a go?" Joaquin asked.

Shannon smiled. "If you're going to make it, then yes."

"What are you going to make?"

"I was thinking about bite-sized ribs, deviled eggs with capers, pot stickers, shrimp cocktail and miniature crab cakes. I also make a kick-ass tuna tartare on kettle-cooked ruffled potato chips and—"

"Say no more," Joaquin interrupted. "That's our menu."

He got up, circled the table and eased Shannon to her feet. Cradling her face in his hands, he brushed a light kiss over her parted lips. "You are incredible."

Shannon's fingers circled his strong wrists and held on to him as if she feared losing her balance. The mere touch of his mouth on hers had her trembling like a leaf in the wind. They'd promised no kissing on the lips, but at that moment, that's exactly what she wanted.

"You just crossed the line," she whispered.

"I know. Will you allow me to do it again?"

The seconds ticked, then she said, "Yes." She wanted him to kiss her over and over as if to make up for all the years she'd told herself even though she'd wanted she didn't need to be kissed or loved.

Shannon lost herself, drowning in a rush of delicious sensations that had her celibate body throbbing for release when Joaquin's arms circled her waist and picked her up. Parting her lips, she moaned when his tongue met hers, and she knew if they did not stop, she would beg him to make love to her.

Somehow, she found Herculean strength to end the kiss and buried her face against his throat. She felt the strong pounding of his heart against her breasts, and Shannon knew the kiss had affected him as much as it had her as she inhaled the lingering scent of his cologne on his neck.

Easing back and lowering Shannon until her feet touched the floor, Joaquin stared at her under lowered lids. Although he'd admitted to her how much he liked her, it was obvious she didn't know how deep it went. And he'd asked himself, *Why her?* What, he wondered, was there about his sister's friend that had him thinking about her when he least expected. Shannon had asked that they take it slow, and he would. And she was right, because neither of them was going anywhere. She lived an acre away from him, a little less than the length and width of the football field. A distance he could run without getting out of breath.

"I'll help you clean up."

"You don't have to."

"But I want to, Shannon."

She exhaled an audible breath. "Okay. Do you want to take any of the leftovers?"

He pressed a kiss to her forehead. "No. I'm just going to take the biscuits."

"I suppose I'm going to have to make a few more to go with the chicken and gravy."

"I can leave some for you."

"That's okay. You can share them with the others. The next time we make them, you're on your own."

"Are you certain I'll be up to the task?"

"Stop it, Joaquin. You know very well that you'll be able to make them without me coaching you."

He winked at her. "Maybe you should write down the steps so they turn out with towering flaky layers like yours."

"Do I really look that gullible?" she said. "You probably know the name of every plant and flower, so I'm not going to fall for the ruse that you don't remember how to make biscuits."

"You can't blame a dude for trying, can you?"

"No, but you have to learn not to be so transparent."

"Not to change the subject, but Taylor doesn't want you to stay here alone if the storm hits us. Why don't you pack a bag, and I'll pick you up tomorrow before it begins raining. And don't look at me like that, Shannon. You know there's more than one bedroom in my house."

"Okay."

Joaquin didn't know why, but Shannon sounded as if she were doing him a favor. It didn't matter if she was, because Taylor had given him a directive that he check on her. And he didn't challenge or debate his brother, because Taylor had assumed responsibility for everything and everyone at Bainbridge House.

He cleared the table while Shannon rinsed the dishes and placed them in the dishwasher. She removed a pan from the freezer with the uncooked biscuits and put them in a resealable bag. He loved watching her move about the kitchen. It was as if there was no wasted motion. She handed him the bag.

"Don't forget to put them in the freezer when you get home."

"I won't."

"Joaquin?"

"What is it?"

"I've changed my mind."

"What about?"

"I'll go home with you tonight instead of waiting for tomorrow."

Joaquin wanted to ask Shannon why she'd changed her mind, but that no longer mattered, because it would be the first and, he hoped not the only, time that she would go to sleep and wake up with him under the same roof.

He smiled. "What do you want for breakfast?"

A dreamy expression flitted over her delicate features. "Surprise me."

Chapter Thirteen

Shannon told Joaquin she'd changed her mind about staying with him because spending the night or the next couple of days with Joaquin was certain to give her a glimpse into who he was and if they could become more than friends.

When she'd questioned him about his relationships with women, he'd been forthcoming when he'd admitted to having encounters that included sleeping with them. And because he hadn't attempted to deny engaging in casual sex, Shannon did appreciate his truthfulness.

She wasn't a prude when it came to sex. It's just that she hadn't found someone who had interested her enough to share a bed since her divorce. She was also aware that she'd given off vibes that communicated to a man that he could look but not touch.

Moving back in with her parents, living with them for a year while rarely venturing out in public had them questioning her mental health. When she'd reassured them that she was all right, Shannon knew she hadn't been completely truthful. She hadn't been all right, because her life had played out in front of the camera. Most people recognized the Black actress with the waist-length straight hair who had been dubbed Naomi Campbell's younger sister.

Shannon may have had a slight resemblance to the beautiful supermodel, but she had had none of her panache or confidence. It was only when Shay was in character that she would become that strong. The day she informed her parents she was leaving Baltimore to stay with her grandparents, she knew she had taken a major step to stabilize her life.

Living on the farm allowed her to bury Shay and resurrect Shannon. Getting up at sunrise to assist her grandfather in caring for the farm animals and then returning to the house to shower and join her grandmother in the kitchen to prepare breakfast had become the highlight of her day. She'd reverted to being a child when she went to the garden to gather fruits and vegetables her grandmother needed for the evening meal.

Nana not only taught her to cook but how to can fruit and vegetables after the last harvest to sustain them during the winter months. Nana claimed there was no need for her to spend money at a supermarket if they grew and raised everything they needed on their family farm. It was after dinner when all the chores were done, then she and Nana would sit on the back porch to talk or occasionally listen to the radio. The one time Nana asked what she wanted to do with the rest of her life, the question had given Shannon pause. She'd been twenty-two and had her entire life ahead of her. And when she said she wanted to become a chef, Nana told her if that was what she wanted, then she had to get up off her behind and go do it. And Shannon did just that when she applied to enroll in culinary school. The first day she walked onto the Charlotte campus had become the first day of her new life as Shannon Younger.

Shannon finished filling a weekender with enough clothes and personal items to last her for at least three days, then slipped on a puffy jacket and walked out of the bedroom and downstairs, where Joaquin waited for her. She found him sitting on a straight-backed chair in the entryway, flipping through one of her cooking magazines. The light from a ceiling fixture shimmered on his dark brown curly hair.

"Ready." She told him she was ready because something told her the moment she walked into Joaquin's home to sleep, she would not be the same woman when she returned.

Joaquin's head popped up. He stood, returned the magazine to the stack and reached for her weekender. "Let's go, sweetie."

Had he called her sweetie because it was a slip of the tongue, or did he think of her as his sweetie? Sitting in his car and staring out the windshield, she told herself not to overthink, something she'd find herself doing much too often.

Joaquin parked in the garage. It would be the second time Shannon would come inside his house, but this time it was different. It was to sleep over. He led Shannon up the steps and opened the door that led into the entryway.

"We're going to have to share a bathroom, and I promise not to leave any hair in the sink once I finish shaving. I would use the one on the first floor, but the shower stall is so small that it's claustrophobic."

"If it's that small, maybe I could use it."

"No, Shannon. The shower stall is so narrow that it's almost impossible to turn around. One of these days, I'm going to have a contractor remove a wall to enlarge the stall and put in a double vanity. I'm going to put you in the bedroom closest to the bathroom so you won't run into me whenever I take the back stairs if I get up earlier than you do."

"Even though I know there is a back staircase in my place, I've never taken it."

"Dom claims the stairs were worn and creaky before they were repaired."

Shannon followed Joaquin to the second floor. "It must have taken countless hours of work on the guesthouses to make them habitable."

"You would have to talk to Dom about that. The man is incredibly knowledgeable about everything at Bainbridge House."

"He should be if he was born and raised here."

"It's a lot more than that, Shannon. You've known Dom a lot longer than I have, and even though I find him a little too taciturn at times, he's growing on me."

"Are you saying that you don't approve of him marrying your sister?"

Joaquin stopped in front of the first bedroom off the staircase. "It's not up to me to approve or disapprove who Viola wants as her husband. I love my sister and only want the best for her, and if she loves Dom and plans to spend the rest of her life with him, then I'm all in."

"You don't believe he loves her?"

"I know for a fact that he loves her, because he's told me that more than a few times. And one of the hardest things for guys to admit is that they are in love with a woman."

"How hard, Joaquin?"

He smiled. "Very hard, Shannon." Reaching around her, he opened the door to the bedroom and tapped a wall switch, flooding the space with soft light from wall sconces. "Your boudoir, mademoiselle."

Shannon took her bag from him and walked into the bedroom. "*Merci, monsieur.* It's lovely."

"It may be a little early for you to turn in, so if you want to stay up you can come downstairs and hang out with me."

Shannon waited for Joaquin to leave before she closed the door. She didn't tell Joaquin she knew Dom was a direct descendant of Charles Bainbridge because that could've been something he hadn't divulged to all the Williamsons.

The bedroom Joaquin had selected for her was awash with shades of blue and white. The floral carpet set the stage for white armchairs, an elegant settee at the foot of a full tester bed with a matching padded headboard draped in off-white linen. Blue-and-white striped throw pillows on the chairs and settee matching the ruffled cloth covering a round table and the window seat.

Joaquin wanted her to join him, when Shannon would've been content to spend every hour she could in the beautifully furnished romantic bedroom. A mahogany highboy and armoire provided more than enough space for her to store her clothes. Working quickly, she emptied the weekender and changed out of her jeans and T-shirt into a pair of gray flannel lounge pants and matching top. Walking on sock-covered feet, she went down the stairs to find Joaquin.

Except for the caretaker's house, the five guesthouses were identical, but it was up to each resident to put their personal touch on the interiors.

And what she'd seen of Joaquin's house she thought reflected a more relaxed style with wood in neutral tones or white that contrasted with shades of blue, black and lavender. His downstairs floors were bare and toile de Jouy patterns were paired with checks and stripes on chairs and window seats. It was obvious his visit to Versailles had influenced him when he'd chosen the furnishings.

She found him in the kitchen standing in front of the refrigerator. All the doors were open. He'd exchanged his jeans and sweater for a pair of black sweatpants and matching short-sleeved cotton tee. "Are you trying to cool off?" she teased.

Joaquin turned and smiled. "No. I'm looking to see what I have so I can figure out what to make for breakfast."

She walked over to him. "Close the doors, Joaquin. You're wasting energy. Making breakfast for me is not that critical."

"What do you normally eat for breakfast?" he asked, closing the doors.

"It all depends on how I feel. It may be toast with peanut butter or preserves, along with coffee. Or if I really want something more substantial, then it will be grits and eggs with bacon, sausage or ham."

"Do you like omelets?"

"Yes."

"Good, because I have enough ingredients to make some." Joaquin smiled. "Now that we've solved that dilemma, would you join me when I turn on a basketball game?"

"Of course." He'd mentioned converting the two downstairs bedrooms into a home office and theater room.

Shannon followed him to a black leather sectional grouping with enough seating room for eight. He picked up a remote and turned on the large flat-screen mounted on the wall over the fireplace. The sounds that filled the space were like those in movie theaters before he lowered the volume. Movie night at Joaquin's was certain to become an adventure with good food, comfortable seating and high-tech electronic equipment.

Shannon looped her arm through his. The playoffs for college basketball teams had begun. "Have you made your brackets?"

Turning his head, Joaquin kissed her hair. "No. I stopped creating brackets for March Madness years ago, because they were busted before the first round. Do you watch basketball?"

"Not too often. I'm more of a baseball and football fan."

"Orioles and Ravens?"

"All the way."

"Do you ever go to the games?" Joaquin asked as he waited for Shannon to sit before he sat next to her.

"Yes, because my father coaches high school football."

"You did say that your parents are teachers."

Shannon nodded. "Dad teaches chemistry, while my mother taught kindergarten and first grades for years before she became an assistant principal at an elementary school. My father will deny it with his last breath, but he is a sports fanatic. Whenever he was home, every TV in the house would be tuned to a game or match, and when I complained to my mother, she said she didn't have a problem with her husband watching sports because he wasn't drinking, drugging or chasing women. During football season, he would take me and my brother to home games. And because I didn't like cold weather, Dad would resort to bribery, saying he would buy me all the hot chocolate I wanted, because he knew I had a weakness for it."

"Do you still like chocolate?"

"Yes."

"I know you'd mentioned hiring a chocolatier, but is there a difference between a pastry chef and one trained in French patisserie?

"French patisserie is food design and what I think of as a master class for professional pastry chefs. When I went to study in Paris, I discovered using Italian meringue in macarons was preferable because the shells were less fragile than if they would've been made with French meringue."

"What's the difference?" Joaquin asked.

"French meringue is uncooked as the sugar is whisked directly into egg whites, while Italian meringue is made with hot sugar syrup. It cooks the egg whites, making the meringue more stable, and that's the reason why the Italian meringue is the method that is more widely used today.

"I plan to make twenty-four color macaron shells filled with different flavored ganache for Viola's wedding. For example, a candied orange filling will be sandwiched between macaron shells made with orange food coloring. I don't want her to know about them until we set them on the dessert table. I'm also planning for candies in edible packaging as wedding favors. Each guest will get a chocolate round or square covered box filled with walnut caramels, mocha and nut creams."

"I'm certain that's going to be a big hit with everyone. Will you also make the cake?"

Shannon shook her head. "Nope. That will be Mara's assignment."

"Why, Shannon? The cake you made for Taylor and Sonja was a work of art."

"There are works of art, Joaquin, and then there are masterpieces. And Mara's creations are what I refer to as the work of a genius. I call her the Picasso of cake decorating."

"There's no need to be self-deprecating, because every dessert you made for my brother's wedding was incredibly delicious. I should know because I sampled every one of them."

Shannon decided not to get into a debate with Joaquin as to her ability as a pastry chef, because she'd studied and worked even harder to hone her craft. She and Viola were very young, thirty and twenty-nine respectively, to run their own kitchens, yet she never doubted whether they would be successful.

"Do you eat a lot of desserts?" she asked him.

"Not normally. But since I've moved back, I find myself indulging a lot more than I used to, because I can't resist whatever you and Viola make."

"Did you grow up eating dessert?"

"Yes, but not every night. My mother was a much better cook than she was a baker. Most times, if we did have dessert, it was store bought."

Shifting slightly, Shannon turned to look directly at him. "How was it being homeschooled? Didn't you miss not having schoolmates as friends?"

Joaquin took Shannon's hand and threaded their fingers together. "I didn't need friends when I had my brothers and sister, and I loved being homeschooled. I can't speak for the others, but I like not having to wait on a corner for the school bus or be looked at differently because I had a multiracial family. Whenever my mother and father would take us out to a restaurant, we would get the strangest looks."

"Did that bother you?"

"It did when I was younger, but after a while, I learned to give them a *What the hell are you looking at?* Stare, and they would avert their eyes. But it was Patrick who had to be restrained if he heard someone talk about us. We couldn't understand why he was so sensitive when he was the only one who could've passed for our parents' biological child."

Joaquin had called Dom taciturn when Shannon thought the term better suited Patrick Williamson. The few times she glimpsed him, he'd appeared to be scowling, and she didn't know if his less than affable mood had anything to do with his fiancée who'd clung to him as if she feared he'd disappear. One thing Shannon did know, or was aware of, was that the Williamsons were not fond of the woman to whom Patrick was engaged. And that included Joaquin's mother. It was probably easier to marry into a royal family, where the union had to be sanctioned by the sovereign, than Andrea getting the approval of her fiancé's family.

"The game's over, so is there anything you want to watch?"

Shannon was tired of sports, so she said, "How about a movie?"

Joaquin let go of her hand, reached for the remote and extended it to her. "I have several streaming services, so select whichever one you want. I'm forgetting my manners. Would you like something to drink? You have a choice of water, soda, beer, wine, scotch, bourbon, gin—"

"Stop, Joaquin," Shannon said, laughing and cutting him off. "I'll have water."

"Fizzy or tap?"

She smiled. He was giving her a choice. "Tap is okay." She'd said "tap," because filters had been installed in all the kitchens.

Shannon waited for Joaquin to return with her drink. A buffet with a hutch in the dining room displayed his extensive liquor collection, along with several sets of china and fragile crystal stemware. The ornate piece matched the rectangular dining table with seating for eight.

Viola had disclosed that her father, Conrad Williamson, as the last surviving Bainbridge, had willed the property to children with the proviso they honor their father's wish to restore it to its former magnificence. Sonja Rios-Martin joined the project as an architectural historian, cataloguing jewelry, furnishings, and dinnerware. Appraisals yielded astonishing totals making the Williamson siblings extremely wealthy. And once the restoration was completed, Viola predicted the property was estimated to be worth a half billion dollars.

Shannon could not have imagined moving into a house that was turnkey and filled with priceless items before Viola had asked her to come to work at the hotel.

Joaquin returned and handed Shannon a glass of chilled water. "Thank you."

He retook his seat next to her. "Have you decided what you want to watch?"

"No. Why don't you choose?"

"Have you seen *Creed*?

"No," she admitted.

"I've seen the first two and planned on watching the third, but I wouldn't mind seeing it again if it's okay with you."

"It's okay."

Joaquin wondered why her response sounded to him

like she did not want to see the film. "We don't have to watch it, Shannon."

"It's okay, Joaquin. I happen to like Michael B. Jordan."

He gave her a skeptical look. "Will the boxing scenes bother you?"

Shifting slightly on her seat, Shannon gave him a direct stare. "No. It's just that you remind me so much of my father."

"Is that good or bad?"

"It's not bad, Joaquin. It's just that you both are into watching sports. First it was basketball and now a boxing movie."

"Your father sounds like my kind of guy. Maybe one of these days, I'll get to meet him so we can trade stories."

"You will get to meet him at the grand opening, because I've invited my entire family. My brother, who is Dom's groomsman, is also coming with his wife and kids."

"So, it's going to be a family affair."

"Not only that, but it is going to be a reunion for Dom and Marcus before his big day. And once my sister-in-law sees Bainbridge House for the first time, she'll probably nag my brother until he agrees that she should start flipping commercial properties."

"She's into real estate?" Joaquin asked, wanting to know more about Shannon's family.

He knew he could probably question Dom but didn't want his sister's fiancé to know the extent of how much he'd come to like Shannon. However, he wasn't certain whether Dom would be that forthcoming with him. He had not developed the same familiarity with Dominic Shaw that his future brother-in-law shared with Taylor. But given time, Joaquin was certain he would come to regard him as another brother.

Shannon nodded. "She taught school for a while, then

decided she wanted to get into real estate, buying and flipping houses."

"Did she flip any?"

"Her first year, she flipped three, and she used the proceeds to buy her dream home."

"How does your brother feel about her getting into real estate?"

"He loves it, because it makes her happy. And Marcus will be the first to tell anyone that a happy wife equals a happy life."

"He sounds like Taylor."

"That's because Taylor knows what to do to make Sonja happy, Joaquin. And it really isn't that hard to find out what a woman needs."

Joaquin wanted to ask Shannon about what a woman wants, that no matter how he'd tried to give Nadine what she wanted, it was never enough. After only six months of marriage, he'd come to the realization she didn't know what she wanted, because it wasn't a husband willing to sacrifice whatever he had to make her happy. What Nadine needed was attention twenty-four hours a day, seven days a week, which had become impossible for him, because he was carrying the maximum allowable credits each semester, and whenever he came home, it was to a surly and often petulant wife who'd spent the day either talking on the phone or watching television.

He hadn't married her to be his maid, but he had expected her to cook a meal and clean their apartment. And whenever he'd asked her why she hadn't cooked, her comeback was, why would she when he was able to cook for himself? However, there was one positive thing to come out of his marriage. He'd become quite adept at doing laundry and housekeeping. His mother had hired a housekeeper, and her children's only responsibility other than keeping up with their coursework was making their beds and putting their clothes away.

Joaquin knew he'd shocked his mother when he told her he was married, then quickly explained it wasn't because he'd gotten a girl pregnant. Elise seemed pleased, because now she could claim another daughter and couldn't wait to meet her, but when Joaquin informed Nadine they were going to New Jersey for Easter, where he would introduce her to his family, she claimed she'd promised her terminally ill mother before she died that she would spend every family holiday with her father. And for more than a year, the Williamsons had believed he was delusional, because they never got to meet his wife, despite him showing photographs of their wedding in Puerto Rico. Once his divorce was final, Joaquin exacted a promise from his family never to mention his marriage ever again.

"What is it you need in a relationship, Shannon?"

The seconds ticked, stretching into a full minute before she said, "I need trust, Joaquin. I need to be able to trust the man who I'm involved with."

"What about love?"

"What about it, Joaquin?"

He smiled. She'd answered his question with one of her own. "Isn't love just as important in any committed relationship?"

There came another pause. "Not to me, because people fall in and out of love. I'd rather trust a man than love him."

Joaquin met her light brown eyes. "Is it because of your ex?"

"Yes. I loved and trusted him enough to marry him, then he shattered that trust when he fathered a child with another woman. A child that should have been ours."

"You want children?"

* * *

Shannon looked at Joaquin as if he'd suddenly grown a third eye. "Of course, I want children. I wouldn't have married Hayden if I didn't. We'd decided to wait a couple of years before becoming parents, but it looked as if he couldn't wait."

"The man was a fool for cheating on you."

"Is that what you think, Joaquin?"

He took the glass from her hand and put it in the cup holder on the arm of the chair. "Yes. You must not have realized how beautiful you are. You were mesmerizing even without saying a word."

"Are you saying you would've been a groupie?"

Throwing back his head, Joaquin laughed. "No. I've never been a groupie. And besides, you were a married woman, and that's a line I never cross."

That's a line Joaquin would never cross, but it hadn't bothered Hayden when he did, because his costar had just broken up with her live-in boyfriend, and when she'd told him she was pregnant, Hayden wasn't certain whether the child was his. It hadn't mattered who had fathered her child, because Shannon told him it was a wrap. That she was divorcing him.

"Do you mind if we talk about something else, because I don't like reliving my past."

Draping an arm over her shoulders, Joaquin pulled her closer. "Of course, I don't mind."

Shannon closed her eyes and tried to imagine what her life would've been like if she'd met Joaquin at nineteen but then quickly banished the thought. He'd had opportunities to marry an actress, yet he claimed being seen with one was only for publicity to grow his business, and what she found odd was that the details of his relationships were never made public. It was as if Joaquin Williamson had carefully monitored his life to reveal what he wanted the public to know and see.

"I'm ready to watch *Creed*."

She wanted to watch the movie, spend the night with Joaquin and discover *if* she was ready to turn another corner in her life to allow a man in.

Chapter Fourteen

Shannon walked into the kitchen the next morning to find Joaquin, his hair covered with a bandanna, dicing ingredients for omelets. After the movie, which she had enjoyed, she'd gone to bed and slept soundly throughout the night, and when she woke and looked out the window, she saw overcast skies.

Joaquin's head popped up. "I didn't expect to see you this early."

"I'm used to getting up to bake bread."

Wiping his hands on a towel, he rounded the island and brushed a kiss over her mouth. "Good morning."

Shannon wondered if this was how she would be greeted every morning if they did live together. With breakfast and a kiss. She smiled. "Good morning to you, too."

Joaquin stared at her under lowered lids. "I could use a sous chef."

"Okay Tupac."

His smile was slow in coming, reminding Shannon of watching the sun as it rose higher. "I suppose you're referring to my bandanna?"

"Yes." He'd tied the bandanna with the ends at the front rather than the back of his head.

"Tupac was my idol. I even have his greatest hits on my playlist."

Shannon laughed softly. "You like Tupac while I'm partial to Biggie Smalls."

Joaquin's eyebrows lifted. "Do I detect an East Coast–West Coast rivalry going on between us?"

Shannon patted his chest over a white tee, encountering solid muscle. "Don't play yourself, Joaquin, because I don't care how long you lived in Cali, but deep down inside, you know you're still an East Coast Jersey boy."

"You're right, Shannon. Whenever I'd come back for family get-togethers I wouldn't stay too long, because if I did, then I knew I would find some excuse not to return to California. And whenever someone mentioned me rushing off, I'd make up an excuse that I had to get back to my business."

Shannon found this disclosure puzzling. "You didn't like living in LA?"

"It wasn't that I didn't like it, but it was about missing my family." He exhaled an audible breath. "It's really about my mother."

She wanted to ask which one. His birth mother or his adopted mother. Viola had mentioned that she and her brothers were adopted but had not gone into detail about the circumstances, and out of respect for her privacy, Shannon hadn't asked.

"What about her, Joaquin?"

"I know it bothered her that she had not one but two

sons who she only got to see three times a year. I left home at eighteen to attend California State Polytechnic University in Pomona, and after graduating, I decided to make Los Angeles my home. Elise resigned herself that I preferred living in California, but when Patrick left to help his girlfriend's family with their vineyard, she thought of it as an act of betrayal."

"But she has two other sons and a daughter."

Joaquin gave her a smile she interpreted as one parents usually gave their children. "Elise would feel the same if she had adopted twice as many children and if two or three decided to leave the nest. She raised us to become independent adults but mandated we gather as a family three times a year. Taylor attended college in New York City, Viola the Culinary Institute of America in Upstate New York, Tariq at Cornell College of Veterinary Medicine in Ithaca, New York, and Patrick at Pace University in New York City. Do you see a pattern?"

Shannon nodded. "Yes. Everyone except you attended a college in New York, which meant she got to see them more often."

"So often that it was as if none had left home."

"Had she encouraged you all to enroll in New York colleges?"

Chuckling, Joaquin shook his head. "No. It just turned out that way. However, I was her only stray sheep until Patrick left."

"What about Tariq? Didn't you say that he must complete some postgraduate courses before he goes back to work on a Kentucky horse farm?"

"Yes, but Tariq had planned to fulfill his commitment to work at the farm before moving back east to get a position as a vet on a horse farm or racetrack on the East Coast before our mother told us about this property."

"It's as if Bainbridge House is responsible for getting the band back together," Shannon teased.

"Elise Williamson calls it a blessing in disguise. Dad died last January, and Mom waited until we all got together for Easter to reveal the details of his will. She had no idea that he owned Bainbridge House, and she was shocked that it now belonged to her. She, in turn, divided it evenly among her five children with the proviso we restore it as was stated in the will.

"Later that day, we came to see the property, and I told her I was all in. Taylor and Tariq were also in agreement. At that time, Viola was the only holdout, while Patrick agreed to come on board if he could monitor the expenditures remotely. Viola finally joined us once she resigned her position at the restaurant, after she was passed over for a promotion."

Shannon thought if Viola had gotten the promotion, then there was the possibility that she never would have met her. That Viola Williamson would have had to weigh becoming a sous chef at a Michelin-star restaurant to working in a kitchen on an abandoned estate that had been in her late father's family since the Gilded Age.

"All's well that ends well," she said, smiling. "Now, what do you need me to do as your sous chef?"

"Do you think you can handle the biscuits?"

"I don't know, Chef."

Joaquin winked at her. "I'm confident that you can bake them so they will be buttery layers of goodness."

Shannon knew she would very easily get used to sharing breakfast with Joaquin as he broiled chicken sausage to accompany fluffy spinach omelets and biscuits. He'd connected the playlist on his cell phone to hidden speakers, and they shared a smile when the infectious baseline beats of "California Love" filled the kitchen.

"Now, you must admit that 'California Love' surpasses anything Biggie recorded," Joaquin said as he picked up his coffee cup.

"I can't, because Biggie's 'Big Poppa' is an anthem."

"I don't think so," Joaquin countered, grinning.

Shannon and Joaquin spent the next few minutes debating the musical genius of two rappers who'd died much too soon, yet their music had survived for future generations. When she thought about having breakfast with Joaquin with what she'd shared with Hayden, there was no comparison. Sitting in the formal dining room at the opposite end of the table, she'd wait for the live-in cook to prepare whatever she'd requested to eat.

At nineteen, she'd been overwhelmed by a much older man who lived in an 8,000-square-foot multilevel house overlooking the ocean with a live-in staff that included a chauffeur, chef and housekeeper. She'd felt like a fairy-tale princess whose prince had taken care of all her wants and needs. Not only did Shannon enjoy cooking with Joaquin, but she also enjoyed his company, and it had nothing to do with the four-year difference in their ages, as opposed to the twenty with Hayden.

"Are you aware that we've spent a lot of time eating together?" she asked him.

"Last night and this morning are the only times we've shared meals with each other. The other times were with our family."

Shannon noticed he'd said "*our* family." It was the second time someone at Bainbridge House had referred to her as a part of their family. First Dom and now Joaquin. Dom was an illegitimate descendant of Charles Bainbridge, while Joaquin and his siblings were heirs to the estate because they were adopted by Conrad Williamson, and she wanted to remind Joaquin that she wasn't family but an employee.

"But isn't that the circle of life, Shannon? You get up, eat breakfast then go to work. You break for the midday meal, then return to work. At the end of the day, you have dinner before going to bed. Then you get up and repeat it the next day. In between the hours, hopefully you'll take time to enjoy your friends and family."

"That works for those who have traditional nine-to-five jobs with weekends off. It's going to be different for me once the hotel opens because many corporate functions and weddings are usually held over weekends."

"I hope you don't plan to work seven days week," Joaquin countered.

"Maybe I will initially until I'm able to set up a schedule for Mara to takeover for me."

"I don't want you to burn out before we're at or close to full capacity."

Annoyance shot through Shannon like an electric current. There was no doubt Joaquin was still smarting because she and Viola had decided to staff an all-female kitchen. "Why do I get the impression that you still don't believe Viola and I can run a successful kitchen?"

"I admit that I was surprised when you claimed you wanted to staff an all-female kitchen, because I'd initially thought of it as sexist, but there was never a time when I doubted your professional training. What the two of you prepared for Taylor and Sonja's wedding was perfect. I said what I did about burning out because I care about you, Shannon. I probably care a lot more than I should."

"How much more?" she whispered.

Joaquin closed his eyes and smiled. "Do you really want to know?"

Shannon couldn't pull her gaze away from eyes that

made him an incredibly magnetic man. When he looked at her, she felt herself drawn into a force field from which there was no escape. It hadn't begun when she'd come to Bainbridge House to bake wedding desserts for his sister but a decade before, when their eyes met across a room when both were living different lives.

"I know it must sound cliché, but you've bewitched me, Shannon Younger, as no other woman has. And it didn't begin when you walked into Bainbridge House to make desserts for my brother's wedding but a long time ago when I saw you with another man, a man who had claimed you as his wife."

A shiver swept over Shannon when she realized Joaquin had unknowingly read her mind. "I was thinking the same thing," she said truthfully. "It had to be fate that we were destined to meet again."

Joaquin nodded. "Meet again under a set of very different circumstances."

"And that is?"

"I don't have to feel guilty about lusting after another man's wife."

Joaquin may have been lusting after her when they first met, but she did now anytime she found them sharing the same space. His presence was a constant reminder of what had been missing in her life. All her professional goals had been met, but it was her personal life that was bland and uneventful.

She was a thirty-year-old single woman who hadn't had a date or slept with a man in almost a decade. Her mother was right when she told Shannon that she had to stop letting her ex control her life. That her divorce should've signaled a clean break so she could move on and start over.

"I'm no man's wife, Joaquin. And I haven't been one in a very long time." Her voice was barely a whisper.

Joaquin realized Shannon was offering him the opportunity to pursue her, but he didn't want her to believe it was all about sex, because it wasn't. Yes, he wanted to make love with her, and he also wanted her to trust him.

"I promise not to cheat on you or take advantage of you."

"Promises can be broken, Joaquin. Just don't do it."

Joaquin felt a calming, almost numbing, comfort that made him feel invincible. As if he'd scaled an impenetrable wall so that he and Shannon would agree that they would eventually take their friendship to another level.

"No promises." He stood up and circled the table to ease Shannon to her feet. He reclaimed her chair and pulled her down to his lap. "Are you okay?" he whispered in her ear.

Shannon looped her arms around his neck. "I'm more than okay—sweetie."

Joaquin smiled. "So, now I'm your sweetie."

Turning her head, she met his eyes. "Right now, you're more than my sweetie."

"What am I, Shannon?"

"Someone who has my brain in tumult, because I don't know whether I'm coming or going with you. My head says no while my body say yes."

Joaquin kissed her ear. "There's no need for us to rush into anything."

Shannon wanted to tell Joaquin that it was so easy to fall in love with him. That she'd felt more comfortable with him than she had when she'd initially met her ex. At that time, she'd been overwhelmed by Hayden's celebrity status, but it was different with Joaquin. Yes, he'd achieved a modicum of acclaim as the landscape architect for Tinseltown's rich and famous, but that hadn't inflated his ego. He'd been willing to give it all up to join his siblings to restore his father's ancestral home. A remote estate bordered by woodlands and only accessible by private roads.

"You're right," she whispered as she struggled to stay in control when she felt the growing hardness under her hips.

"How long has it been for you, babe?"

Shannon's breath caught in her lungs. She wondered if he'd asked because Viola had mentioned it to him. "Why?"

"Because I need to know how we should proceed, Shannon. That maybe you need more time before we agree to sleep together."

She exhaled an inaudible sigh of relief. It was obvious his sister hadn't discussed her sex life with him. "It's been a long time."

"How long is a long time?"

"Eight years," she said as she buried her face against the column of his neck.

A pregnant silence filled the kitchen as beats of time passed slowly. "What the hell did he do to you?" Joaquin asked.

She pressed her mouth to his ear. "It's not what he did but what I wouldn't allow myself to do, and that is trust a man not to cheat on me."

"I told you I won't—"

"I don't want you to say it," Shannon said, as she cut him off. "Just don't do it."

Sitting on Joaquin's lap and feeling his erection under her buttocks had turned her on to the point she wanted to beg him to make love to her. That she hadn't known when their eyes met ten years ago that she'd want to feel him inside her. That it had been the first and only time a man had seduced her with a glance.

"Babe?"

"What is it?"

"You're going to have to get off my lap before I embarrass myself."

Shannon tightened her hold around his neck. "Do you have protection?"

"Yeah."

"Then, let's take this upstairs."

"Are you sure?"

She smiled. "I've never been surer of anything in my life."

Shannon knew once she made love with Joaquin, she would change. Everything in her life would change—forever. It wasn't about happily ever after. Joaquin would become her Mr. Right Now. And because she did not want history to repeat itself when she'd allowed her heart to overrule her head.

She lost track of time when Joaquin pushed off the chair with her in his arms, carried her out of the kitchen and headed in the direction of the back staircase. Everything about the man holding her to his heart seeped into her. His warmth. The cloying hypnotic scent of his masculine cologne. Shannon could not have predicted she was about to sleep with a man she'd glimpsed in a room crowded with people who'd attended to be seen and photographed as invited guests of an award-winning movie director.

She felt the unyielding power in his arms as he effortlessly held her against his chest. The tapping sound against the window at the end of the upstairs hallway signaled it had begun raining.

* * *

Joaquin walked into his bedroom and placed Shannon on the mattress, his body following hers down. It was storming outside the house and inside the bedroom. He could not remember when he had not wanted to make love to Shannon. It hadn't begun when she'd first come to Bainbridge House last Christmas or briefly for the week last month or even now that she was living on the estate. And he hadn't lied when he said he didn't want to continue to covet another man's wife, because it was exactly what he'd done.

He'd overheard someone remark that she'd recently been nominated for a Daytime Emmy as an actress for an outstanding supporting performance in a drama he'd never watched. But that changed when he began to DVR the show just to see her. Joaquin was mesmerized when her image filled the screen, then he rebuked himself for acting like an obsessed fan. He didn't want to believe he was behaving like an adolescent boy worshipping a girl who didn't know he existed.

Even attending the dinner party had not been planned. His mentor Claude Eccles had been too ill and had insisted he go. Joaquin's name had been linked with the famed landscape architect when Eccles had transferred most of his client list to him.

Joaquin buried his face in Shannon's hair, breathing a kiss on the coconut-scented strands. His mouth moved slowly to the side of her neck, pressing a kiss to the velvety flesh. He moved lower, down to her throat, tasting the sweetness of her skin. The sounds coming from her were almost his undoing when blood rushed to the area between his thighs, hardening his sex so quickly that it left him light-headed. He had to slow down, or it would be over before it began. His hand slipped under her shirt and covered a firm breast. Reaching around her back, he undid her bra. Slowly, methodically, he removed her tee, bra, jeans and panties. She lay completely naked in his bed, and he couldn't pull his gaze away from her perfectly formed full breasts. Joaquin loved her smell, the way she tasted, and he knew that he was falling in love with her.

He wanted to kiss and taste every inch of Shannon's fragrant body, bury his face between her legs. She may have had sexual intercourse but wondered if she'd ever been made love to. And that's what he wanted to do—make love to and with her.

Shannon felt as if she were drowning in erotic sensations that heated the blood coursing through her veins when Joaquin's mouth trailed kisses from her throat to her belly. He was taking her to a place where she'd never been. She only had one man to compare Joaquin's lovemaking to, and there was no comparison. This was no frantic coupling, but a slow, measured seduction that had her craving his caress, his kiss.

His touch and kisses became bolder as his tongue dipped into the indentation of her belly button. Attuned to the changes in her breathing, the slightest movement of her body, he took his time giving and receiving pleasure. Her hands went to his hair when he put his face between her legs to inhale her distinctive feminine heat and scent. Her fingers tightened on his head as she tried to grip his cropped hair as her hips lifted.

"Easy, baby," he crooned softly. "Let me make you feel good."

She arched off the mattress. Everywhere he touched her, he ignited a burning passion that grew hotter and hotter until she found herself gasping in the sweetest agony. The barrier she'd erected after ending her marriage was swept away with the onslaught of desire that weakened her defenses, and she opened herself to welcome the pleasure that had eluded her for years. Shannon tried to sit up, but the hand splayed over her belly stopped her. The intense pulsing she'd long forgotten returned, stronger than she had ever experienced in her life.

"Joaquin!" she screamed, not recognizing her own voice.

"Relax, darling. I'm not going to hurt you."

How was she going to relax when she felt as if she were coming out of her skin? And how could she relax with his head between her thighs. Joaquin applied the slightest pressure to keep her from closing her legs as his tongue searched for the opening he sought. A single sob escaped her before it dissolved in hoarse gasps.

He was relentless, his tongue flicking over the swollen bud of flesh until it seemed to swell to twice its size. Her gasps were replaced by a low keening that made Shannon feel as if she were losing her grip on reality.

Joaquin lessened his sensual possession of her body when he reached over to the bedside table and opened the drawer to remove a condom. It took only seconds to slip the latex sheath over his erect penis. Moving up her moist, trembling body, he kissed her throat.

"Breathe, baby. Just breathe," he crooned over and over, hoping to get her to relax so he could penetrate her.

Shannon felt his hardness, the increasing pressure, as he slowly eased his penis inside her. Her body flamed with fire for one minute, and then she trembled uncontrollably from the shiver of cold. The hot and cold sensations continued until the heat won out and love flowed through her like thick, warm, sweet honey.

Her arms circled his waist, holding him where they'd become one. Heart to heart, flesh to flesh and soul to soul. Establishing a rhythm as if they'd choreographed their dance of desire, Shannon discovered a pleasure that sent waves of delight up and down her spine. Joaquin had promised to make her feel good, and she did.

She felt the contractions. They began slowly, increasing and growing stronger until she was mindless with an ecstasy that hurtled her beyond everything she'd ever known. She screamed! Once, twice and then lost count as her orgasms kept coming and overlapping with one another. She dissolved into an abyss of satisfaction that swallowed her whole, and Shannon was too caught up in her own whirling sensations of fulfillment to register the low growl exploding from Joaquin as he, too, climaxed. They lay together, savoring the aftermath that had made them one.

Shannon moaned in protest when Joaquin withdrew from her. Turning over on her side, she lay drowning in a maelstrom of a lingering passion that lulled her into a sated drowsiness reserved for lovers. She wasn't aware when Joaquin left the bed to discard the condom. She stirred slightly when he returned to the bed and pulled her against his body and fell asleep.

When Joaquin woke hours later, the storm had intensified with increasing wind gusts and driving rain. He managed to pick up the clothes he'd discarded and leave the bedroom without waking Shannon. After a quick shower, he went downstairs to clean up the remains of breakfast. He'd just finished rinsing plates and stacking them in the dishwasher when his cell phone chimed a familiar ringtone.

"Yes, Viola."

"Is Shannon there with you?"

"Yes. She's upstairs sleeping."

"Is she okay?"

Joaquin smiled. "She's okay, Viola. We were up late last night watching a movie, so she decided to take a nap."

He'd told his sister a half truth. It was after ten when the movie ended, and they'd spent another hour critiquing the film before they'd retired to their respective bedrooms. There was no way he was going to tell Viola that they'd spent the morning making love.

"I was just checking on my friend."

"Don't worry about your friend. I will take good care of her."

"I'm counting on you to do that."

"Shannon doesn't need a babysitter, Viola. In case you haven't noticed, she is a grown woman."

"And I'm sure you've also noticed that big brother."

"What's that supposed to mean?"

"You know exactly what I'm talking about, Joaquin. Only someone visually impaired wouldn't see how you look at her."

"Does that bother you?" Joaquin was becoming more than annoyed with his sister's innuendos.

"Not in the least. If Shannon was to become involved with someone, then I'd prefer it be you, because you both deserve a second chance at love."

"Look at you, Miss Wannabe Love Guru. Just because you're in love, you feel the need to play matchmaker."

"Are you saying you're not opposed to having a relationship with Shannon?"

"Goodbye, Viola."

"You didn't answer my question."

"And I'm not going to. I'm going to hang up now. You and Dom stay safe."

Joaquin hung up before his sister could continue with her inquisition. The family joke was Viola was like a dog with a bone. Once she latched on, she refused to let go until she got the answer she wanted.

He would leave it up to Shannon to decide if she wanted to go public with their relationship, while he was willing to go along with whatever she wanted because he loved her.

Chapter Fifteen

Shannon woke up totally disoriented. She knew she was in Joaquin's bed because she could detect his cologne on the linens. What she couldn't discern was the time of day. A soft moan escaped her when she straightened her leg. The slight discomfort was the result of muscles she hadn't had to use in years.

Sitting up, she swung her legs over the side of the bed and noticed her underwear at the foot of the bed. Walking gingerly, she picked up her clothes and headed in the direction of the bathroom. She'd decided to take a warm bath instead of a shower in the hope that it would help ease the tightness.

Forty minutes later, she went downstairs and found Joaquin sitting at a desk in his office. She noticed he was talking to someone on the phone and took a backward step, but the motion caught his attention, and he beckoned her in. Smiling and nodding, Shannon sat on a daybed covered in a woven fabric depicting hunting scenes and waited for him to finish his call. His replies were short, almost curt, and it was apparent he wasn't pleased with whoever he was speaking to.

Sitting and watching Joaquin made her realize what she felt wasn't infatuation. She liked him—enough to possibly fall in love with him. Lovemaking notwithstanding, he possessed all the positive traits she looked for in someone who she could have a relationship with. His loyalty to his family was without question, and she'd come to respect his candor whenever he answered her questions.

Shannon glanced around the room and observed an office with a classic European-style desk, matching armchairs and woven baskets filled with tubes of blueprints. He'd turned on the gas fireplace, filling the space with an inviting warmth. She was surprised to find a half-finished puzzle on a mahogany table in a corner. She bit back a smile; she never would've figured Joaquin would be into puzzles. Several glass globes were filled with jigsaw pieces, grouped by colors. It was apparent he had a system.

Joaquin ended his call and joined her on the daybed. A shiver eddied through her when he gave her a direct stare, and Shannon wondered what was going on behind the dark orbs. A hint of a smile parted her lips when he leaned forward and brushed his mouth over hers. "Hey, you," he whispered.

"Hey, yourself."

Shannon closed her eyes, inhaling the scent of body wash on Joaquin's throat as his arms circled her waist and pulled her closer. In that moment, she'd felt loved, protected, something she now realized had been missing in her marriage.

She had married Hayden believing he loved her

enough to be a loyal husband, but Shannon had concluded the man had married her because it enhanced his image as a one of Hollywood's most eligible bachelors and also inflated his ego that he was able to claim a young glamorous wife.

"How are you feeling?" Joaquin said in her ear.

"Good."

"No pain?"

"Just a little discomfort from muscles I haven't had to use for a while."

Joaquin eased back and met her eyes. "I'm sorry I hurt you."

"You didn't hurt me, Joaquin." Shannon rested her hand alongside his jaw. "I love making love with you."

Smiling, he pressed a kiss to her forehead. "And I you. But we should wait a while before we do again."

Shannon wanted to tell Joaquin that she didn't want to wait, that she'd wanted to make up for all the years she'd experienced a self-imposed sexual drought. She was willing to wait because they had time to discover what the other person needed and wanted.

"Okay," she agreed.

"Viola called to ask about you, and I told her you were sleeping."

Shannon went still. "Did you tell her about us?"

"If you're asking if I told her about us sleeping together, then no. Firstly, I don't kiss and tell, and secondly, I'm going to leave it up to you to disclose our relationship to my sister and anyone else you choose."

Shannon didn't know why she thought Joaquin had wanted her to be the point person to tell others about their association. Was his posture a holdover from when he'd dated women in California? He'd dated women yet refused to grant interviews.

"I'm not going to lie and pretend there's nothing going on between us, Joaquin. I'm too old to play games. If you're ashamed about us going public, then please let me know now, and we can end it right here, right now."

Joaquin cradled Shannon's face, unable to believe he would be ashamed of her and whatever he wanted to share with her. "Have you lost your mind? Me ashamed of you? I was being ttruthful when I told you that you're different from any other woman I've ever met or known. I don't know what that is, but given time, I will discover it for myself. If you want, I'll call a family meeting and tell everyone that we're a couple."

"That's not necessary, Joaquin. What I'm saying is that we're both too old to sneak around to be together. And because both of us profess to like being single, let's just enjoy the ride for as long as it lasts."

Joaquin didn't know why, but Shannon made it sound as if she were looking for a relationship that had an expiration date. "Do you want it to last, Shannon? Or do you want a wham bam, thank you, ma'am?"

"I'm a realist, Joaquin, and we both know that nothing lasts forever."

A beat passed. "Why are you looking to end something that has just begun? Something I believe is good to and for us."

"I— That's not true," she stammered.

"Yes, it is. And I'm willing to bet that you will be the first one to walk away because you don't believe you deserve to be happy."

"That's not true," Shannon repeated. This time her voice rose slightly.

"Let's hope I'm wrong, but if I'm not, then I promise not to tell you that I told you so."

Joaquin wanted in his heart of hearts to be wrong about Shannon looking for a reason or an excuse for them to break up. He knew his initial attraction to her was her natural beauty. But then he discovered she had a brilliant culinary talent. If her assistant was Picasso, then Shannon was Leonardo da Vinci, and once the hotel opened for business, he predicted she would be touted as a pastry prodigy.

"I didn't know you were into puzzles," she said after a swollen silence, pointing to puzzle pieces on a side table.

Joaquin smiled. "Yes. It's a holdover from my childhood. I always liked putting together puzzles as a kid. It began with two hundred, then five hundred and eventually a thousand pieces. I order them from a company in Vermont, and once I'm finished, I donate them along with a check to Big Brothers and Sisters."

"How long does it take for you to complete one?"

"Usually a month. That's how long I give myself to finish it, and even if I don't, I still donate a thousand dollars to my favorite charity. When we were kids, my mother would preach 'To whom much is given, much will be required.' That was her way of telling us that because we were blessed with wealth and talent, she expected us to give back to those less fortunate."

Shannon snuggled closer to his side. "Tell me about Elise Williamson and why she decided to adopt you, your brothers and your sister."

"When my mother married Conrad Williamson, she didn't know that she would never give him children. But he told her if she wanted children, then he would support her if they were going to adopt. She got in touch with a college friend who was a social worker with Child and Protective Services who convinced her to become a foster parent, because the adoption process could be a lengthy one. My mother, who'd earned a graduate degree in education and as a teacher was certified to teach kindergarten through high school, decided to homeschool Taylor. She loved fostering Taylor so much that she decided to do it over and over when she became a foster mother to me, Patrick, Tariq and Viola."

"How was she able to homeschool five children at the same time?"

"Once Mom decided to homeschool us, she converted the library into a one-room schoolhouse. Each of us had computers, and after instruction, we would work independently on our assignments or homework. She'd hired a housekeeper, so that freed her up from doing laundry and housework. She got up early to prepare breakfast and lunch. After the school day ended, she would fix dinner."

"She had to be a superwoman teaching and cooking for five kids."

Joaquin chuckled softly. "Elise Williamson had developed a system for food preparation. She also set up a schedule where each of us had to sit with her one night a week to watch her prepare dinner, because she claimed her children had to learn to cook rather than depend on someone else to feed them. Especially her sons."

Shannon patted his chest. "Your mama did good."

"Yes, she did, but Elise Williamson is a mama lioness who still feels the need to protect her cubs who are now adult lions and lionesses."

"Are you talking about her encounter with Dom about Viola?"

"Yes. She made a truce with Dom, but I doubt whether she will ever accept Patrick's fiancée as her daughter-in-law."

"I'd heard she made a fuss about her suite at the château, but it couldn't have been that critical."

"It was more than a fuss, Shannon. She was totally disrespectful. So much so that Pat refused to even talk or listen to her. It ended when Viola took her aside, and whatever she said to her did the trick. After that, Andrea was all smiles and sweetness."

"How did she react to Taylor marrying Sonja?"

"It was different with Sonja because she's carrying Elise's first grandchild."

"Are you saying that Andrea would have to become pregnant to win over her future mother-in-law?"

"I don't know if another Williamson baby would change my family's opinion of Andrea."

Shannon shifted on the daybed and gave him a direct stare. "You don't like her, do you?"

"I'm indecisive when it comes to Andrea, because even if she's the woman my brother has chosen as his life partner, I believe he needs to be with someone with less drama."

"How do you think your mother will react when she discovers one of her sons is dating a chef?"

Joaquin knew Shannon was referring to herself. He didn't believe Elise would have the same reaction she'd had once she heard her nineteen-year-old son had married a girl she hadn't met. And during their brief liaison, Elise would never come to meet Nadine, while in hindsight he was fortunate she hadn't, because Joaquin doubted if Elise or even Conrad would've been able to conceal their distaste for the entitled young woman. That she hadn't had to cook, clean or do laundry because her husband had grown up with help. What she did not know was that Joaquin still relied on his parents to pay for his tuition and off-campus apartment. And the money he'd earned working at her father's nursery he'd deposited into a savings account.

"When you talk about us being too old to play games, then it's the same with me, babe. I'm too old to even think about seeking my mother's approval of who I get involved with."

"It wouldn't bother you if she didn't like me, Joaquin?"

"No."

"It wouldn't bother me, either," Shannon said, "because I'll be sleeping with you and not your family."

Joaquin sat cradling Shannon while Mother Nature unleashed her fury with strong winds and driving rain. The mood inside the house was one of calm and warmth, and for Joaquin, it was a promise of wonderful days and nights to come with the woman in his arms who had become his everything.

The property had sustained moderate damage from the storm; there were several downed trees, power lines and lampposts along the road leading to the château. It had taken nearly a week before everything was back to normal and for work to resume on the château's interiors.

Dom had assisted Joaquin with installing the irrigation systems in the two greenhouses, and once completed they would program it to regulate the interior temperature and humidity. Viola wanted to grow a variety of vegetables. She also wanted him to cultivate a collection of melons, along with citrus trees.

Dom removed a bandanna from the back pocket of his jeans and wiped his forehead. "I hope your sister will be satisfied now that we've set up two greenhouses."

"Why is she my sister and not your fiancée?" Joaquin asked Dom.

"Because she's still your sister and not my wife."

Joaquin shook his head. "Viola is living with you and

wearing your ring, so you have more dog in that hunt than I do."

A smile crinkled the minute lines around Dom's dark green eyes. "I like having your sister live with me even though she can be a little bossy."

"If she's bossy, it's because it's taken her a while to come into her own, and I'm confident she's going to be able to use her training to do what she's always wanted."

"The same can be said for her partner, Joaquin. Viola said Shannon has always wanted to supervise her own pastry kitchen."

Joaquin picked up a hygrometer to measure the humidity inside the structure. "Well, it looks as if the ladies will be able to do their thing in a couple of months. Shannon told me she has selected her assistant."

"She's one up on Viola. She said she's going to start interviewing her staff after the Easter break." Dom paused. "What about you, Joaquin?"

"What about me?"

"Have you begun hiring your landscaping crew?"

"Not yet. I've been talking to this dude who's been jerking me around about hiring some of his workers he's looking to let go."

"Is he or isn't he firing them?"

Joaquin blew out his breath. "I don't know. What's the expression? He needs to either shit or get off the pot."

"Is it too late for you to contact someone else for workers?"

"No. The problem is this place is so out of the way that it's not as if you can see your neighbor's landscaping crew and ask if they can take on another client. I'm going to give my contact one more week before I'm forced to make a few more phone calls."

Even before moving back to New Jersey, Joaquin had

contacted a man who headed a landscaping franchise, with locations throughout the country, and he'd promised to give Joaquin the names of workers in the region looking for employment.

"Good luck, brother. If I can be of help, then let me know, and I'll try to pitch in anywhere I can."

Joaquin nodded, smiling. "Thanks. Let's hope it won't come to that, because you'll be busy interviewing and training restaurant staff."

Sitting on a stool, Dom stretched out his legs. "I never knew when I used to watch my grandmother run the kitchen and supervise the staff waiting on the Bainbridges that I would grow up and do it myself. My grandmother was like a drill sergeant barking orders to everyone who did everything to stay out of her way. And when I asked why she intimidated her workers, she said she had to act tough, or they wouldn't do what she wanted them to do."

"So, it was an act for her?"

"My grandmother would give an award-winning performance because she took her position seriously. She had been hired to run the kitchen of one of the wealthiest families in New Jersey. She also traveled with them when they spent the fall and winter months at their Brooklyn Heights townhouse."

"It's amazing that you know more about my father's family than we do."

"That's because I'm related to your father," Dom stated.

"Don't you think it's kind of weird that you're planning to marry your distant relative's adopted daughter?"

"It's too weird to even imagine."

Joaquin shook his head as he folded his body down on the stool, facing Dom. Although he hadn't known his biological parents, he doubted whether he'd become involved with a distant relative, and if he had, then he'd hoped it would've been very, very distant.

"Well, you probably don't have to concern yourself with that when you marry Shannon."

Joaquin jumped as if something sharp had been jammed under his fingernail. "What the hell are you talking about?"

Smiling, and seemingly ignoring Joaquin's scowl and angry tone, Dom said, "It's as plain as the nose on your face that you're in love with her."

Smothering a curse, Joaquin shook his head. "That's where you're wrong, *brother.* I'll admit that I like Shannon, a lot, but I'm not in love with her."

He realized he was in denial because he knew the hardest thing for him was to admit to someone that he was in love with woman. What he could not and did not want to admit to Dom was that he *was* falling in love with the pastry chef. For Joaquin, *falling in love* and being *in love* wasn't the same, and there wasn't a time during the day when he did not think about her. And there were nights following the storm when she had stayed over at his house and he at hers. What they hadn't done was make love again.

Dom sandwiched his hands between his jean-covered knees. "I need to have my say, and when it's done, I promise never to bring it up again. I don't know if Viola told you that I was married before. It didn't work out, and I'd told myself never again. But life and fate are mysterious, and when we least expect it, someone will come into our lives and make liars of us. There was something about your sister the first time I saw her that made me want to run in the opposite direction because I knew she was so different not only from my ex but any other woman I'd been with. Fast-forward, Joaquin, I've watched you around Shannon. You have that same look in your eyes that I had whenever I was with Viola. You claim that you and Shannon are friends, but when Viola and I first met, we also agreed to be friends.

"We were friends when I took her with me to Shannon's family Halloween party and we were forced to sleep in the same bed. Nothing happened, and when we came back here, she would occasionally sleep at my place because it was too late for her to go back to your mother's condo, and again she slept in a different bedroom, and nothing happened. I suppose it had to happen that way for her to trust me enough not to take advantage of her.

"Now, there's Shannon. Her brother and I were college roommates, so I knew her before she left home to be an actress. And when the news broke about what that dog of a husband had done to her, I pleaded with Marcus not to go to California, because he was threatening to put the man in the ground."

"I know about that, Dom. What does this have to do with me?"

"I'd visit the Youngers off and on after Shannon came back, and I found her to be a shadow of the vibrant young girl with a lust for life. It was as if the light had gone out behind her eyes, as if she were searching for something to make her whole again. She found some of it when she decided to become a chef. And when I saw her last October and again in December for Taylor's wedding, I said to myself, 'She's almost back.'"

"I'm going to ask you again. What does this have to do with me?"

"Being around you as put that light back in her eyes. She appears happier that she has been in years. You are the last piece in the puzzle, and I hope you'll give Shannon what she deserves.

Joaquin leaned forward. "How do you know this?"

"If you repeat what I'm going to tell you, then I'm going to lie and say I don't know what you're talking about. I overhead Shannon tell Viola that she believes she's falling in love with you." Dom paused. "Now, what say you?"

Joaquin wanted to lie but couldn't, because what he felt for Shannon went beyond friendship or sex. "I feel the same way about her."

Dom's raven-black eyebrows lifted questioningly. "And that is?"

Suddenly, feeling as if he'd been put on the spot, Joaquin glared at Dom. "What do you want me to say?"

"Come on, bro. That you're in love with the woman, and if you wait too long, you could lose her. Once the hotel opens, there will be a parade of men coming and going, and she might change her mind about you and move on. Sonja happens to have a collection of jewelry that was worn by several generations of Bainbridge women, and you should ask her to see some so you can select a ring for Shannon."

"Whoa! Hold up! You're rushing things, Dom."

"I don't think so. It's a known fact that you and Shannon weren't strangers when she came here during Christmas."

"That's where you're wrong," Joaquin argued softly. "I *saw* Shannon ten years ago at a Hollywood party, and we never spoke because she had attended with her then husband, and I was with a date. I was quite surprised when I showed up here for Christmas and discovered she was hired to make wedding desserts. Even though I tried to get her attention, she wasn't having any of it, because she was at work, and I had to respect that. Now it's different because we're both living on the estate. She's no longer a movie star, and I'm no longer the landscape architect to the rich and famous. And only now have we been given the chance to get to know each other, so you suggesting I propose to her is definitely out of the question."

"So, you're not going to tell her that you love her?"

"I will when the time is right. My focus, along with everyone else involved in the restoration, is getting this place ready for the grand opening. I'm certain between that time and after your wedding, we will know what direction to take."

"Sounds good."

Joaquin and Dom wouldn't be having this conversation if Shannon hadn't revealed how she felt about him to Viola. They'd made love once, but it was enough to know what they felt for each other wasn't predicated on sex.

And if they were to reach the point in their relationship where marriage was a topic for discussion, then Joaquin knew he had to tell Shannon about Nadine. He did not want to plan a future with her while keeping secrets.

Chapter Sixteen

Shannon dipped a spoon in the soup in the large Dutch oven and extended it to Viola. "Have a taste."

Viola took the spoon and slowly took a sip, her eyes widening as she slowly chewed the creamy soup. "Oh my gosh! That's delicious. I don't know how you do it, Shannon."

"Do what?"

"You cook as well as you bake."

"I like to experiment with different dishes, but my preference is baking."

Viola picked up a ladle and filled a small bowl with the soup. "This tastes like it came out of an Italian nonna's kitchen." She ate another spoonful. "Yup. This is authentic creamy potato soup with Italian sausage. It's as delicious as the soups I had in Italy."

Shannon felt a warm glow flow through her. When Viola had mentioned testing Italian recipes, not including pasta dishes, she'd thought about soup. The potato soup with sausage was a favorite of hers. Not only was it hearty, but the broth made with chicken and beef broth, cream and white wine could be enjoyed on its own.

"Do you want to put it on the menu?" she asked Viola.

"Are you kidding? I bet once we do, it will become as popular and maybe even more popular than the ubiquitous baked potato soup."

Shannon had made the dish with potatoes, spinach, sausage, diced tomatoes, heavy cream, sprigs of fresh thyme—which she removed before serving—and grated parmesan cheese. Her first year in cooking school, she'd befriended another student who invited her to her grandmother's house for dinner. The instant she'd tasted the flavorful soup, she knew she wanted to make it.

"Cup or bowl?" she asked because she and Viola had to decide on the servings.

"Definitely a cup. Offering it as a bowl will make it a meal."

Shannon stared at the dishes lining the countertop. Joaquin woke her up at dawn to tell her he had to meet Dom to begin installing the irrigation system in the second greenhouse and that he would see her later that evening.

They didn't get to see much of each other during the day because Joaquin got up early to work outdoors while she spent her day testing recipes for her pastry kitchen. Shannon would have preferred working in the château's kitchen, but that wouldn't be possible for at least another month. Taylor had predicted mid-April for most of the work to be completed, but the cleanup after the storm had changed it to late April. The storm had also preempted her baking desserts for Jameson's St. Patrick's celebration because the pub was forced to close for several days after the wind had blown off roofing, which resulted in water damage in the main dining room.

J.J. had also suspended her making desserts for the sports bar. He'd apologized because he'd forgotten the rider on contract with his current supplier was scheduled to expire at the end of September because of he had to give them six months' notice before termination. The delay did not bother Shannon because it gave her more time to concentrate on baking for the hotel. And by that time, she'd planned to be fully staffed.

"I'm going to bake the bread, then we can break for lunch."

Viola nodded. "What do you want to eat?"

Shannon scrunched up her nose. Whenever she and Viola cooked together, they always made enough for lunch and dinner. "A cup of soup with bread, honey chipotle chicken skewers and deviled egg potato salad. What are you thinking about?"

"I'm leaning toward the soup, potato salad and the meatballs."

"Why can't we have all of them?" asked a deep voice.

Shannon and Viola turned around to find Dom and Joaquin standing at the entrance to the kitchen. "Because we wanted to save some for dinner," Shannon told Joaquin.

He walked into the kitchen and stared at the plates on the countertop. "There's enough food here for lunch, dinner and a late-night snack."

"Word," Dom drawled, joining him.

Shannon shared a glance with Viola who gave her a barely perceptible nod. "Okay, but you guys are cooking tonight." Shannon smiled when the two men shared a fist bump.

"We're going to clean up, then we'll be back," Dom said as he headed to the bathroom off the kitchen, Joaquin following.

* * *

Fifty minutes later, Shannon sat next to Joaquin on the bench seat with her plate filled with meatballs, shrimp and potato salad. Dom and Joaquin raved about the soup and asked for seconds. The honey grilled chicken made with chicken thighs that melted on her tongue competed with the grilled bacon-wrapped shrimp for deliciousness.

Joaquin nudged her softly in the ribs. "You and Viola are a dynamic duo in the kitchen."

"Yup," Dom agreed after swallowing a mouthful of potato salad. "They are definitely superheroines."

Viola elbowed him. "I'm glad you said 'heroines.'"

Dom winked at her. "I'm not about to put my foot in my mouth like brother Joaquin did when you talked about staffing an all-female kitchen."

Joaquin lowered his eyes. "Did you really have to bring that up, Dom?"

An expression of innocence flitted across Dom's features. "I'm just saying."

Shannon touched a napkin to her mouth as she cleared her throat. She knew Joaquin was still smarting about his sexist remark and was trying to live it down. "Viola, have you thought about a color scheme for your wedding?" she asked smoothly.

In keeping with the Christmas theme for Taylor and Sonja's wedding colors of red, green and white, Shannon had baked samples of red velvet, pistachio and white cakes.

Viola and Dom looked at each other. "Dom mentioned he wants something that represents his Irish and Scottish ancestry."

Shannon smiled. "Are you talking about a tartan?" She recalled the plaid banner on the doors of Viola's red pickup.

Dom nodded. "I was thinking of black watch, but that may be too dark for a summer wedding."

"There are different shades of the tartan," Shannon said. "I've seen plaids with dark blue, medium green, light green and black."

"What color would you make the cake?" Viola asked.

"Probably a light green, but I'd have to confer with Mara to see what she suggests."

Viola's hazel eyes lit up. "I like those colors. What do you think, Dom?"

He lifted broad shoulders under a sweatshirt. "It doesn't matter to me, love. Choose whatever you want and just let me know when you want me to show up."

"When are you going to send out invitations?" Shannon asked Viola.

"I'm going to talk to my mother as soon as she gets back. I know I want colorful invitations with flowers. Joaquin, you're going to have to help me select the flowers that will go on the invitations so they'll match my bouquet."

Ideas tumbled over each other in Shannon's head as she tried visualizing the wedding cake. "Your cake topper can be a bow of ribbon in the tartan plaid cradling edible flowers that match your bouquet."

"You are a creative genius," Viola gushed.

"I try."

"Cut the BS, Shannon," Dom said. "You do more than try. Marcus told me you were wasting your time working for other folks when you should've gone into business for yourself as a personal caterer."

"I'm glad she didn't," Viola interjected, "because then I never would've been able to convince to come work at Bainbridge House."

Shannon nodded, smiling. "And I wouldn't have met

you if Dom hadn't brought you to Baltimore as his plus-one last year."

"Speaking of your family," Dom said, "Viola and I want to invite all of them to the grand opening. My folks have already committed to coming, and so are Sonja's."

"My family wouldn't miss it," Shannon said.

"It looks as if we're going to have quite a turnout," Joaquin remarked.

"I know Taylor is tired of me asking when everything is going to be ready," Viola said, "but I don't think he realizes that Shannon and I need get into the kitchens to set everything up for when we begin training our assistants."

"You don't need to put any more pressure on our brother, Viola, because he has enough to do with supervising the restoration and taking care of his pregnant wife."

A rush of color darkened Viola's face after Joaquin's reprimand. "I was asking, not pressuring him."

"Then please stop asking," Joaquin countered, "because the storm has shifted some of the timelines."

"Taylor gives me an update on everything, Viola, so if you want to know how things are progressing, just ask me," Dom told his fiancée.

Viola narrowed her eyes. "So, you want me to *ask* you?"

Dropping an arm over her shoulders, Dom pulled her close and pressed his mouth to her hair. "You can ask me any and everything, babe."

"Yeah, until you tune me out, *babe*," she teased.

Dom smiled, dipped his head and brushed a kiss over Viola's mouth. "That will never happen."

Joaquin glared at Dom. "Do you really have to do that in front of me. After all, she is my sister."

Shannon caught Joaquin's arm. "Let it go, sweetie," she whispered softly. "They're living together and will be married in a few months, so you can stop playing the protective big brother."

Joaquin stared at her under lowered lids. "Do you think your brother would appreciate seeing me kiss his sister in his presence?"

"I don't think he would mind if I told him that we were a couple."

"Are we a couple?" he asked in her ear.

"Yes, we are a couple," Shannon said loud enough for Viola and Dom to hear.

Viola applauded. "Congratulations. I was hoping you two would end up together."

Shannon felt unburdened. She'd admitted not only to herself but to others that she wanted an ongoing relationship with Joaquin Williamson. He was everything Hayden wasn't and couldn't be, and the long wait to find someone like him was worth it. She rested her head against Joaquin's shoulder, smiling when he placed a hand on her thigh under the table.

A smug grin touched Dom's mouth as he stared at Joaquin. "Well done, brother."

Joaquin inclined his head. "Thank you."

Knowing she'd openly acknowledged Joaquin as someone in her life fueled Shannon's passion for him when he joined her in bed later that night. Bending her knees, she looped her legs around his waist, holding him fast as he rotated his hips, each thrust deeper, harder.

Shannon felt the pulsing that began like gentle waves washing up on the beach. They grew stronger, more turbulent, as gusts of fiery desire shook her from head to toe. She trembled like a fragile leaf in a storm as the hot tide of passion took over completely, and she and Joaquin surrendered simultaneously to the uncontrollable joy that made them one with each other. As she lay savoring the aftermath of the lingering passion, Shannon knew for certain that not only had she fallen in love with Joaquin but that she also loved him.

She loved Joaquin Williamson, and as much as she wanted to tell him, something wouldn't allow her to speak the words aloud. They would remain her secret until the time came when she wouldn't be able to hide what lay in her heart. A moan of protest slipped past her lips when Joaquin pulled out of her still pulsing body.

"Don't leave," he said in her ear.

Shannon smiled. "Where would I go?" she whispered.

After they had said goodbye to Viola and Dom, Shannon had wanted go home to clean the kitchen and bathroom and dust, but Joaquin had insisted she come home with him.

"Back home to dust and vacuum."

She rested a hand on his stubble. "That's where you're wrong. After making love, all I want to do is sleep."

Joaquin kissed her. "Go to sleep. After I get rid of the condom, I'll be back to join you."

Shannon managed to stay awake long enough for Joaquin to join her in bed. Making love with him was like a stimulant that took her to heights she'd never experienced before bringing her down where she wanted nothing more than to sleep—the sleep of a sated lover.

She loved Joaquin because she felt comfortable enough to say whatever came to mind without censoring herself as she had with her ex-husband. There were occasions when she felt more like a daughter than a wife when Hayden chastised her for something she'd said. Even when she'd attempted to defend herself, he'd hush her with an angry glance or place his finger over her mouth. The second time he'd put his hand over her mouth was the last when she grabbed his finger and bent it back until he howled in pain. There hadn't been a need to say anything when he walked out of the house and didn't come back until a week later. And when he did return, he was apologetic and remorseful and promised it would never happen again.

Once her divorce was finalized, Shannon blamed herself for marrying a man so much older when she was barely out of her teens. At thirty and thirty-four respectively, she and Joaquin were better suited for each other.

She felt the warmth of Joaquin's body when he got into the bed. She sighed, and seconds later Morpheus claimed her as she fell asleep in the arms of the man holding her to his heart.

"Leave it to Mr. and Ms. Hollywood to make movie night spectacular," Viola crooned when she walked into Joaquin's house amid the flowery fragrance from diffusers and the flickering glow of electric candles on the table in the entryway.

"I think it's very romantic, Viola," Sonja said, greeting Shannon with a kiss on the cheek.

"Joaquin and I decided on romantic ambience because the theme of *West Side Story* is love."

Taylor made a snorting sound. "I just don't see my brother as the romantic type."

"Cool your jets, brother. I can be romantic when I want to be. Just ask Shannon."

Shannon glared at Joaquin. She didn't want to believe he would call her out like that. "Only when he brings me flowers."

"That's because he's the plant man," Taylor teased.

"Stop it, Taylor," Sonja whispered loudly. "There's no need to embarrass the man."

Dipping his head, Joaquin brushed a light kiss over Shannon's mouth. "Do I embarrass easily, babe?"

Her face flamed with heat. "No, because you have no shame."

Dom cocked his head. "Is that the instrumental version of the *West Side Story* soundtrack I hear?"

Shannon nodded. "Yes. Joaquin and I decided to get you into the mood by playing the soundtrack while you eat. Please come into the dining room and select whatever you want to eat before we watch the movie."

She stood in the dining room next to Joaquin, watching the reactions of Taylor, Dom, Sonja and Viola when they saw the buffet dinner they'd set out for them. "I think they like it," she whispered.

Sonja extended her hand to her husband. "Pay up, Taylor."

Joaquin shared a glance with Shannon. "Are we missing something?"

Sonja took the bill Taylor handed her and slipped it into the pocket of her flowing smock. "I bet your brother that you and Shannon would go all out when hosting movie night, but he didn't believe me.'

"Dammmn," Viola said, drawing the word out. "You guys really went over the top with this spread."

Dom selected a plate from a stack at the end of the table. "Y'all keep talking, but I'm about to get my eat on."

Shannon and Joaquin gave each other low fives as they stood in line behind their guests waiting to fill their plates. They'd decided to serve a mocktail punch that made it difficult to differentiate it from a classic Jamaican rum punch.

"How long did it take you to make the honey garlic baked pork bites?" Sonja asked Shannon.

"About three hours for a four-pound pork shoulder."

"That's how long it takes whenever I make perñil," Sonja said.

"Which is something that you don't make enough of," Taylor complained.

Sonja blew him an air kiss. "I'll make it for you for Christmas. It isn't Christmas in a Puerto Rican home unless there's perñil, rice with pigeon peas and pasteles. But making the vegetable and meat tamales is a marathon affair with at least three people putting them together."

Shannon ate and drank as she listened to the conversations about food floating around the table. She'd admitted to Joaquin that every time they'd gotten together with his family, it was over a meal, but then she had to acknowledge that she and Viola were chefs, and talking about food was relevant to their professions. And their chatter would've probably bothered Joaquin, Taylor and even Dom if they didn't cook themselves or had little or no involvement in the hotel.

The Dirty Dozen and a Greek salad were enjoyed by all who'd openly admitted they'd eaten too much.

"I hope everyone saved room for coffee and dessert?"

"What did you make?" Viola questioned.

"Petit fours. I made a few with crystallized ginger, orange almond paste, Black Forest, raspberry brandy, coffee and cognac, rum and orange marmalade, and nougat and amaretto. And I used liquor-flavored extracts for the brandy, cognac, rum and amaretto."

Slumping in his chair, Taylor groaned. "It's a good thing we're going to be here for a few more hours, because I'm going to have to wait for my food to settle before I'm able to move."

Viola stood to help Shannon bring out the dessert. "Joaquin, you and Shannon should host Easter dinner this year."

Joaquin shook his head. "Nope. As the eldest, the honor goes to Taylor. I'll host it next year."

"And because my sister is with child, I'm offering to prepare all the meat," Viola volunteered.

Shannon noticed everyone staring at her. "I suppose I'll make the desserts."

"No!" everyone chorused, laughing uncontrollably.

"These look almost too pretty to eat," Viola said when she saw the petit fours.

"Have you contacted everyone you want to work with you?" Sonja asked.

Shannon nodded. "I sent out emails to three girls I went to pastry school with, and hopefully I'll hear from at least two."

"Dom kept bugging me, so I did contact those I thought we would be able to work well together with. My last resort will be to post a listing with the CIA for a possible referral for an intern," Viola stated.

Sonja picked up a petit four. "You claim Patrick hasn't given you a budget for your personnel, so if you're willing to offer the kitchen staff a little more than the prevailing going wage, then you shouldn't have a problem hiring who you need."

Viola smiled at her sister-in-law. "That's what I plan to do even if I must negotiate when it comes to the starting salary."

Viola hadn't hesitated when Shannon told her what she'd wanted as a starting salary and respected her for acknowledging her training and experience.

Dessert had become a leisurely affair, with no one wanting to move away from the table. After coffee, tea and the petit fours, Joaquin invited everyone to move into the theater room, where they claimed butter-soft leather reclining chairs. He handed them movie night gift tubs filled with popular candies and packages of microwave popcorn.

"Compliments of the establishment," he teased before dimming the lights.

When Shannon had announced they were showing *West Side Story*, she insisted they view the latest Steven Spielberg version. Joaquin claimed a chair next to her and held her hand as the opening credits filled the large screen.

And it wasn't the first time that he wondered what would have happened if he'd met Shannon years ago and married her instead of Nadine. Would they still be together, and if they were, how many children would they have?

He knew thinking about marriage wasn't an option for Shannon because of her stance that she'd been there, done that, while he was open to trying it again, because he knew he'd been too young and immature to have been a good husband. He was as wrong for Nadine as she was for him, and in the end, both expressed no regrets once the divorce was finalized.

Joaquin told Viola that he liked being single, but that was before he had come to know Shannon, and before he was able to witness the affection between Taylor and Sonja, and Viola and Dom. The two couples didn't appear reticent as they openly exhibited their love for each other, which reminded him of his parents.

He missed his father, and he knew his mother missed her husband of nearly fifty years, and he knew she'd booked consecutive cruises to put distance between her and the place where she had shared so many memories with Conrad Williamson.

And when Joaquin thought about it, he realized he'd

spent too many years away from his family and probably would've continued to live nearly three thousand miles away if he hadn't inherited a share of Bainbridge House.

He'd come back, and this time it was to stay, because he was looking forward to becoming an uncle and to witness his sister marry a man who'd promised to love and protect her with his life.

His thoughts about Shannon would remain his until the time came when he would say what he needed to say to her, and hopefully, it was what she wanted to hear.

Chapter Seventeen

"I hope I didn't overdo it," Shannon said. It had been two weeks since she and Joaquin had hosted movie night when she'd volunteered to bake desserts for Easter.

She stood in her kitchen staring at cakes, pies, tarts and a tray of cookies. She hadn't made up her mind as to what she'd wanted to make, but once she started, she found she couldn't stop baking until she'd run out of flour. And she knew if the hotel's pastry kitchen was open and fully stocked, she would've continued until exhausted.

Elise Williamson had come back to the States three days ago, and Viola said her mother was resting in her condo, while Tariq was driving up from Alabama to stay with Elise. She'd also revealed that her veterinarian brother did not like flying and always drove whenever possible.

The day before Joaquin had driven to the airport to pick up Patrick, who was flying in from California. He'd informed her that Patrick and his fiancée would be staying at his house during their visit. Later that night Joaquin had sent her a text that Patrick had flown in alone and had refused to talk about Andrea.

Shannon did not have an opinion of Patrick's fiancée one way or the other because she'd been too busy working Sonja's wedding to interact with the woman. Her interaction with all the Williamsons was limited, because her sole focus when she'd come to Bainbridge House was to create desserts that would highlight her training and experience.

Staring at her cell phone, she noted the time. She had a little more than an hour to shower, wash her hair and get dressed before Viola came to help her transport the desserts to Taylor's house. Sonja had decided on a buffet rather than a sit-down dinner, which was a stark departure from traditional Williamson holiday get-togethers.

Her straight hair was longer than it had been in a while, and Shannon hadn't decided whether to let it grow or cut it again. When blown out, the thick strands now reached her jawline. However, she knew for certain that she would never go back to the style that garnered so much attention during her acting days. Her hair and her eyes had become her signature when she'd auditioned for parts, and she'd been asked constantly if she was wearing hair extensions and contact lenses, and the answer was always the same: no.

To be compared to Naomi Campbell did wonders for her ego, but it was her acting ability she'd wanted to take precedence over her resemblance to the supermodel.

She left the kitchen and went upstairs to her bedroom. When Viola mentioned that the gatherings were always informal, Shannon had decided to wear a pair of black pants with a white wrap long-sleeve shirt that tied in the front, and black three-inch leather boots.

She'd blown out her hair, parted it off-center and run a large-barreled curling iron through the ends before applying a light cover of makeup. It was the first time in a long time since she'd made up her face. The doorbell rang as she hurried down the staircase. Viola was right on time. Shannon opened the door to find her and Dom smiling back.

"Happy Easter. Please come in."

"Happy Easter to you, too," Viola said, pressing her cheek to Shannon's.

"Hey, kid," Dom said, smiling. "Viola brought me so I could do the heavy lifting. We just came from dropping off meat at Taylor's."

"I don't know about heavy, but there is a lot of stuff."

He narrowed his green eyes. "How much, Shannon?"

"Go in the kitchen and you'll see."

She followed Dom into the kitchen to see Viola standing with her mouth open, but no words came out. "I didn't know what to make, so it was a little bit of this and that."

"How long did it take you make everything?" Viola said when she recovered her voice.

Shannon smiled. "A couple of days." She'd had time on her hands, because with Patrick staying with Joaquin, she wasn't sleeping at his house or him at hers.

"Pound and Black Forest cake, apple and sweet potato pies, peach cobbler, mini key lime tarts and checkerboard cookies," Viola intoned as she identified each one."

"Shiiiit!" Dom said, gasped. "Who's going to eat all of this?"

Viola turned to look at him. "It may take a few days, but I'm willing to bet there will be nothing left midweek."

Shannon smiled. She'd observed whenever the Williamsons got together to eat, there were very few leftovers.

"I prefer making too much to not having enough."

"I agree," Viola said. "There's nothing worse than running out of food."

"I see that you came in Lollipop, but I'm going to suggest we take my vehicle, because I have racks in the cargo area that will stabilize the containers so that they don't shift."

"Where are your car keys?" Dom asked.

"They're in a basket on the table in the entryway."

Once the desserts were loaded in the SUV, Shannon locked up the house and joined Viola as Dom drove to Taylor's house. The weather had cooperated with bright sunshine and afternoon temperatures in the midseventies. Spring had come to the Northeast with warm days and cooler nights, while daffodils, crocuses and tulips had appeared, along with leaves on many of the younger trees on the estate.

The door to Taylor's house opened when Dom maneuvered into the driveway next to a Subaru and behind Joaquin's sports car. Shannon got out at the same time Taylor came over to greet her.

"Happy Easter."

"Happy Easter to you, too," she said, smiling.

"Go inside. Everyone's in the sunroom."

Shannon walked in, made her way toward the rear of the house and was met with mouthwatering aromas coming from the warming trays lining a long table. A banquet table with cushioned folding chairs was set up at the opposite the end of the room facing the buffet.

She saw Joaquin talking to his mother, and she nodded when meeting his eyes across the room. The scene was so reminiscent of that moment years ago, but this time it was different. She wasn't married and he hadn't attended with another woman. They were no longer strangers but lovers, and not seeing him for two days made her aware of how much she'd missed spending nights with him.

Shannon waited for Joaquin's approach after he'd excused him from his mother. He was casually dressed in a shirt, dress pants and a pair of leather loafers. She smiled when he dipped his head and kissed her cheek.

"How are you?" she whispered.

"Much better now that you're here," he said in her ear. "Come, let me reintroduce you to my mother."

Shannon noticed the tall, slender woman with dark blue eyes and coiffed wavy gray hair that still had a trace of red who was staring at her as she and Joaquin approached, wondering what the older woman was thinking.

Elise angled her head and smiled. "I almost didn't recognize you as the chef who made the desserts for my son's wedding."

Shannon knew she looked different out of her chef whites. "It's nice seeing you again, Mrs. Williamson."

Elise shook her head. "None of that 'Mrs. Williamson' business. Please call me Elise."

"Okay. Then it's Elise," Shannon confirmed.

She wanted to tell Elise that if her mother and grandmother heard her address an older woman by her first name without prefacing it with Mrs., they would've given her a tongue-lashing she would've remembered all her life. Although Maryland wasn't geographically the South, culturally they were very close. And not only had she spent her summer vacations in North Carolina, but she'd also attended culinary school in the Tar Heel State.

"That's better. And I want to welcome you to the family."

Shannon went still when she replayed Elise's words.

She forced herself not to look at Joaquin. Had he told his mother that they were sleeping together, or had she just assumed because she was living and working on the estate that she'd thought of her as family?

She forced a smile. "Thank you."

Elise reached over and took her hand. "I've heard so many wonderful things about you, and now that I'm going to be around for a while, I hope we will get to see more of each other."

"I'm sure we will," Shannon said, smiling.

"That went well," Joaquin said when Elise walked away to say something to Dom when he came in with containers of dessert.

"Did you tell her about *us*?"

"No, Shannon, but she knows because my brother and sister were talking to her about us being together."

"What did she say to you about *us*?" Shannon asked Joaquin.

"She said she's happy for me."

Shannon let out a sigh of relief. Even though she was sleeping with Joaquin, it was something she didn't want to flaunt to his mother.

"Can I get you something from the bar?"

She glanced over where Patrick was pouring drinks. "I'd like a white wine."

Joaquin dropped a kiss on her hair. "I meant to tell you that you look beautiful. Beautiful and very sexy."

Shannon lowered her eyes, but not before she noticed Elise staring at her and Joaquin. It was obvious that the woman saw her son kiss Shannon's hair. Elise smiled and Shannon nodded and smiled. She felt comfortable now that she knew Joaquin's mother was aware that she was dating her son.

"I'll go with you," she said, looping her arm through

Joaquin's, who covered her hand with his. The proprietary gesture wasn't lost on Patrick when he smiled at her.

"Welcome to the family, Chef. What can I get you to drink?"

Shannon responded with a friendly smile with one of her own. "A white wine, please." She tried not to react to his greeting welcoming her to the family. First Elise and now Patrick.

Patrick expertly uncorked a bottle of chilled white zinfandel and filled a glass. "How have you been?"

"Wonderful," she answered truthfully. And she was. Everything was right in her world. She had fallen in love with Joaquin, and she was counting down the time when she would assume her position as the head pastry chef at Bainbridge House.

It was the first time Shannon shared a family get-together with the entire Williamson family, and she felt as if she were a spectator at a stand-up comedy show. Tariq, Patrick and Joaquin teased Taylor incessantly with expectant father jokes. They even went as far as to place wagers that he would faint once Sonja announced that she was in labor. And despite the teasing from his brothers, Taylor took it all in stride, claiming he had one up on them, because with the birth of his son or daughter they would all become uncles.

"Don't worry about Taylor fainting," Viola said, "because I told Sonja that I would be her backup."

Tariq bore a striking resemblance to Taylor because they shared the same dark complexion. His large dark eyes seemed to miss nothing as he stared at Shannon before glancing away. He'd shaved his head, and his smooth pate reminded her of dark chocolate.

Viola and Sonja had outdone themselves when they'd

prepared an herb-crusted leg of lamb, honey ham, collard greens with cornmeal dumplings, Cajun red beans and sausage, and rice. Bottles of wine, pitchers of beer and sparkling water lined the table for liquid refreshment.

"Shannon, my children tell me you've created some spectacular dishes for the hotel's menu," said Elise.

Shannon glanced at the succulent sliced lamb on her plate. "They're just a few of my favorites."

"Mama, Shannon is being modest. She's trained as a chef *and* a pastry chef, and that makes her an amazing talent." Viola said.

"Mom, now that you're going to be here for the next three months, you'll get a chance to sample some of the dishes Viola and Shannon have produced for the menus," Joaquin said.

Elise smiled, and her eyes seemed to appear even bluer in her sun-browned complexion. "I'm looking forward to it."

"Aren't you tired of cruising?" Taylor asked.

"A little, but not enough to stop until I see every continent," Elise said. "I told my friends that I'm going to be stateside through the summer, and if things change, then I'll join them for their next adventure."

Elise looked at Shannon. "Do your parents have grandchildren?"

"Yes. They have three. Right now, they're on a Disney cruise."

Viola rested a hand on Elise's shoulder. "Mama, as soon as you've recovered from your trip, I need you to help me with the invitations, because my wedding is a little more than three months away."

Elise nodded. "Have you decided on a color scheme?"

Viola smiled at Shannon. "Yes. I want blues and greens."

Elise smiled. "Nice. Will there be any tartan?"

Viola couldn't control her burst of laughter. "Yes, Mama, there will be tartan as a nod to Daddy's and Dom's ancestors."

A smile softened Elise's mouth. "When you marry Dom, I will be able to claim another son. That's five." She glanced around the table at her three single sons. "What's the holdup? Other than Viola and Sonja, I would like to have another daughter."

"Please give it a rest, Mom," Taylor said under his breath. "Your sons will marry when they're ready to take that step."

"Step, Taylor! Right now, your brothers are frozen in place."

"Mama," Viola whispered, "first it was grandbabies and now it's daughters-in-law. You must stop fixating on what you can't control."

Joaquin stared at Shannon, wondering what she was thinking when witnessing his mother's new campaign about wanting to see her sons married. Patrick hadn't brought his fiancée, and he hadn't mentioned that they had split up. When Joaquin asked him about Andrea, he said she didn't want to come, and he'd left it at that.

"What's on your agenda for your next trip, Mom?"

Elise touched a fingertip to the corner of her eye. "I don't know. That all depends on my children."

Joaquin frowned. "What's that supposed to mean?"

Elise took her time looking around the table and giving each of her unmarried sons a long penetrating stare. "If I can look forward to another wedding or grandbaby, then I won't leave."

"Patrick's next," Tariq said. His pronouncement was met with silence as Elise's dour expression communicated what she refused to say, and after an uncomfortable pause, conversation resumed.

Joaquin glared at Tariq and shook his head. A beat passed before he nodded. Patrick's relationship with Andrea was not up for discussion.

Joaquin picked up his wineglass and took a swallow of rosé. He preferred the more informal buffet setting to one where everyone sat around the table passing dishes. Not only had it saved time, but he was able to select whatever he wanted to eat.

There had been a time when he'd returned to New Jersey three times a year to reunite with his family, but this time was different. He was back to stay and hopefully he would be able convince a beautiful pastry chef to trust him to where they would eventually share a future.

Joaquin found his mother sitting next to him when Shannon got up to help Viola and Sonja prepare to serve coffee and dessert. "I'm glad you're going to take a break from globe-trotting with your wild bunch friends."

Elise rested her head against his shoulder. "I must admit that I do get tired, and when I do, I stay on board the ship rather than go sightseeing. Now that Sonja's expecting to have her baby next month and Viola's planning her wedding for the end of June, I'm going to be home for a while. Enough about my travels. How are you adjusting to moving back?"

"It's been a lot easier than I'd anticipated."

"You don't miss the Hollywood nightlife?"

Joaquin gave her a sidelong glance. "Now, you know that was all for show."

"If it was, then you gave an award-winning performance. Speaking of performances, I'd heard from the others that you're dating Shannon, but is what you have with that pretty pastry chef all for show?"

Joaquin laughed softly. "So, you noticed?"

Elise also laughed. "Of course, I noticed, Joaquin.
I don't know why my children think they can fool
me. The minute I saw Viola and Dominic Shaw, I knew
something was going on between them."

"And what they had, Mom, almost blew up in your
face, didn't it?"

"Please don't remind me how foolish I reacted about
the whole thing when I thought Dominic was after Viola's
money."

"Dom doesn't need Viola's money, and you have to
stop suspecting that every person your children choose
as their life partner is a gold digger."

His father's death had left his wife and children extremely wealthy. Conrad had also established a trust to
restore Bainbridge House with the proceeds from the
sale of his investment company totaling more than a half
billion dollars.

Elise nodded. "Viola has chosen well. Now, back to
you, Joaquin?"

"What about me?"

"Have you told her how you feel about her?"

"Not yet."

"If you wait too long, you must might lose her."

First Dom, and now his mother was warning him
about Shannon. "Shannon's not going anywhere, Mom.
She lives *and* works here."

"Do you really believe that would make a difference
when a woman decides she wants nothing to do with you?
She can sleep in the same bed with you and still act as
if you don't exist."

Joaquin wanted to tell his mom what he'd shared with
Shannon was too new to reveal his true feelings. "I don't

want a repeat of what I had with Nadine. I want to take my time to see if it's going to last a lifetime."

"The difference is Shannon is nothing like your first wife. Nadine saw you as prey and went in for the kill. But when she discovered that you weren't financially independent and that you had to rely on your father for support, she wanted out. Shannon is an independent, professional, educated woman who doesn't have to rely on a man to take care of her. She doesn't need you, Joaquin—not for anything. Don't get up," she said as she pushed to her feet. "I'm going inside to help bring out the dessert."

Joaquin was still seated when Tariq took the chair their mother had vacated. "Are you okay?"

"Why?"

"Because I was watching your face when you were talking with Mom."

"We were talking about things that happened a long time ago."

"Did it have anything to do with your ex?"

"Yes, and you know that's something we don't talk about."

"But you were talking about it with Mom."

"That's because she is our mother, and I can't just shut her down like I'm going to do with you."

Tariq put up both hands. "No problem."

Knowing Tariq was nonconfrontational, Joaquin said, "I'm sorry I came at you like that, but I have a few things on my mind."

"It's looks as if you're not my only brother who has a few things on his mind."

"Are you talking about Pat?"

"Yup. Hopefully he'll get to straighten out his life before it's too late. I know the two of you are close because you both lived in California, but it's Mom who is really worried about him."

"Pat's staying with me, so I'm not going to bring up Andrea unless he does. Then I'm just going to listen."

Tariq patted Joaquin's shoulder. "That's why I prefer dealing with horses. They don't talk back and they have never given me grief."

"You're still young, bro. Once you finish your education and find the time to wine and dine a woman, you'll change your mind."

Tariq smiled. "That will only happen if I can find someone who likes animals as much as I do."

"She's out there, Tariq. You're just not looking for her."

"True. But right now, I'm going inside to look for something stronger than water and wine. I know Taylor has some bourbon. Do you want me to bring you a glass?"

Joaquin stood. "Nah, bro. I'm coming with you." Tariq wasn't the only one who needed something stronger to drink.

Chapter Eighteen

It was the first week in May, and Bainbridge House, shimmering in the bright spring sunlight, resembled an enormous, fancy, vivid pink diamond plucked from Australia's Argyle Mine surrounded by a collection of rare Colombian emeralds. It was as magnificent as it had been when first constructed centuries ago.

The formal gardens bordering the château were restored to their original structure with geometric shapes and a symmetrical arrangement of box hedges and flower borders. But Shannon preferred the informal gardens with flowers, herbs, ferns and ornamental grasses growing in seeming abandonment, where she'd begun sharing lunch with Joaquin when he and his landscaping crew broke for the midday meal. She enjoyed sitting on a blanket under the branches of flowering fruit trees while watching the antic of the ducks and swans who'd returned to their home on the ponds.

The bridge, erected over the lily pond, was an exact replica of the one in Monet's painting, and a stone path on the other side of the bridge led to a gazebo with an intricately detailed wrought iron frame painted all white. Inside the gazebo was a matching table and cushioned chairs that beckoned guests to come and sit for a while. As predicted, Joaquin had wrapped the wrought iron arches with climbing roses.

There had been an undercurrent of excitement from everyone involved in the restoration, and Shannon had been no exception. Mara Lewis had convinced two women who'd worked with her at her old job in DC, one a chocolatier, to join her at Bainbridge House. A Realtor had found Mara a three-bedroom rental house less than four miles away, and Mara promised she and her cohorts would move in to their new home in time for staff training.

Shannon's pastry kitchen wasn't the only kitchen fully staffed. Viola had hired a butcher, sous chef, broiler, fry and sauté cooks, and bussers. Dom was doing double duty as business and dining room manager when he scheduled interviews for three weeks before selecting those he would train and supervise. There was also a steady stream of applicants applying for positions in housekeeping, the front desk, bartenders, bellhops, security, sales, room service, and banquet manager. May 17 was established as training day for all Bainbridge House personnel.

Resting her head on folded arms, Shannon stared up at the trees that would soon bear apples. She had requested and Joaquin had planted four more Granny Smith trees to add to ones already growing in the orchard because she needed them for pies and other desserts.

"I could fall asleep right here," she said in a quiet voice.

Joaquin, turning over on his side, smiled. "I wouldn't chance it, because some of the female swans are sitting on eggs, and there's no doubt she will attack you if she suspects you will harm her babies."

"I can't wait to see the babies once they hatch when they'll settle on the backs of their mothers as she takes them on a ride on the pond."

"Are you aware that swans mate for life?"

Shannon shifted until her nose was only inches from Joaquin's. "Yes. Unlike humans who profess their undying love for each other, then turn around and try to figure out why they'd given the other person even the time of day."

"Tariq claims he prefers interacting with horses because they don't argue with him and will never break his heart."

"That's the perfect excuse for not getting into a relationship."

"Not really. Tariq has had relationships in the past, but now he's focusing on earning a postgraduate degree. He's scheduled to graduate next week."

"Are you still going to the ceremony?" Joaquin had mentioned in passing that he could possibly fly down to Alabama for his brother's graduation.

"Yes. I told my mother I would go with her. Taylor can't leave because Sonja could have her baby any day now, and Viola has volunteered to stay and act as the conduit between Sonja and her parents. Sonja claims she doesn't want her mother to come down before she has the baby because she wants to remain as calm as she can until the delivery."

"What about Patrick?" Shannon asked.

"Pat plans to fly into Tuskegee, Alabama, two days

before the ceremony and return to California the following morning."

Shannon closed her eyes for several seconds. "It's as if everything is compressed into two months. First there's Sonja's baby, then the grand opening and finally Viola's wedding."

"Are you ready to get on and ride the Williamson roller coaster?" Joaquin said.

She scrunched up her nose. "I wouldn't miss it for all the money in the world." Shannon had been truthful because she preferred being busy to sitting around and waiting for something to happen.

Viola had solicited her input when she wanted to select designs for her wedding invitation and response card once she confirmed she'd wanted blues, greens and lavender for her color scheme, while Elise had contacted Dom's family in Arizona and spoke at length to his stepmother about the plans she'd made for her daughter's wedding and the reception to follow.

Shannon, knowing she would have to supervise the kitchen staff once again because this time Viola would be a bride, planned for Mara and the assistants to monitor wedding desserts. Viola's wedding would differ from Sonja's because they would not have to use a caterer for logistics. The in-house banquet manager would assume that responsibility.

"How are the flowers in the greenhouse doing?"

Joaquin ran a finger down the length of her nose. "They're doing quite well. I know Viola wants blue and green hydrangeas and baby white roses, so I'm going to make certain they will be enough for the floral designer to make boutonnieres and bouquets for her and Sonja."

Shannon knew Viola wanted to be a June bride and hoped the small window between the grand opening and wedding was enough time to make it a success. And hopefully Viola wouldn't have a meltdown before she was to become Mrs. Dominic Shaw, because on occasion, Shannon had noticed her exhibiting premarital anxiety.

"How are the repairs coming on the golf course?" she asked Joaquin.

"They're going well."

She smiled. "So, everything's well?"

Joaquin rested a hand over her hip at the same time he kissed her mouth. "As well as it could be under the circumstances."

"Are you saying it could be better?"

"Yes."

Shannon stared into eyes that were as dark as black coffee. "What would make it better?"

"Making love to you right now. I can't believe you've put me on a sex diet."

Shannon buried her face against his chest. "It's only been three days, so you're going to have to wait for at least another three before we're able to make love again."

"What do you expect me to do in the meantime?"

"Take cold showers, Joaquin, or whatever you dudes do when you're horny."

"You're a cold-hearted woman, Shannon Younger."

"You're contradicting yourself, Joaquin, because a few days ago, you told me I was hot."

He chuckled. "You are when you prance around in panties that barely cover your goodies."

"I wasn't prancing, just getting ready to take a shower when you invaded my boudoir. But that's what I get for not locking the door." Joaquin had stripped off his clothes in seemingly 1.2 seconds and joined her in the shower. Their passionate coupling stopped short of him penetrating her because he didn't have protection.

Joaquin's expression suddenly grew serious. "I told you that you're going to have to begin locking your front door at all times, because we now have people working around the property at different hours."

Not only had Joaquin frightened her when he'd walked into the bathroom, but she hadn't expected to come to her house that night because they'd agreed to take a few days off from each other. Since they'd begun sharing a bed, they'd spend the night either at her house or his. The exception was Easter when Patrick had extended his stay for a week to reconnect with his family.

Shannon had noticed no one had mentioned Andrea Fincher's name whenever she was present, and she found it odd that the woman Patrick was engaged to had suddenly become persona non grata. This left her wondering if they were still together. She was aware that families claimed in-laws and outlaws, and there was no doubt that Andrea was the latter when it wasn't the same with Sonja and Dom.

She didn't place herself in either category. Although she'd found herself falling in love with him, Shannon was more than content for them to continue as lovers. And she doubted if they would continue to sleep together as often once she moved out of the guesthouse to take up residence in her apartment at the château.

Reaching for her cell phone on the blanket, she noted the time. "I need to get back because Viola wants to meet to discuss what she wants for her reception."

"She's not getting married for weeks, so why can't that wait?"

Shannon sat up. "No. Have you forgotten that the hotel will be open for business, and when it comes to an event, we must plan weeks in advance? We just finalized the menu for the grand opening weekend that's less than four weeks away."

Joaquin also stood, then extended his hand to help Shannon to her feet. His arms encircled her waist. "Thanks again for lunch."

Tilting her chin, she smiled. "You're welcome. I'm going back now."

"Will I see you later tonight?"

"Sure. I'll make dinner."

Lowering his head, Joaquin covered her mouth with his until her lips parted. "Later, babe."

"Later," she whispered.

She packed the remains of their lunch in the wicker basket and then folded the blanket before she walked over to the golf cart. The carts had become the temporary mode of transportation on the estate because the roads were being repaired and paved. Barriers were set up at different intervals to prevent vehicular traffic and to allow the cement to dry before the cover of blacktop.

Shannon took Mara, Chelsey Stuart and Lisa Vaughn on a tour of Bainbridge House before they took the elevator to the lower level and the pastry kitchen. The three women were speechless when riding the elevator to the suites in the turrets before taking the staircase down to the third- and second-floor suites. And if Taylor hadn't taken her on the same tour several days ago, Shannon's reaction would have been the same: speechless.

There were two guest elevators and one for food service. The lobby with twin massive chandeliers and an enormous round table to display fresh flowers set the stage for elegant dining and lodging. The three restaurants—one for the public, another for hotel guests and a third reserved for private parties were as ornate as those in royal castles.

The bars and lounges claimed brick walls, coffered ceilings, leather seating, ginger-colored paving-stone floors, old iron chandeliers and a vast array of wines and liquors for leisurely sampling. The setup in the meeting rooms was reminiscent of nightclubs, where chairs were positioned around tables rather than theater style. Monitors were positioned around the room for easy viewing of the stage. Powder rooms were decorated with antique mirrors, flanked by shaded sconces and stunning onyx sinks with twenty-four-karat gold-plated fixtures.

Shannon gave each woman a direct stare. "Well, how do you like Bainbridge House?"

"It's breathtaking," Mara said.

Chelsey Stuart nodded. She was a thirtysomething woman with a pale complexion and dark hair and eyes who'd been a stay-at-home wife for twelve years, divorced her husband and enrolled in culinary school to become a chocolatier. "It's beyond anything I've seen. It's like going back in time when nobility lived in castles."

"Bainbridge House has retained many of its original features," Shannon explained. "The exception is plumbing and heating. What had been one hundred bedrooms was reduced to seventy-five suites while two ballrooms were converted into restaurants and meetings rooms.

Lisa Vaughn nodded. "I feel like Cinderella at the ball."

Lisa reminded Shannon of her younger self with her long straight hair. However, she did not want to remind the Black woman who appeared to be barely out of her teens that when working in the kitchen, she had to cover her hair.

"What we want is for Cinderella to find her prince at Bainbridge House and share his suite, not run away once the clock strikes twelve," Shannon teased. "I wanted you to see the hotel before I give you an overview of what is our kitchen. I say 'our' because it belongs to all of us. Mara and I will work closely together making desserts for private parties, while Chelsey will be our bread maker and at times assist with French patisserie." Shannon paused. "I hope you won't have a problem with this."

Chelsey shook her head. "Of course not. I love working with dough."

Shannon breathed an inaudible sigh. She was hoping her assistants would agree to what she'd assigned them. "Lisa, chocolatier extraordinaire. You will be responsible for all things chocolate, and that includes desserts, cakes and candies. One of the owners will be married on-site at the end of June, and I want to fill you in on what we are expected to prepare."

It took Shannon less than twenty minutes to outline the dessert menu for Viola's wedding, beginning with the color scheme and what she'd planned for various desserts, concluding with wedding favors. Mara was excited because she'd been given the task of decorating the cake with layers of pistachio green, lavender and light blue. It was when Shannon explained the significance of the tartan that the other three pastry chefs were willing to offer their input on incorporating the plaid into other desserts.

They spent several hours discussing and sketching miniature pastries, fancy cookies made from short pastry and couverture, tarts, tortes and exotic treats with varying fillings and decorations, and Shannon knew for certain, based on Mara's recommendation, she had hired the talented and experience chefs she needed for her kitchen.

"I'm going to need everyone to be here around nine in the morning so we can make samples of everything we plan to offer hotel guests. That includes bread, muffins, biscuits and cupcakes. The following day will be sweetbreads and scones. And any other thing we can come up with before Bainbridge House opens for business. I don't want anything left to chance once it's listed on the menu."

"You say the grand opening is the Memorial Day weekend?" Lisa asked.

Shannon nodded. "Yes. Some guests will check in Friday afternoon, and the festivities for the ribbon cutting are scheduled for Saturday at noon. Once that's concluded, there will be lunch, and for those who booked afternoon tea, it will be served in the solarium with finger sandwiches and tea cakes."

"Welcome to Bainbridge House!"

Shannon swiveled on the stool to find Viola standing at the entrance. "Mara, Lisa and Chelsey, I'd like you to meet Bainbridge House's executive chef, Viola Williamson."

Applauding, Viola walked into the kitchen. "My pleasure. I think it's time you met your counterparts. Please follow me."

The pastry chefs followed Viola, and Shannon trailed behind them as they walked to the main kitchen. There were gasps once the chefs realized there wasn't a man among them.

Viola stood off to the side. "I'm going give everyone time to introduce themselves to one another before we sit down to eat. Shannon and I were up early this morning preparing a little repast to welcome you to Bainbridge House." She shared a smile with Shannon as the women cheerfully greeted one another with handshakes and others with hugs. "Shannon and I are equal partners in the kitchens. If I'm not here to answer a question, then feel free to go to her. We'll use the kitchen on this floor when we must prepare banquets for large parties of fifty or more; otherwise, we'll use the kitchen on the first floor. Pastry chefs will always work down here. I'm certain you've noticed that we're an all-female kitchen, and you can thank Shannon for that concept. I had to agree with her because I was passed over a few times at a Michelin-star restaurant because of my sex, and that's when I said never again. It's time I stop running my mouth and let my partner have her say."

Shannon nodded. "Thank you, Shannon. Our grand opening is in two weeks, and we're going to take that time to make every item listed on the menus, and you will also evaluate them before the hotel opens for business so we can decide what to serve out guests that weekend."

"You're going to leave it up to us to make that decision?" Lisa asked, wide-eyed.

"Yes. There's no *I* in team, Lisa. And Viola and I want you all to work together as a team. What we do expect is for you to come in on time and cover your hair. I know I may sound a little picky, but please leave your jewelry at home. Rings with sharp edges are known to tear disposable gloves. If you are feeling unwell, please do not come in. Your work schedule won't be finalized until several days before we open. If there aren't any questions, then we're going upstairs. We will be eating in one of the lounges where everything has been set up in advance. I hope y'all like Italian because that's what we'll be eating today."

"How do you think it went?" Shannon asked Viola when they sat across from each other in the pastry kitchen.

Viola took a sip of sparkling water. "Better than I could've ever imagined. "I think you really put everyone at ease, where they don't think of you as a boss but a coworker."

"That's because I worked for a man everyone called Beast, and I swore if I was ever in a supervisory position, I would never bully or intimidate those I had to work with. But I must admit that your idea to prepare a welcoming lunch for the staff was genius. I don't think they were expecting us to cook for them."

She and Viola had prepared cannelloni, spaghetti pomodoro, ravioli with spinach and ricotta, grilled asparagus with pecorino Romano, veal saltimbocca and chicken parmigiana. Dessert was peaches and prosecco with almond cream, cannoli, gelato and almond cake.

"What do you think about beginning with soup and salad, then appetizers before we cover every item on all menus?" Viola asked.

"It's a good idea. Start small and end big."

"I know we've talked ad nauseam about what I want to serve for my wedding guests, and I've changed my mind again. Because the wedding is going to be held in the afternoon, I was thinking about an informal outdoor buffet."

Shannon angled her head. "Are you thinking about a cookout?"

"That's exactly what I'm thinking. We've got the smoker, so the butcher can dress a whole hog and smoke it along with slabs of ribs, chickens and brisket. Having a barbecue reception will be a refreshing departure from the ubiquitous sit-down wedding reception. If the weather holds, then we'll have it outdoors, or if not, then we'll have it in the banquet room with a DJ playing cookout tunes."

"Have you discussed this with Dom?"

"Dom refuses to get involved. He says all he wants to do is show up, repeat his vows and become my husband."

"That's because Dom is no nonsense, Viola. He doesn't like conflict."

"That's the reason I fell in love with him. He was willing to walk away rather than come between me and my mother when she called him hired help."

"I'm glad they were able to resolve that. Now are you sure you want a cookout menu?

Because if I'm going to be responsible for supervising the kitchens, then I need a firm commitment now."

Viola nodded. "Yes."

"Yes what, Viola?"

"Yes, I want a cookout menu."

A beat passed. "I swear, if you change your mind again, then you'll either hire an outside caterer or cook yourself."

A rush of color darkened Viola's face. "I promise not to change my mind again."

Viola didn't know her choice made it easier for Shannon to prepare food for the wedding reception. Once the meat was in the smokers, she just had to concentrate on making desserts and side dishes. "Good."

A cell phone pinged, and Viola reached into the pocket of her slacks. "Oh my goodness. Taylor just sent me a text that he's taking Sonja to the hospital because her water broke. I'm going to be an auntie!"

Shannon smiled. The Williamsons had a lot of celebrating to do with the birth of a new baby, the opening of the hotel and Viola's wedding.

Joaquin watched Shannon greet her family as they entered the hotel lobby. She'd told him her parents, brother and his family would check in late Friday afternoon, and he'd held back from asking her to introduce him to them because he still wasn't ready to go public with their relationship. Shannon had revealed her feelings for him to Viola, and Joaquin was surprised that his sister had been mute on the subject. If it hadn't been for Dom, he never would've known her feelings.

He'd noticed his mother giving him questioning looks whenever she joined the family for movie nights, but she hadn't said anything to him about Shannon since Easter. Shannon had moved out of the guesthouse and into her apartment at the château, and not sharing meals or a bed made him realize just how much he loved her.

Dom and his mother had urged him to tell Shannon what lay in his heart, but he wanted to wait until the time was right. The official grand opening was scheduled for noon the next day, and then they had to prepare for his sister's wedding. Joaquin didn't want to shift the spotlight from Viola once he revealed his true feelings for the hotel's pastry chef.

"She won't know your thoughts unless you tell her."

Joaquin turned. He hadn't heard Tariq come up behind him. There was a family joke that Tariq had ghostly tendencies because he could appear and disappear without anyone noticing him.

"All in due time, bro."

"What's the holdup, Joaquin?"

"I'll tell her after Viola's wedding. We've had enough excitement with Sonja giving birth to our niece, and now it's the hotel's grand opening."

Tariq patted his back. "Suit yourself."

Shannon bit back a smile when she lined up with the other chefs wearing white coats with black-and-white pin-striped pants and white chef skull caps. The coat cuffs and collars were trimmed in Black Watch tartan matching the embroidered Bainbridge House logo on the breast pocket. She affected an impassive expression as photographers captured the historic moment of a new hotel with an all-female staff.

The waitstaff, housekeeping, the banquet manager, and security had also assembled on the steps of the château for the grand opening photographs. Taylor, Patrick, Tariq, and Joaquin, wearing royal blue business suits with tartan plaid ties and pocket squares were available for the ribbon-cutting ceremony along with several local elected officials. Members of the media, who were on hand to document the restoration of a property listed on the National Register of Historic Places and the reopening of upscale luxury lodgings.

The Memorial Day weekend was the official kickoff to the summer season, and the weather had cooperated for the Williamsons to host the festivities outdoors under a large white tent. Taylor, who'd been interviewed earlier, escorted Sonja into the tent. Three-week-old Maria Elise Violet Williamson slept in a suite with her grandmothers sharing babysitting duties.

Sonja had named her daughter after her mother, Taylor's mother and her best friend who'd been responsible for her meeting and falling in love with her brother.

Shannon felt as if she could finally exhale, because all was right in her world. She had her own pastry kitchen, was a part of a history-making event with the restoration, and she had fallen in love with one of the owners of the estate.

She approached her parents under the tent, exchanging hugs with them. Annette Younger blinked back tears, and Shannon hoped her mother wouldn't lost her composure because she always cried when becoming emotional.

"You did good, baby girl," Marcus Younger told his daughter. Everything is wonderful, and I told your mother that we have to come back during the summer for vacation to take advantage of some of the amenities like swimming, golfing, and the on-site health club and spa."

"Y'all come back whenever you want," Shannon told them.

Marcus and Dom ignored everyone, appearing to be joined at the hip when they had settled into chairs at the far end of the tent. They were probably catching up on what had been going on in their lives and Dom's upcoming wedding.

Mara had struggled to contain her excitement when her parents arrived, along with her brother, his wife and two children, and her father's business associates and their wives. Shannon noticed that Patrick, who again had returned to Bainbridge without his fiancée, appeared quite interested in her assistant. Mara was helpless to hide her blushing whenever Patrick said something to her, and Shannon wondered if anything was going on between the two, because Viola had mentioned that Patrick was planning not to return to California until after her wedding. And if Patrick was no longer in a relationship with Andrea, and wanted Mara as a friend, then it was good for her because he didn't need her money. Patrick Williamson was wealthy in his own right and didn't need any woman's money.

It wasn't until late Monday afternoon that Joaquin managed to find Shannon alone. Every time he'd wanted to approach her, there were others around, and he hadn't wanted to encroach on the limited time she had to spend with her family.

"Hey, stranger," he said smiling.

Shannon rested a hand on the sleeve of his shirt. "I've wanted to talk to you, but it's been hectic these past few days."

"I know, because I've been watching you work your magic. You and your fellow chefs are phenomenal."

She lowered her eyes. "Thanks."

"I wanted to ask…" His words trailed off when his cell phone rang, and he cursed the timing. Reaching for the phone, he recognized the name and number on the screen. It was Nadine's father. It had been years since he'd spoken to the man. "Excuse me, babe, but I need to answer this."

"I'll talk to you later."

"No. Stay," he said quickly. Tapping the screen, he said, "Hello." His greeting was followed by inconsolable sobbing. "What is it?"

"It's my father. He's dead. I didn't know who to call."

Joaquin saw Shannon staring at him. "What do you want me to do?" he asked his ex-wife.

"Can you come? I found a letter Daddy had written, saying if anything happened to him, he wanted you to take care of his business. I have enough money to bury him, but I don't know anything about selling the nursery."

Joaquin closed his eyes, and he wanted to tell Nadine to go to hell, but he knew he had to honor the last wishes of a man who had been good to him. "Okay, I can't come now, because I'm involved with some family business. I'll call you tomorrow to let you know when I'll be able to come."

"Thank you, Joaquin."

He ended the call and sighed. "I have to go to California. An old friend just passed away and his daughter needs me to help her negotiate the sale of his business."

Shannon took a step closer. "It's okay, babe. Don't worry about me. Go and help her out. I'll be here when you get back."

Dipping his head, Joaquin kissed her cheek when it was her mouth he wanted to taste. Turning on his heels, he walked away before he reneged on his promise to help a duplicitous woman who he'd relegated to his past but had resurfaced at the wrong time. He would do what he could to assist the sale of Harry Phillips's business and then return to New Jersey and to the woman he loved enough to make his wife and hopefully the mother of their children.

Chapter Nineteen

Joaquin's flight landed at LAX two days later, and he picked up a rental and drove to a hotel in a neighborhood not far from where Harry Phillips had lived all his life. He checked in and called Shannon to let her know he'd arrived safely but hadn't reserved a return flight. He didn't tell her that the business he would negotiate to sell had belonged to his ex-wife's father. Nadine was his past and that's where she would stay, while he wondered if he was making a mistake not telling Shannon that he was in California meeting with his ex-wife. However, he'd told himself it wasn't about her, but her father.

After showering, he changed his clothes, drove to the modest home on a well-kept tree-lined street and pulled into the driveway. The front door opened before he got out, and the woman standing in there looked nothing like the one he remembered. It wasn't that she'd gained weight, but she appeared bloated, and he wondered if she was ill.

Nadine was a year younger than he was, but at thirty-three, she looked so much older. The pretty young woman with a winning smile and flawless nut-brown complexion was gone and in her place was someone he hardly recognized.

"Thank you for coming," Nadine said.

Joaquin nodded. Even her voice had changed. It was as if she'd spent too many years smoking, something he'd never seen her do when they were married. "I came for your father. Where is he?"

Nadine opened the door wider and stepped aside. "He's at the funeral parlor. I prepared a room where you can stay while you're here."

"That's not necessary, because I've checked into a hotel not far from here."

"Okay. Come in and sit while I get the papers Daddy left."

Joaquin sat, glancing around the living room where Nadine had grown up with her parents. It was clean, neat, unlike the apartment where they'd lived after they were married. And it wasn't the first time he wondered if she'd resented him for not hiring a housekeeper because he'd grown up with one.

Nadine returned and handed him a legal envelope. "Can I get you something to eat or drink?"

"No, thank you." Joaquin wanted to take care of whatever it was he'd come to California for and then return home to Shannon and his family.

The envelope was filled with tax returns, an insurance policy listing him and Nadine as beneficiaries, and a copy of his will. "Are you aware that I'm listed as a beneficiary along with you on his insurance policy? And that he's left the nursery to me?"

"Are you saying I don't own any of the nursery?" Nadine asked.

"That's exactly how the will reads. I don't want or need your father's money. I'm going to give you everything. I'm not certain how much the nursery will sell for, but whatever it is, you will get the money."

As a college student Joaquin had answered an ad to work at the nursery, and as a horticulture major, he'd learned more from Harry Phillips than he did in class. Harry could identify what was wrong with a plant or grass with a single glance. And when he met the man's daughter, there was something he couldn't resist and had convinced himself that she was his soulmate. However, their fairy-tale romance didn't last long enough to make it to their second anniversary, and Joaquin knew he had to end it to save himself emotionally.

A wry smile parted Nadine's lip. "I suppose you don't need money, because not only were you born with a platinum spoon in your mouth, but you also made a name for yourself sucking up to rich movie stars."

Joaquin wanted to tell her he wasn't born into wealth but to a woman who had a revolving door of boyfriends who had used her as a punching bag until one killed her. If it hadn't been for Elise and Conrad Williamson, he probably would've also become a victim of domestic violence.

"You asked me to fly across the country to help you with your father's finances, and if you continue spewing venom, then I'm going to walk out of here and go home. You can always pay a lawyer to straighten out everything. And I'm not going to change my mind about not taking a penny of your father's money. What's it going to be, Nadine?"

"I'm sorry, Joaquin. I suppose I'm still angry that you didn't want to stay married."

"It's been more than a decade, so I suggest you let it go and get on with your life. The money you'll get from Harry's life insurance and what I'm going to give you after the sale of the nursery should allow you to live comfortably if you don't squander it."

Nadine nodded. "Okay. Daddy wanted to be buried next to my mother, so I made the arrangements for that to happen midweek. Once I get the death certificate, I will send it to the insurance company. I also have the names of a few people who'd been asking to buy the business, so I'll leave that up to you, because I have no idea what it's worth."

"Give me the names and I'll contact them. I'll call you from the hotel to let you know when I've set up appointments because I want you to be present."

"Okay. Will you be at the graveside service when they bury Daddy?"

"Yes. Text me the time and I'll be there."

Shannon had begun counting down the days since Joaquin had flown to California. It was now five days going on six, and she wondered how long it would take to bury someone, but then she'd recalled him saying he had to help his friend's daughter sell her father's business, and that was something that could not be accomplished in a week. He'd called her when he'd landed, but she hadn't heard his voice since that time, because he'd gotten into a habit of sending her text messages giving her updates on what he was doing to negotiate the sale of a nursery.

She was tempted to ask Viola if she'd heard from him but stopped herself because she didn't want to appear like some needy woman who didn't want her man out of her sight for any appreciable length of time.

One week stretched into two, and then on impulse when she got a break in the kitchen, she dialed his number. It rang three times before there was a break in the connection, and Shannon froze when she heard a woman's voice answer.

"I must have dialed the wrong number."

"If you're looking for Joaquin Williamson, then you didn't dial the wrong number. I'm Nadine, and he can't come to the phone because he's in the shower. Do you want to leave a message for him?"

"No, thank you. I'll call him back later."

Shannon ended the call and struggled to breathe normally. Not again. She couldn't believe a man who she'd fallen in love with had deceived her with another woman.

She shocked herself when she turned off the ringer on the phone and slipped it into her pocket. She was tempted to block Joaquin's number, but Shannon decided against that, because she wasn't a coward. When he called, then it would go directly to voicemail because she didn't want to hear his excuse as to why he hadn't called her and when she did call him, why a woman had answered his phone.

Joaquin felt as if he'd been through an emotional mincer when the jet lifted off for his return trip to the East Coast, and he fell into a deep sleep, only to awaken when he had to deplane at O'Hare to catch a connection to Newark International Airport. He'd forgotten how mentally draining Nadine could be. She vacillated between anger and tears because not only had she lost her mother as a young girl, but now she felt as if her father had abandoned her. She claimed she didn't want the money if she could only have him back.

Joaquin knew he couldn't leave California until he settled everything because he didn't want to come back and relive his life with a woman who didn't know what she wanted or needed. And the few times he'd tried to call Shannon, it was either too early or too late given the three-hour time difference, so he'd sent her text messages.

It was past midnight when the driver drove through the gates of Bainbridge House and came to a stop at his house. He tapped his phone, giving the man a generous tip, thanked him and went inside. Joaquin managed to shower before collapsing face down on the bed and falling into a deep, dreamless sleep.

He woke hours later, drank water and then returned to bed and did not wake up again until early in the evening. After shaving and showering, he drove to the hotel. Even though it was midweek, there were a few guests checking in, and he nodded to a bellhop who'd recognized him. Using a keycard, he rode the kitchen elevator to the lower level and didn't find anyone in either kitchen.

Joaquin left the kitchen and walked down a hallway to the resident apartments. He knocked on Shannon's door and waited. He knocked again, and when she finally opened the door, he hadn't realized how much he'd missed her until that moment.

"Hey, sweetie."

"What the hell are you doing here?"

"I came back to see you."

"No, you didn't!" Shannon spit out. "You came back because you got tired of playing with your Cali hoochie."

Joaquin couldn't believe what he was hearing. "What are you talking about?"

"I called you, Joaquin, and Nadine told me you were in the shower. Was it because you'd just finished making love to her?"

Joaquin cursed raw ugly invectives under his breath. "No."

"Who is Nadine, Joaquin?"

He had planned to tell Shannon about Nadine before asking her whether she would marry him. "She's my ex-wife."

Shannon covered her mouth with her hand to keep from screaming. Her heart was beating so fast she was certain Joaquin could see it through her tee. "Why did I have to find out like this? Why couldn't you have told me that you had been married before we slept together? I told you I had a problem trusting men, and now I know why."

"I was going to tell you, Shannon."

"When Joaquin? And why was it such a secret?"

"It wasn't secret but something I wanted to forget."

"Men don't forget their ex-wives, Joaquin. And why didn't someone in your family mention that you'd been married."

"Because I made them promise never to talk about it. Just like we promised one another not to tell anyone why we were in foster care."

"But...but you told me." Shannon was so angry that she found it hard to get the words out.

"I told you because I love you."

"You love me, Joaquin? You claim you love me when you can't trust me enough to tell me about your past when you know all about mine."

A vein throbbed in Joaquin's forehead. "That's because your life was played out in public, Shannon. It was different for me and my family."

"Well, you can keep your family secrets, because we're through.

"No, Shannon."

"Yes, Joaquin."

"But I'd planned to tell you before asking you to marry me."

She moved to close the door. "Sorry, but that's never going to happen. Now I want you to leave."

"Don't—"

Whatever he intended to say was cut off when Shannon closed the door in his face. She wanted to cry, but something inside her wouldn't permit the tears to come. She cried enough in the past over a man who wasn't worth her love, and she refused to do it now. What she did do was pick up a pillow off the bed and punch it. And when she began, she discovered she couldn't stop until feathers were flying everywhere.

They were in her hair, ears and a few had gone up her nose, which prompted a sneezing fit. She pummeled a good pillow when it had done nothing but provide her a wonderful night's rest. Shannon felt foolish when she saw the mess she'd made of her bedroom. There was no doubt housekeeping would be faced with the task of vacuuming them up.

Taking another pillow and blanket off the bed, she went into the living room and lay on the sofa. Joaquin didn't or couldn't tell her he'd been married before, while he had the audacity to talk about marrying her when he had waited until she'd forced him into proverbial corner to say that he loved her. She recalled him saying that one of the hardest things for dudes to admit is to tell a woman that they are in love with her.

Well, she was sorry, but not for herself. She was glad she had ended it before she'd found herself in too deep.

Shannon walked into the kitchen a week after Joaquin had returned from California to find Mara waiting for her. She was always in the kitchen at least an hour before the others arrived.

"What brought you in so early?" she asked Mara.

"I wanted to talk to you before the others got here."

Shannon sat on a stool at the prep table. "What about?"

"You, Shannon."

"What about me?"

"Are you pregnant?"

Shannon's jaw dropped. "What!"

"You heard me. Are you pregnant?"

"Of course not," she retorted. "What made you ask me that?"

"Because your hormones are all over the place. First, you're cheerful, then you look and act as if you've lost your best friend. What's up?"

Shannon wondered how much she should tell her friend, then decided to come clean about her relationship with Joaquin. She'd thought about talking to Viola, but then again, Joaquin was her brother, and she would no doubt take his side. And it wasn't that she hadn't unburdened herself to Mara about her marriage to Hayden when they were roommates. She told her friend everything from the first time she saw Joaquin Williamson across a crowded room to his revelation that he'd been married before.

"What I don't understand, Shannon, is why wouldn't he tell you when he knew you had been married? What's the big flipping secret?"

"I don't know, Mara. Maybe she's one of those women who was in jail, and he married her after she was paroled."

"Oh, you mean *Love After Lockup*. I love that show."

Shannon wanted to laugh but thought maybe there was a possibility that Joaquin had married an ex-con, and that's why she hadn't heard anyone mention that he'd been married before. That it had become the Williamsons' best kept secret.

"I try not to watch reality TV, because some of the episodes remind me of my past life."

Mara rested her elbows on the table. "What are you going to do?"

"Nothing. I told Joaquin I'm not going to marry him, and that's that."

"Do you love him, Shannon?"

"Yes, I love him, but not enough to marry a man I can't trust to be open and honest with me. He knows what happened when I was married to Hayden."

"That's because it was all over the tabloids and social media. You couldn't hide because the whole world knew. What if he tells you that he loves you?"

Shannon closed her eyes as she pondered Mara's question. "He did tell me that he loves me, but I don't understand why he had to wait until I confronted him about hiding his ex-wife. He had to have loved the woman enough to marry her, so I don't understand what the big deal is about her being a secret."

Mara's eyes grew large. "He actually came out and said that he loved you?"

Shannon nodded. "Yes. I believe he said out of desperation because I told him we were through."

"Men would rather go through a root canal procedure without anesthesia rather than admit to a woman that he loves her, Shannon." Mara paused. "I know you're upset, but there has to be good reason why Joaquin doesn't want to talk about his ex." She paused again. "Have you thought that maybe she cheated on him?"

"And if she did, why not tell me. He's not the first man with a cheating wife and he certainly won't be the last. It happens every day."

"I don't want you to give up on him, Shannon, because something tells me you're made for each other. Will you think about?"

Shannon wanted to tell Mara "hell no," but said instead, "I'll have to think about it."

Mara smiled. "That's my girl."

Shannon returned her smile. "Thanks."

"For what?"

"For your concern. I had no idea that I was acting crazy."

"Being in love makes one crazy. Remember Beyoncé's 'Crazy in Love'?"

Shannon laughed. "You should've majored in theater instead of accounting."

"I didn't have the talent to make it in theater. I can't sing or dance, but I was always good in math, so I took the easy way out and decided to become an accountant."

Chelsea walked in, and Shannon and Mara deftly changed the topic of conversation to what they wanted to bake for afternoon tea.

Joaquin sat on stone bench near the waterfall across from Dom. He'd asked Dom to meet him because he needed his advice on a personal matter. His sister's fiancé's expression did not change when he talked about what had transpired between him and Shannon.

"What do you want me to say, Joaquin? That I told you so?"

"Maybe that's what I need to hear."

"I'm not going to tell you that, but I'm going to call you a jackass. You knew you're in love with the woman long before now, but then you tell yourself that you wanted to wait to tell her. What's up with time limits?"

"I don't want to make the same mistake with Shannon that I made with Nadine. I met her, then boom, three months later we were married."

"Who did the proposing, Joaquin? Did you or Nadine?"

"Now, that I think back she was the one that brought it up."

"And you with your randy ass thought if you marry her, then you didn't have go trolling for girls to sleep with."

Joaquin gave Dom a threatening stare. "You really like running off at the mouth and saying things that can get you into trouble, don't you?"

Dom smiled. "You're bothered by what I say because you know it's the truth. And what you've just told me about your ex answering your phone means she is still trying to mess with you. And that when she called you using her father's phone, she knew you would answer the call. Face it, Joaquin, the woman knows you better than you know yourself."

"Now that's really the past because there's no need for her to ever contact me again. I wrote her a check for the sale of the nursery and my share of the life insurance payout. She married me for money, and now we're even."

"What about Shannon?" Dom asked.

"What about her?"

"When are you going to square things with her?"

"I don't know. Right now she's not willing to listen to anything I have to say. It can't be before you marry my sister."

"That's less than two weeks away."

Joaquin gave Dom a direct stare. "Two weeks is like a second compared to the years I plan to share with Shannon as husband and wife."

"That sounds like a plan, brother."

"And thanks for lending me your ear when I bitch and moan about what a mess I've made of something that's so simple."

"That's where you're wrong, Joaquin. Love is never simple, and that's what makes it so exciting *and* unpredictable."

Shannon didn't realize how much she'd missed Joaquin when she went to bed and woke up alone. During the day, she'd managed to stay busy so as not to think about him. She'd spent two full days making six dozen color macarons for Viola's wedding, while Mara had put the finishing touches on the cake with Russian piped flowers atop tartan ribbon on the three-tiered cake covered in pale blue buttercream. Chelsea had painstakingly made sixty chocolate candies in edible packaging as souvenirs. The edible boxes were filled with walnut caramels and mocha and nut creams.

It was only four days before the Fourth of July, but the Williamsons had decided to celebrate early with a backyard barbecue wedding reception.

Shannon had just removed a tray of potato salad from the fridge and handed it to one of the servers when Joaquin walked in. He wore a pale blue shirt, opened at the collar and navy dress pants. A boutonniere made with sprigs of lavender was pinned to the pocket.

"Well, it's finally here," she said, hoping she sounded normal when her heart was beating so fast that it made her feel slightly light-headed. "Viola will become a Shaw."

"I didn't come here to talk about my sister, Shannon."

She let out a breath. "What did you come to talk about, Joaquin?"

"Us."

"What about us?"

He angled his head. "I know I've made a mess of what we have—had," he said, correcting himself, "but I want to make things right."

"How are you going to do that?"

Joaquin stared at something over her head. "By being completely honest with you."

"Okay. I'm listening."

"I love you. It's something I should've told you weeks—no—months ago, but I didn't want to make the same mistake I made with Nadine."

"Your ex-wife."

He nodded. "Yes, my ex-wife. I married her after knowing her for only three months, and I lived to regret it because I didn't take the time to know who she was, and she didn't know who I was. Our marriage didn't last two years, and even though she never met my family, I made them promise never to speak about it." Joaquin recognized disbelief flit across Shannon's features when he mentioned that no one in his family had ever met his ex.

"Why wouldn't she want to meet them?"

"I don't know. Whenever I came home for holidays, she claimed she didn't want to leave her father, she said she'd promised her mother before she died she would always be with him. And when I mentioned this to my mother, she said Nadine was selfish and manipulative and she wanted nothing to do with her. It didn't take me long to realize she only married me because she thought I had a lot of money because I'd mentioned I'd grown up in a big house and that my mother had employed a housekeeper." Joaquin stopped talking when another server came into the kitchen and Shannon gave him a tray of baked beans to take outside. "When I left California, I left everything I'd ever shared with Nadine behind—forever. She has enough money to take her into old age if she doesn't squander it."

"She's your past, but where does that leave us, Joaquin?"

"I want us to start over—this time with no secrets. I love you."

"You love me, but I don't believe you. Say it like you mean it, Joaquin Williamson."

"I love you with every breath I take, and I want to marry you, but that will have to be your decision, not mine."

Shannon heard the passion in his voice and struggled not to break down. "I do love you, Joaquin, but if we do marry—I'm not saying I will—but I must think about it."

"How long will you have to think about it?

"A year."

Joaquin blew out his breath. "That's a long time to think about something."

"Yes it is. However, it isn't that long if it's worth it."

He smiled. "You're right. And you're more than worth it, Shannon Younger."

"There's something else," she said.

Joaquin sighed. "What now?"

"We live together before we marry so we can decide if it is what we really want."

"That also works." Joaquin took a step, bringing them less than a foot apart. "Now, I'd like to ask you something."

"What's that?"

"Are you willing to accept something from me while you spend the next year thinking about us?"

Her eyes narrowed. "What is it?"

Reaching into the pocket of his pants, Joaquin took out a delicate gold tennis bracelet with alternating diamonds and sapphires and slipped it on her left wrist. "I know your birthday is in September, so I thought I'd give you an early present," he said, securing the clasp.

Shannon couldn't stop smiling. "I think you just cut six months off my thinking." Going on tiptoe, she put her arms around his neck and kissed him. "Thank you. It's beautiful."

"So are you, Shannon Younger."

"Now, please get out of my kitchen, because I have to make the reception special for my friend and the woman who will eventually become my sister."

Viola got her wish to have a garden wedding and reception as she exchanged vows with the direct descendant of the man whose dream of restoring Bainbridge House to its original magnificence had become a reality. Elise Williamson dabbed her eyes with a lace-trimmed handkerchief when Dominic Shaw, wearing a tartan jacket, kilt, and tie, dipped his head and kissed her daughter.

"We've done well, Conrad. Two down and three to go," she whispered under her breath. She glanced at Joaquin sitting next to her. Now, if she could only get him to see that he and that beautiful pastry chef were perfect for each other, then she'd only have to work on her other two sons.

"What are you whispering about?" Joaquin asked.

"Nothing, my son. I'm just happy because my children are happy." Joaquin took her hand and kissed the back of it. "I think I'm going to stay home for a while because I don't want to miss seeing my granddaughter grow up. And now that Viola's married, I'm hoping she will give me another grandbaby sometime soon."

"Don't rush her, Mom. She has time."

"But I don't. I'm seventy-three, so I'd like at least a half dozen before I turn eighty."

Joaquin stood and helped Elise to stand as Viola and Dom proceeded down the white carpet under a shower of flower petals. The newlyweds smiled at family and friends who'd come to Bainbridge House to witness their special day.

* * * * *

COMING NEXT MONTH FROM

⬢ HARLEQUIN
SPECIAL EDITION

#3031 BIG SKY COWBOY
The Brands of Montana • by Joanna Sims

Charlotte "Charlie" Brand has three months, one Montana summer and Wayne Westbrook's help to turn her struggling homestead into a corporate destination. The handsome horse trainer is the perfect man to make her professional dreams a reality. But what about her romantic ones?

#3032 HER NEW YORK MINUTE
The Friendship Chronicles • by Darby Baham

British investment guru Olivia Robinson is in New York for one reason—to become the youngest head of her global company's portfolio division. But when charming attorney Thomas Wright sweeps her off her feet, she wonders if another relationship will become collateral damage.

#3033 THE RANCHER'S LOVE SONG
The Women of Dalton Ranch • by Makenna Lee

Ranch foreman Travis Taylor is busy caring for an orphaned baby. He doesn't have time for opera singers on vacation. Even bubbly, beautiful ones like Lizzy Dalton. But when Lizzy falls for the baby *and* Travis, he'll have to overcome past trauma in order to build a family.

#3034 A DEAL WITH MR. WRONG
Sisterhood of Chocolate & Wine • by Anna James

Piper Kavanaugh needs a fake boyfriend pronto! Her art gallery is opening soon and her mother's matchmaking schemes are in overdrive. Fortunately, convincing her enemy turned contractor Cooper Turner to play the role is easier than expected. Unfortunately, so is falling for him...

HSECNM1223